Banished IN THE HIGHLANDS

Other Books by Anna Durand

Dangerous in a Kilt (Hot Scots, Book One)
Wicked in a Kilt (Hot Scots, Book Two)
Scandalous in a Kilt (Hot Scots, Book Three)
The MacTaggart Brothers Trilogy (Hot Scots, Books 1-3)
Gift-Wrapped in a Kilt (Hot Scots, Book Four)
Notorious in a Kilt (Hot Scots, Book Five)
Insatiable in a Kilt (Hot Scots, Book Six)
Lethal in a Kilt (Hot Scots, Book Seven)
Irresistible in a Kilt (Hot Scots, Book Eight)
Devastating in a Kilt (Hot Scots, Book Nine)
Spellbound in a Kilt (Hot Scots, Book Ten)
Relentless in a Kilt (Hot Scots, Book Eleven)
Incendiary in a Kilt (Hot Scots, Book Twelve)
Wild in a Kilt (Hot Scots, Book Thirteen)
Lachlan in a Kilt (The Ballachulish Trilogy, Book One)
Aidan in a Kilt (The Ballachulish Trilogy, Book Two)
Rory in a Kilt (The Ballachulish Trilogy, Book Three)
The American Wives Club (A Hot Brits/Hot Scots/Au Naturel Crossover)
Brit vs. Scot (A Hot Brits/Hot Scots/Au Naturel Crossover)
A Novel Secret (A Hot Brits/Hot Scots/Au Naturel Crossover)
The Dixon Brothers Trilogy (Hot Brits, Books 1-3)
One Hot Escape (Hot Brits, Book Four)
One Hot Rumor (Hot Brits, Book Five)
One Hot Christmas (Hot Brits, Book Six)
One Hot Scandal (Hot Brits, Book Seven)
One Hot Deal (Hot Brits, Book Eight)
One Hot Favor (Hot Brits, Book Nine)
Natural Obsession (Au Naturel Nights, Book One)
Natural Passion (Au Naturel Trilogy, Book One)
Natural Impulse (Au Naturel Trilogy, Book Two)
Natural Satisfaction (Au Naturel Trilogy, Book Three)
Fired Up (standalone romance)
Echo Power (Echo Power Trilogy, Book One)
Echo Dominion (Echo Power Trilogy, Book Two)
Echo Unbound (Echo Power Trilogy, Book Three)
The Janusite Trilogy (Undercover Elementals, Books 1-3)
Obsidian Hunger (Undercover Elementals, Book Four)
Unbidden Hunger (Undercover Elementals, Book Five)
The Thirteenth Fae (Undercover Elementals, Book Six)
Cyneric (Undercover Elementals, Book Seven)

Banished in the Highlands

A Hot Scots Prequel

ANNA DURAND

JACOBSVILLE BOOKS · MARIETTA, OHIO

BANISHED IN THE HIGHLANDS
Copyright © 2023 by Lisa A. Shiel
All rights reserved.

ISBN: 978-1-958144-14-5 (paperback)
ISBN: 978-1-958144-15-2 (ebook)
ISBN:978-1-958144-16-9 (audiobook)

Manufactured in the United States.

Jacobsville Books
www.JacobsvilleBooks.com

Publisher's Cataloging-in-Publication Data
provided by Five Rainbows Cataloging Services

Names: Durand, Anna, author.
Title: Banished in the Highlands / Anna Durand.
Description: Marietta, OH : Jacobsville Books, 2023. | Series: Hot Scots prequel, bk. 3.
Identifiers: ISBN 978-1-958144-14-5 (paperback) | ISBN 978-1-958144-15-2 (ebook) | ISBN 978-1-958144-16-9 (audiobook)
Subjects: LCSH: Highlands (Scotland)--Fiction. |Time travel--Fiction. | Middle Ages--Fiction. | Man-woman relationships--Fiction. | Historical fiction. | Romance fiction. | BISAC: FICTION / Romance / Time Travel. | FICTION / Romance / Historical / Scottish. | FICTION / Romance / Historical / Medieval. | Paranormal /Witches. | GSAFD: Love stories. | Historical fiction.
Classification: LCC PS3604.U724 W55 2023 (print) | LCC PS3604.U724 (ebook) | DDC 813/.6--dc23.

Chapter One

Alyssa

'm a fugitive, but no one is chasing me and I haven't broken any laws. I've escaped from my life and committed the crime of giving a damn about a man who destroyed me, wasting everything I had—money, energy, love—on trying to ensure he didn't suffer. What else could I do? Even a bad man shouldn't languish in agony. Compassion was my downfall.

And now I have nothing.

Well, not quite nothing. I blew the last of my savings on the once-in-a-lifetime trip I'd dreamed of taking since I was a little girl. The movie *Brigadoon* had made me long for the romantic world the people in that movie lived in, minus the "sleeping for a hundred years" thing. Maybe I would like to sleep for that long, though. By the time I woke up, I might have forgotten all the bad stuff.

"Ma'am? Your key?"

The clerk behind the car rental counter shakes the key ring at me while politely smiling. I had kind of sunk into a trance. Must be jet lag. The young man's accent reminds me that I am not hallucinating. I've actually landed in Scotland, in the Highlands—at the Inverness airport.

I accept the keys. "Thank you. Sorry I zoned out for a minute there."

"Don't worry, I've seen everything in my job."

"Yeah, I imagine you have. Airports are windows to the world."

"Enjoy your stay in Scotland. Do you need help finding your car?"

I hold up the rental company's brochure. "Got this. It tells me where to go."

"Aye, it does."

The wheels on my suitcase rumble across the hard floor as I make my way out of the building and to the rental car lot. I have no trouble finding my vehicle, a small, four-door model. I toss my suitcase onto the passenger seat and open the maps app on my phone to figure out where I'm going. I made a reservation at a castle that was described as "part medieval fortress, part museum, part bed-and-breakfast." That sounded intriguing, and the photos of the grounds and the interior sealed the deal. I had to go there.

Dùndubhan, here I come.

The maps app tells me my journey will take approximately three and a half hours. Along the way, I plan to stop at touristy places. Might as well make the most of my last hurrah. What comes after this…heaven only knows.

I make my first few stops before leaving town, visiting Inverness Castle and the Victorian Market, as well as getting some lunch at a Scottish pub that sells fish and chips. Okay, every pub here is Scottish. But I love the atmosphere and the way people talk, and I mean more than their accent. Every last person I meet is cheerful, which makes me feel like smiling too.

Naturally, as a gauche tourist, I stop at Loch Ness and wait for half an hour in the hopes I'll glimpse Nessie even though I don't believe in monsters. No luck, anyway. The only monster I see is the truck sort with four wheels and huge tires. Though I had planned to stop often along the main roads, I find myself just veering off into the countryside now and then to admire the stunning scenery. By the time I reach Ballachulish, I've lost interest in sightseeing, at least for today, and decide to get to the castle as soon as possible. After one more stop, at a petrol station where I gas up my car, I head out into the hinterlands.

Wow, the landscape is stunning. Tomorrow, I plan on exploring all the areas I bypassed today.

Just as the sun begins to set, I turn off the main road and go down a narrow two-track through a dense forest. The foliage forms a canopy above me, so I can't see the first stars or the moon. Then I come to a metal gate. The woman I'd spoken to when I made my reservation had told me the gate would be open and that I should drive right through it. She didn't lie. I continue through that gate where the driveway turns to gravel.

I emerge from the woods, and suddenly, I feel as if I've been transported back in time. Though the twilight makes it harder to see, I can tell the castle is enormous and boxy with a high wall surrounding it. The brilliant glow of what must be a huge floodlight spills out from the courtyard inside the massive wooden gates, which hang open. As I pass through the entrance, I spy turrets atop a tower.

But when I park inside the courtyard, I don't see carriages or horses. No, I park right next to a sleek Jaguar convertible. It makes my little sedan seem like a clunker.

I've barely climbed out of my car when two people rush out of the castle to greet me.

A blonde woman pulls me into a hug and kisses my cheek. "Welcome to Dùndubhan, Alyssa. We're thrilled to have you staying with us for the next two weeks."

"I'm excited to be here. This place is amazing."

"You'll love it here. I'm Emery, by the way."

The muscular man beside her seems mildly amused by her behavior. "Take it easy with the lass, Em, she must have jet lag." He offers me his hand. "I'm Rory MacTaggart. My wife and I own Dùndubhan."

Emery wraps an arm around Rory's waist. "We live in Ballachulish, but we wanted to be here to greet you. Our staff will take care of you during your stay, and you might see a few of my hubby's relatives too."

Rory sighs and smiles at his wife with gentle affection. "Our 'staff' consists of my relatives and their loved ones."

"Mrs. Brody too. Oh, and her husband Tavish." Emery's expression mutates from excited to sheepish. "I have a confession to make, and I hope you won't be upset about it. But you are our very first b&b guest."

"Really? No, I don't mind. I wanted to get away from it all."

"This is the perfect place to do that." Emery waves toward the door she and Rory had come out of a moment ago. "Let's go inside. We'll give you the grand tour of the interior, then tomorrow, you'll get the whole shebang."

"Sounds good."

My hosts lead me into the vestibule and through a doorway that takes us into the main hall of the ground floor. They honestly do give me the grand tour. I get to see every room on every floor, except for Rory's office. Every hallway features displays of antiques and ancient artifacts, all related to Scotland, accompanied by placards that explain each item's origins and historical relevance.

On the second floor, which is the third level of the castle, we enter the long gallery. The walls here feature historic paintings as well as photographs of what Dùndubhan looked like at various times in the last two hundred years or so. The center of the gallery contains glass cases full of antiquities, everything from eighteenth century coins to Viking artifacts.

I'm too tired to absorb everything I see.

Rory and Emery seem to notice that since they usher me into a bedroom, the one they had selected for me.

"You can choose a different room if you don't like this one," Emery says. "But this room has the best view and the cushiest bed."

"I'll take this one. You've decorated it so beautifully." I amble over to the four-poster bed and flop my bottom onto it. Wow, this is a wonderful mattress. I might sleep for days just because I'm so comfy. "Thank you both for the tour. I love this castle, and I can't wait to explore it more. I'm also looking forward to seeing the rest of the Highlands."

"You'll have plenty of time for that."

Rory clears his throat. "Em, why don't we let Alyssa rest now? She's had a long journey."

My hosts graciously exit the room, shutting it behind them.

I change into my nightie and crawl under the covers, feeling more at ease than I have in a long time. The quiet atmosphere in this castle is like nothing I've experienced in ages. Decades of living in one city or another gave me a kind of amnesia about what life should really be like. Bumper-to-bumper traffic on freeways had become my normal. I've got one last chance to experience a new normal, here in another country.

Then what? I have no clue.

In the morning, I wake up having no idea when I fell asleep. Guess I was more exhausted than I realized. Now, I stretch and yawn and smile. A satisfied sigh rushes out of me. If this isn't heaven, it must be the next best thing. I get dressed and amble down to the dining room, where the castle's website had said I would find a buffet. Since I'm the first and only guest, I kind of doubt anybody will go to that much trouble.

But when I walk into the dining room, I see a genuine feast awaiting me.

A gray-haired woman smiles with her cheeks dimpled when she notices me. "Come, dearie, sit down. I'm Mrs. Brody."

I shuffle over to the table and try to sit down, but Mrs. Brody shoos me away. "Not that one. Take the chair at the head of the table."

"Are you sure?"

"You are our guest, Alyssa."

She must know my name because Rory and Emery told her. Well, a good b&b host would want to make sure every guest is treated like royalty. So I take the seat at the head of the table, the one Mrs. Brody pulled out for me. I survey the large amount of food arrayed on the table.

"Um, this is an awful lot for one person," I say. "Did you invite your friends to breakfast?"

"No, dearie. Eat whatever you like. The leftovers will feed the staff. And feel free to use the kitchen whenever you want, to have a piece or just to get something to drink."

After breakfast, I go upstairs to the long gallery so I can examine the artifacts there. Last night, I'd been too tired to fully enjoy them. Fifteen minutes into my perusal, I come to one item that causes me to stop and study it in greater detail than I'd done with any of the other artifacts. The glass case houses a sword. Something about it transfixes me, though I can't explain why. As far as swords go, this one is relatively plain. But when I lean in, I can see odd markings on it. The placard explains that this is the claymore that once belonged to Ciaran mac in tSagairt, the Gaelic version of the name Kieran MacTaggart. Not sure how that's pronounced. The placard also states that the MacTaggart clan only recently discovered that their ancestor had once lived at Dùndubhan.

That's interesting, but hardly earth-shattering. Why, then, do I seem incapable of tearing my gaze away from the sword? I slowly walk around the case to examine every angle.

It's just a sword, dummy. Stop gawking.

Shaking off my bizarre stupor, I drag myself out of the castle and to my rental car. Time for some sightseeing. I bump into Mrs. Brody on my way out and let her know I'll be gone for most of the day. Then, I jump into my car and head out. But instead of stopping at every touristy spot, I bypass all of that stuff and keep driving, not sure where I'm going or why I want to go to wherever my destination might be. Must still be jet lag.

Eventually, I wind up in a village called Loch Fairbairn. I don't stop there either, though. Something compels me to drive past the village, down a narrow road that takes me to…a cemetery. A chill shimmies up my spine, raising goosebumps on my arms. I need to go into the burial ground. So I get out of the car and stare at the headstones that litter the graveyard. A small sign declares it to be "The MacTaggart Family Cemetery."

That's a bizarre coincidence. No, it's not strange at all. There must be lots of MacTaggarts around here. I am in Scotland, after all.

I want to leave the cemetery. I should leave. But my feet won't let me climb back into my car. Instead, I find myself wandering through the rows of headstones until I come upon the one that had drawn me here. Can't catch my breath. Can't comprehend what I see. The headstone in front of me belongs to… No, it can't be. But it is. I snap a picture of it with my phone, though I still feel like I must be dreaming.

Because the gravestone reads, "Kieran Aulay MacTaggart. Died 1598."

Chapter Two

Alyssa

I slump to my knees and stare at the gravestone without blinking. How could I have known where Kieran was buried? What is happening to me? There must be a rational explanation. The placard at Dùndubhan must have mentioned it, and I just forgot I saw that. Yeah, I've lost my ability to remember things I read an hour ago. Well, I'm probably jet-lagged. No mystery here. Just a tired mind in need of more sleep.

But I'd slept for ten hours last night. How many times can I reasonably claim I have jet lag?

Oh, this is ridiculous. The fact I happened to come here, to this cemetery and one specific grave, means nothing. I rise and dust off my jeans, then turn to leave.

I can't do it. My feet refuse to budge. And as I stand here trying to move away, even one inch, a strange tingle sweeps over my skin from head to toe. I glance back at the headstone, and my heart begins to pound, making me feel lightheaded. I shuffle around to face the grave again. Suddenly, all the strange symptoms I'd experienced evaporate. It feels as if a giant weight has been lifted off my chest. I take several slow, deep breaths until my pulse returns to normal.

"Good morning."

I jerk and spin around to see who just spoke to me.

A man and woman stand there watching me, seeming rather confused by the fact I'm hovering over the grave of a man who died hundreds of years ago. Yeah, I'm confused too.

"Oh," I say. "I didn't know anyone else was here."

"Aye, that was clear." He holds out his hand to me. "I'm Munro Mac-Taggart. The man whose grave you're studying was my ancestor."

What am I doing? I lost my mind, at least temporarily, and I don't care to tell these two strangers why I was staring at Kieran MacTaggart's headstone. So instead, I move away from it. "I should go. This was a bad idea."

"What was?" the woman asks, and she sounds American. "You seem fascinated by the inscription."

"No, I—" Suddenly cold, I hug myself and rub my arms. "I have no idea why I came here. Had this crazy impulse to come to Scotland, and I dropped everything to do it. When I saw the sign that said this is the Mac-Taggart family cemetery, I couldn't stop myself from having a look."

"You must have seen every headstone in this cemetery. This one is in the oldest section which is furthest from the entrance."

"I walked straight to this spot." I gaze at the headstone, biting my lip. "I think I've lost my mind."

Munro MacTaggart lifts his brows. "Why would you say that, lass?"

"Because I can't explain anything I've done lately. I felt...drawn here." I shake my head, trying like hell to forget what I experienced a few minutes earlier. "Sorry. I should go."

I race past the couple and don't stop running until I get back inside the safety of my rental car. My heart is pounding again, but only because I sprinted across the whole cemetery. Whatever took hold of me in that graveyard, I will never experience it again because I will never return to this place. Can't even think about sightseeing. But I would look like such a moron if I returned to the castle before lunch. I need to waste time somehow.

I do up my seatbelt and clamp my hands around the steering wheel. *Put the key in the ignition, dummy.* Right, duh, that's kind of required. I fumble with the key, dropping it three times before I finally manage to start the car. As I'm driving back through Loch Fairbairn, I force myself to stop in at a café. Though it's only eleven o'clock, I suddenly feel ravenous, like I haven't eaten in days. A sweet young woman escorts me to a table in the outdoor patio section of the café, and I order fish and chips like I had yesterday. That seems like more of a British thing than a Scottish thing, but I don't care. I need to eat, if only to distract myself from the weird morning I've had so far.

The food is good, and I do feel better after eating. Then I order some warm homemade scones with raspberry jam for dessert. *Mm, yum.* I've almost returned to normal and shaken off those eerie sensations that overtook me back in the cemetery. Never again will I visit any kind of burial ground.

Luckily, when I arrive back at Dùndubhan, I don't see anyone, though I can hear someone in the kitchen humming. I guess that must be Mrs. Brody baking or cleaning up or something. So I sneak back upstairs without bothering her. As I reach the second-floor landing, I veer away from the long gallery and all those artifacts without even glancing back. A moment later, I'm safely ensconced in my room.

By the next morning, I feel fine again. No strange urge to study a sword. No spooky need to look at a medieval grave. I am myself again, and that chick wants to do some real sightseeing today that does not involve moldering corpses or antique weapons.

For the next two days, I do just that.

On the third day, I have dinner with Rory and Emery as well as Evelyn and Tavish Brody. Yeah, I finally asked what Mrs. Brody's first name was on the second day. The four of us have a great time, laughing and eating and enjoying a bottle of Cabernet. Rory and Emery tell me stories about their clan, all the crazy things they've done that aren't secrets because they did them in public. Rory himself tried to strip naked on the village square in Loch Fairbairn simply to make his wife smile. Emery stopped him from going all the way.

I feel like I know the whole clan. That's how good the stories are.

Rory and Emery leave after dinner, but Evelyn and Tavish are on duty tonight, which means they will sleep in one of the bedrooms in the ground-floor guest wing. I say goodnight to them in the vestibule.

But I don't feel tired enough to go to sleep yet. Evelyn had mentioned that the sliver moon will be visible tonight, so I wander out into the courtyard and gaze up at the sky. Stars twinkle. An owl hoots. Crickets chirp. I scan the heavens until I spot the sliver of a moon, then tip my head back more. I've never seen a sky like this, so clear and free of light pollution. Every star in the galaxy must be on display tonight and probably quite a few from further away too.

A creaking noise draws my attention to the castle.

I trot over to the side of the building, where a doorway hangs open, creaking as it turns on its hinges as if a strong breeze has caught it. Getting out the flashlight on my phone, I shine it into the darkness below. A flight of stairs leads down to some kind of room. Is that the wine cellar? Maybe Rory forgot to shut the door. I creep down the steps until I reach the bottom. Now I can tell there's a small window at the level of the stairs.

And yeah, I was right. This is the wine cellar.

Maybe I should grab a bottle just in case. Never know when I might need a little vino to put me to sleep. Besides, Rory and Emery said I should think of Dùndubhan as my home until the day I fly back to America. What the heck. I reach out to grasp the neck of a bottle.

And everything goes black. I can't move, can't scream, can't do anything except listen to my pulse thundering in my ears. A force like a whirlwind seizes me, and I go tumbling into absolute darkness.

Then I thump down on a solid surface.

A flash of white light blinds me as my eyes struggle to recover from the shock, and goosebumps raise all over my body. Voices whisper. A glow flickers nearby. My ears are ringing, but as I sit here in shock, that fades away. Now I can see three figures who squat on stools near a small, round table. Three women. I blink several times rapidly. These women wear old-timey clothes—long dresses and ankle boots. But that's not the weirdest thing.

They seem to be chattering in another language.

"Hello?" I say. But my throat is dry, and I need to swallow a few times before I can speak loud enough for the strangers to hear me. Then I try again. "Hello? Who are you?"

The trio stare at me blankly. One of them whispers something, and the other two nod their agreement.

A plump, gray-haired woman who seems older than her companions, based on her wrinkles, toddles over to me and drops a necklace down over my head. The pendant attached to the silver chain has a pattern I recognize. I think it's called a Trinity Knot or maybe a triquetra. I've heard both terms. The complex design is a combination of two ovals and one circle, and it's composed of silver like the chain.

The gray-haired woman pats my hand. "There, *gràidh*, can you understand me now?"

"Uh, yes, I think so." My words came out haltingly, probably because I'm confused and slightly groggy. "Where am I?"

"Dùndubhan."

"The castle? This must be some part of the building that I haven't seen. But I was in the wine cellar when everything went wonky."

The woman's brows knit together over her nose. "Dùndubhan has no wine cellar, though I dearly wish it did. I do not understand 'wonky,' but I should explain how you came to be here."

"Yeah, please do."

"We summoned you."

I might've actually done a double take. "You did what?"

"Summoned you. We invoked the spirits of our ancestors to bring you to this place. Please know that we wish you no harm."

"Who are you people?"

"I am Efrica MacTaggart." She gestures toward her two friends in turn, a slender woman with gray-streaked dark hair and another who has dark-blonde hair and a wide mouth. "These are my sisters, Lachina and Morna."

"Tell the lass why we summoned her," Lachina says. "You are confounding her, Efrica."

"Oh, aye, of course." Efrica rolls her shoulders back and looks straight at me. "You are to be the bride of our beloved nephew. He is a good man, and you will grow to love him, of that we are certain."

"Uh-huh." I must've inhaled some spores from a hallucinogenic mushroom when I was in the wine cellar. But I might as well roll with the wackadoodle daydream, for now. I touch the pendant Efrica had given me. "Does this make it so I can understand you?"

"Yes, dearie, it does. We speak Scots Gaelic, not to be confused with Irish Gaelic."

"But you said a word I don't recognize. *Gràidh*? That's what it sounded like."

"*Gràidh* is Gaelic. The occasional word in our native tongue may break through the translation enchantment, particularly if the word has emotion or fear attached to it in your mind. Conniving might also interfere."

"Sure, whatever."

A banging erupts from the closed doorway. "What are you three doing in there?"

"Oh dear," Efrica says, rising from her chair. "Our nephew has found us a wee bit sooner than expected." She shouts toward the door, "Dinnae fash, Kieran!"

More banging.

Efrica rushes to the door and swings it open.

A tall, muscular figure stands there with one fist raised as if to slam it into the door again. The man has fur pelts draped over his body to form a kind of patchwork coat that extends down his thighs but doesn't quite conceal his kilt. He seems to be shirtless, though well-worn boots cover his feet. The thing that makes me recoil slightly is not his muscles or the fact that he seems enraged. No, I cringe because blood stains those fur pelts as well as his face and arms. The hand not raised to bang on the door grips a large knife while he has a bow and a quiver of arrows slung over one shoulder.

Did I mention the dirt and blood and who knows what is also caked in his hair? The man seems like a beast straight out of the epic of Beowulf.

Efrica seems unfazed. "Before ye shout at us, at least meet the lass. We summoned her for you."

"Summoned?" His eyes narrow, then his gaze veers to me. He glances down at the pendant that hangs over my chest. The man's nostrils flare, and he glowers at his aunts. "I will deal with you later."

"Kieran, please—"

He stomps up to me, leans in, and rips the pendant away. I can smell the blood now too. Tossing the necklace onto the floor, he throws me over his shoulder and storms out the door.

Chapter Three

Kieran

I climb the cellar stairs and cross the courtyard, marching straight through the open wooden doors of the fortress. Barely glancing at the raised portcullis above me, I stalk over the drawbridge to go down the well-worn path I've traveled many times. I do not look back at the gatehouse. The woman slung over my shoulder tries to kick me. When that accomplishes nothing, she pounds her wee fists on my erse, but that also accomplishes nothing save to vex me. During the entirety of her attempt to free herself, she snarls many words, most of which seem to be gibberish.

The pendant my aunts had gifted to the woman apparently allowed her to comprehend Gaelic, which suggests she does not know the language. Mayhap she is English. If so, I do not wish to allow her into my home. If she were Scottish, I still would not welcome her. Lasses cause nothing but trouble.

The braies she wears look like none I have seen before. Their rough blue fabric clings to her thighs and extends to her ankles.

"Let go of me, jerk-off," she says. "You probably don't speak English because you're a big, rude, evil moron. I don't understand Gaelic, but even if you understood what I was saying, you probably wouldn't explain anything."

I continue walking down the path while I ponder the problem of how to rid myself of this creature. If I throw her into the river, she might drown. As much as I disdain the woman, I have no desire to end her life. I want her away, not dead.

She once again beats her wee fists on my erse. "I hate you. If you're the nephew those three women thought I'd want to marry, they're as nuts as you are. You're the most obnoxious man I have ever met, and you stink of blood and filth. It's a damn good thing you don't understand me. Might as well speak my mind, huh? Okay, here goes. I hope you catch a horrible disease, like scurvy, and then you fall into a big hole and can't get out. Oh, and I hope you land in a pile of bat shit and then those bats start gnawing on your face."

I can't stop myself from laughing. She might be a troublesome wench, but she knows how to craft unusual curses. I do not believe for one moment that she has supernatural powers, though.

She moans. "I'm getting dizzy. If I vomit, I'll try to aim it at your calf. That's what you get for wearing a skirt."

The lass does sound unwell. I might not want to invite her into my home, but even I am not enough of a knave to refuse assistance. What should I do with her? For the moment, I have but one choice. I toss her onto the ground.

She lands face-first on the earthen trail and twists her head to the side to glower at me.

"You may now vomit," I announce. "My kilt will not be damaged."

"Gee, I'm so frigging glad your skirt won't get barf all over it."

I wave my arm. "Arise, wench, and be on your way."

She pushes up onto her straight arms. Blowing hair away from her face, she glares at me for a moment, then rises to a kneeling position. Since her clothing has become caked with dirt, she attempts to brush it off. "You bastard."

"My mother and father were wedded before I was conceived."

"Well, isn't that great for you." She rises to her feet. "Don't ever call me 'wench' again, or I'll make sure you're singing soprano from now on."

"You are implying you will castrate me, but that shall never come to pass." I wave toward the trail ahead. "Be away, and dinnae fash me again."

She glances around, and her forehead wrinkles. "Where are we? Efrica said it was Dùndubhan, but that can't be right. I mean, there's a moat and a drawbridge. I saw a huge gateway of some sort too. But Dùndubhan doesn't have any of that."

"How could know what my home looks like? You had never visited it before today. I know this because I live here." I slant toward her only enough to intimidate the woman. "I am Kieran MacTaggart, the Laird of Dùndubhan. I know the name of everyone who resides in my castle, and you are not among them. If you had visited Dùndubhan in the past, you would know that it is a castle with many fortifications."

She stares at me as her eyes gradually widen. "You're Kieran MacTaggart?"

"Aye. Have ye lost your sense of hearing? Mayhap you are simply an idiot."

The lass swivels her head as if she is looking for something that she cannot find. "This can't be—I can't be—No, I must be in a coma or something."

"You speak nonsense."

I turn and stride back down the path.

But the wench races after me, coming up alongside me. "This might sound insane, but I think I know what happened. How I got here."

"My aunts cast a spell to summon you."

"And you actually believe that."

"Silence. I have no need of your company."

When I increase my pace of walking, she trots to keep up with me. "Here's something you don't know, Mr. Smartypants. I'm from the twenty-first century. Your aunts didn't only summon me, they brought me back in time."

"Even my aunts can't cast such a spell. You are insane."

She reaches into her coat and produces a strange item from an interior pocket. After poking it with her finger several times, she offers me the rectangular object. "Look at this."

I snatch the object from her. "This is an extraordinarily detailed rendering. It seems to have been painted on smooth stone that's very thin."

"That is not a painting. It's a photograph taken by a smartphone. But the part I wanted you to notice was the background."

I squint at the wee painting. "I see nothing."

"Look closely." She points at something. "That's a gravestone."

"Aye, that I can see."

She holds her thumb and forefinger in a pinching gesture and touches them to the painting, then spreads them wide. "Read the name on it."

The rendering had grown larger when she touched it. This is some variety of magics, but ne'er have I seen anything like it before. When I at last read the words in the painting, I feel my brows cinch together. "What am I meant to glean from this? You created a painting with my name in it."

"It's not a painting."

I hand the rectangular stone back to her. "Away, wench. You are a demon's mistress, for only the spawn of Satan would create such a thing."

When I resume walking, increasing my pace in the hopes she will not follow, my hopes are dashed. The lass catches up to me and maintains an equal pace despite breathing harder. "I'm from the future, jackass. But even if you refuse to believe that, you know your aunts brought me here. That means I can't go home. I'm stranded at Dùndubhan."

As we reach the gatehouse doors, my aunts emerge from the courtyard. Lachina shouts, "Kieran! Dinnae send her away. The poor lass needs our help, and the spirits chose her for you."

"Haud yer wheesht, Lachina," I snarl. "You three orchestrated this event without my permission."

I thrust an arm out to prevent the wench from going any further. "Remain here. I will return once I have discussed the matter with my aunts."

"Yeah, whatever. And my name is Alyssa Vescovi, not 'wench.' If you call me that again, I really will castrate you."

I grunt and stalk to the other side of the compound, far from the vexing woman, with my aunts in tow. "You summoned that lass, now send her back to whence she came."

My aunts exchange glances, then Morna speaks. "We can't, *gràidh*."

"Of course you can."

"Nay, we cannot. Once the spell was cast, nothing could reverse it." She pats my arm. "You need a wife, Kieran. Our spell was conceived out of love for you, and we asked the spirits to send you a woman who would fulfill your every need and desire. Dinnae send Alyssa away. Give her a chance."

"What sort of name is 'Alyssa'? Never have I heard its like before."

"Mayhap she tells the truth," Efrica says. "She was transported here from a world yet unseen that exists in the future."

Lachina clasps my hand. "We beg you, Kieran. Give the lass a chance. She has been banished in a way not dissimilar to how you were."

I groan and rub my eyes. "As you wish."

Efrica whirls about and cups her hands around her mouth. "Come hither, lass! You are not banished, Alyssa. The laird of Dùndubhan bids you to stay."

Though I did not bid the woman to stay, I see no value in arguing with my aunt. I said the lass can stay, not that I invited her to do so. Does the slight difference matter? Either way, I am doomed to host a strange woman in my domain.

Alyssa approaches me with her arms crossed. "I suppose you expect me to thank you."

"I expect you to behave like a proper lady. No more cursing at me."

She squints her eyes and flattens her lips. "You don't own me."

Mayhap I wish I did because then I could order the lass to do what I say without arguments. The thought also arouses me.

Alyssa continues to stand there wearing that haughty expression.

I seize her arm and drag her to me. "You are my property now. The moment you set foot in Dùndubhan, you lost all rights to self-governance, because this is my castle and my land. You will obey the laird."

"Go to hell, Cro-Magnon."

Whatever that means, I don't care to ask her. I grip her arm more tightly. "If you wish to leave Dùndubhan, you may do so. But another laird will claim you, and I doubt he will treat you as well as I would."

"Please. I'd do better with a dog than you."

I release her. "Leave this place, then. But do not return and beg me to allow you back into my home."

She spins on her heels and marches toward the open gates. There, she halts. For a moment, mayhap two, she does not move except to tap her fingers on her thighs. Then, the wench glances back at me once and marches off down the path to nowhere. I know to where that path leads, but she does not. By God's bones, the woman is stubborn.

"What will you do now, Kieran?" Morna asks. "You've driven the poor lass away. She will starve at best or be defiled by the first foul man who meets her. Even you haven't sunk low enough to send a woman out into the world alone."

"Dinnae question my decisions," I snarl. "You brought her to Dùndubhan. If you want to save her, summon her back from whence she came."

Efrica lifts her chin. "We will leave you to consider your actions. But if you make the wrong decision, you won't be welcome at Dùndubhan any longer."

My aunts march into the castle single file, heads held high, refusing to look back at me. The last one to enter the house, Morna, slams the door so powerfully that the harsh sound echoes in the courtyard.

I try to walk toward the door, to go inside and forget about that unwanted guest. But my feet refuse to move. This is nonsense. I have the ability to move my feet. I can't be hesitating because I feel...guilt over what I've done to Alyssa. She speaks like no other woman I have ever met, in her accent or in the words she chooses. Mayhap she is—No. I do not need or want a woman who was conjured by my aunts. I am the laird. No one contradicts my edicts.

Alyssa has long, bonnie hair in a shade of auburn like none I have seen and eyes as blue as a sapphire from India that I'd seen once during my travels. The shape of her body makes my cock ache. I have never seen a woman with hips that seem designed to drive a man mad, and her breasts make my mouth water from thoughts of what she might look like naked. Aye, I want to fuck her. But I have enough problems without complicating my life further simply to appease my lust.

Yet I've gone too long without a woman. What if resisting the urge proves too much for me? If I take her as my wife, then mayhap... No, I cannot do that.

Movement at the casement on the second floor draws my attention there. Though I can't see them well, I know the shapes hovering behind the glass panes belong to my aunts. One of them opens the casement and thrusts her hand out, showing me her middle finger.

That must have been Morna.

Mhac na galla. They will not leave me be, and I abruptly realize they've been right all along. I am the one who needs to repent. So I stomp out of the courtyard and break into a sprint as I head down the trail.

Chapter Four

Alyssa

The rat bastard booted me out of his precious castle, which quite frankly, doesn't look like much in the sixteenth century. The version of Dùndubhan I'd seen in the twenty-first century was beautiful and majestic and didn't smell like something died in the cellar. Kieran treated me like dirt, so I say good riddance. He can frown and glower and growl at somebody else. I don't know how his aunts can put up with the man. They seem like nice ladies, but I guess somebody had to watch over the cretin so he wouldn't tear the castle down when he had a hissy fit.

But damn, I can't deny he's hot. How did a sixteenth-century man get as ripped as a modern bodybuilder? He must lift a lot of cabers or toss a lot of women over his shoulder. Since I had to stare at his calves for what felt like hours but was probably ten minutes, I got a good look at those muscles. Thick. Powerful. Impressive. Don't even get me started on his biceps. He also has the most beautiful golden-brown eyes I've ever seen and gorgeous hair the color of sinfully dark chocolate streaked with golden highlights. Okay, yeah, I might not mind getting it on with Kieran, except that he's such a jerk.

As I stop and turn in a circle, I try to figure out where I am. Away from Dùndubhan, that's all I know. He ordered me to "leave this place." *Thanks a lot, Cro-Magnon.* Do medieval people know about Cro-Magnons? Not sure when that term was first used. Well, if Kieran didn't understand what I said, good. Serves him right.

When did I revert to behaving like a twelve-year-old? That man drives me crazy, but I'm too old to react this way.

I glance down at my jeans and realize I've got splotches of dirt on them, probably from when Kieran tossed me onto the ground face-down. I start picking at the caked-on grime.

"*Madainn mhath, bòidheach boireannach.*"

The unfamiliar voice makes me straighten and stare at the man who stands no more than a dozen feet from me. Whatever he said, it didn't sound like English. How did he sneak up like that? Well, I had been engrossed in cleaning off my jeans.

I clear my throat. "Do you speak English?"

"Aye, I do." He has fiery red hair but tanned skin, which I assume comes from spending a lot of time outdoors. The man wears a kilt with a shirt too, unlike shirtless Kieran. "I am Simidh Gunn."

Should I tell him my name? That seems like a bad idea. My first encounter with a medieval Scot hadn't gone so well.

I guess I've accepted that I'm in the past. How bizarre.

"What is your name, lass?" Simidh Gunn asks.

"Um…"

Footfalls pound behind me, and I whirl around to see who's coming up the trail. Kieran pushes past me to place his body between me and Simidh Gunn.

"Stay away from her," Kieran snarls. "She belongs to me."

"Is that true?" Gunn asks, leaning sideways to see me. "A woman walking alone would seem to have no ties. Or she is exceedingly foolish. Mayhap both."

"Haud yer wheesht, Simidh." Kieran backs up until his backside is flush with my front. "I have claimed this woman."

Earlier when he announced that I belong to him, I'd wanted to smack him hard. But I don't mind him saying it now because I get a wriggly feeling in my gut whenever Simidh Gunn looks at me with lustful intent. I might be reading too much into his expression, but I don't think so. When he licks his lips while staring hungrily at my body, that wriggly feeling turns into a sensation like a hundred worms burrowing into my soul.

"Let's go home, Kieran."

He glances down at me without bowing his head, and surprise flickers in his eyes briefly. Yeah, I can't believe I said that either. I've wanted to escape from Kieran since the moment I met him. This is a special circumstance, though, and I will get away from the laird of Dùndubhan somehow.

Simidh Gunn smirks. "You cannot keep her forever, MacTaggart. If I want her, she will be mine eventually."

Kieran snarls something that I don't understand, which probably means it's Gaelic. Based on his tone, I think he must be cursing like a drunken sailor. Then he sweeps me up in his arms, though he doesn't fling me over his shoulder this time, and stalks back up the path to the castle. Over his shoulder, I can see Gunn still standing there while a breeze flutters his shoulder-length red hair. The intensity of his focus on me sends a shiver rattling up my spine. Who is he? What is he? I need to get away from him, that's all I know for sure.

The Laird of Dùndubhan sets me down and lowers the massive metal grille, which I think is called a portcullis. Once he has finished that task, he pushes the huge wooden doors closed one by one. Then he drops a thick wooden cross-bar into a slot that essentially locks the horizontal piece in place. His biceps had flexed with every movement, and his jaw remains firmly set. I'd noticed earlier that both halves of the wooden doors are at least as thick as my skull and feature layers of vertical and horizontal boards. I guess that must make the structure harder to breach.

Kieran seizes my wrist and drags me into the house, though "house" doesn't seem like the right way to describe this castle. I can't make myself keep calling it that. It's too weird. I'm in a castle. With a nasty "laird." The entryway is taken up mostly by a big spiral staircase fashioned from stone with no hand-rails and a utilitarian design. A chilly draft wafts through the space.

Yeah, I wish I were trapped in the modern version of Dùndubhan. At least that incarnation had a nice staircase and insulation, not to mention electric lights and hot water.

My captor gives me a shove toward the stairs. "Walk."

"Why don't you go first? I'm not sure where you want me to turn."

"Follow the steps until I tell you to stop."

I hike up the steps with the jerk following two paces behind me. My thighs have started to ache by the time we reach the second floor, which I assume is what I should call it since that's how Rory and Emery had told me I should refer to the levels in this structure. The second floor is actually the third level. But we don't stop there. I glance back at Kieran, who gives my ass a shove.

We're going to the top floor, apparently.

"Halt," Kieran says. "This is our destination."

"But we're in between floors."

"Aye. And this is where you shall remain."

He digs a keyring out of a hidden pocket in his kilt and shoves a big skeleton key into the wall. When he twists the key, a thunk indicates he has unlocked something. Kieran returns the key to his pocket and places both hands on the stone wall, then gives it a shove. A rectangular section swings open. The grinding of stone on stone sends vibrations through the stairs beneath my feet.

Kieran raises an arm toward the now-revealed doorway. "Your quarters."

I peek around the door—and my stomach drops. What do I see? A bare stone room with no rugs, furnished with only an equally bare wood bed frame and flimsy-looking mattress. A tiny window positioned high on the wall allows a meager amount of light into the space. Beside the bed, I see a brown ceramic bowl.

"What is this room?" I ask. "You can't be expecting me to sleep here."

"Nay." He lays a hand on my back, giving me a slight push to force me to enter the room. "This is your home until I decide what to do with you."

"You mean I'll sleep here. In the daytime, I'd rather be outside as much as possible."

He shakes his head. "You shall remain in this room at all times. My aunts will provide food for you."

"What if need to, you know, relieve myself?"

"Sleep if you are tired."

"No, I meant—Ugh. What if I need to empty my bowels or bladder? Do you at least understand what those words mean? Probably not."

"Of course I understand 'bowel' and 'bladder.' Everyone comprehends the terms for such organs and their bodily functions. But you spoke of relieving yourself, which I assumed meant you want to sleep."

Now that I've at least figured out what he calls the need to relieve oneself, I have to get an answer from him. "So tell me, what should I do when I need to empty my bowels or bladder?"

He waves toward the general area of the bed, where it meets the wall. "Use that."

"Uh, what? I'm not doing that on the floor."

Kieran scowls and stomps over to the bed. He picks up the brown ceramic bowl that had lain on the floor and thrusts it in my direction. "Piss and shit in this container."

A chamber pot? That's what the ceramic bowl is for? Oh, hell no. I cannot squat over a little brown pot.

"What then?" I ask. "After I relieve myself in that pot, what am I supposed to do with the, um, contents of it?"

"Discard them by throwing everything out the window."

I march over to the tiny window that lies several inches above my head. And I gape at him. "You have got to be kidding me. I can barely reach that window. If I try to dump the contents of that pot out here"—I stretch as far up as I can, raising onto my tiptoes—"it'll fall onto my head."

He shrugs one shoulder. "Not my concern."

The laird of Dùndubhan saunters out of the room and shuts the door. I hear a click as he locks it.

I clench my fists and my jaw. That bastard. He left me here in this lovely little prison cell. I clomp over to the bed and drop onto the mattress. The frame creaks. Something stabs into my bottom. Several somethings. I get up and study the spot where I'd sat down, noticing strands of...straw. They stick out of the rough fabric that makes up the mattress. That's what poked me. *Oh, great.* I get to live in a crappy cell in a dingy old castle, and I have to use a window I can barely reach as my toilet.

Maybe I can climb out the window. It's not very big, but I might be able to squeeze through the opening. Then what? I'd need to climb down the side of the castle. From outside, it looked like a sheer drop with no hand-holds or footholds. I'd probably tumble out the window and go splat in the courtyard.

What year is this, anyway? The gravestone I'd seen in the MacTaggart clan cemetery stated that Kieran died in fifteen ninety-eight. He's alive and healthy right now. Too damn healthy. I wish he'd contract a terrible dis-ease and kick the bucket today. No, I don't really wish that. He might be a monumental jackass, but I could never wish for another person to die, despite what I said earlier.

Efrica had claimed that her nephew "bid" me to stay. But he clearly wants me gone—or at least trapped in this crummy room.

Shouts erupt outside in the courtyard. More than one person is hollering out there, but I can't understand the words.

I rush over to the wall below the window. Still can't hear what they're saying. If it's Gaelic, I really won't be able to tell. I grab the chamber pot and stand on it. That gives me just enough extra height that I can grip the lower edge of the window with both hands and raise onto my tiptoes to see what's going on in the courtyard. The words I hear make no sense, but their actions are clear.

Kieran's three aunts are giving him a good reaming. I see lots of finger-stabbing, hand-waving, chest-smacking, foot-stomping, and many other types of angry gesturing. To my utter shock, though, Kieran seems cowed by his aunts. He bows his head, and his shoulders slump.

Efrica grasps his face and tells him something that makes the jerk grip the back of his head, bowing it even more. Then she kisses the top of his head. She smiles with obvious affection and ruffles his hair. I take that to mean she forgives him because he admitted he screwed up and apologized to his aunts.

Damn, those ladies are amazing.

Morna starts talking, and Kieran nods in agreement.

The chamber pot I'm balanced on suddenly shatters. I let out a sharp cry as I tumble to the hard floor. A pain stabs through my hip. I wince and struggle to get up, with all the shards of the chamber pot crushed beneath me. Is this really my life now? Trapped in a castle with a jackass. An alien living among medieval people who speak a different language and have strange customs. I might as well have landed on Mars.

I sniffle, struggling not to cry. But tears sting my eyes, and my throat constricts. No, no, no, I will not cry. When I suck in a breath, it's ragged. And I can't fight the tears anymore. They stream down my cheeks while I sob and fall into a human puddle on the floor.

The door is thrown open.

And Kieran glowers at me.

Chapter Five

Kieran

Mhac na galla. The lass is lying on the floor, sobbing and hiccuping, surrounded by shards of what seems to be the chamber pot. By God's bones, what is the woman trying to do to me? I will not feel empathy for her. She burst into my life without warning, without my consent, and I refuse to have anything to do with her. Yet here I am, hovering just inside the door to her chamber. I ran here because I heard a commotion that originated in her room.

Alyssa tries to sit up, but her arms give out and she slumps onto the floor again. Her sobbing seems to have escalated.

Bod an Donais. I trudge over to the lass and push my arms beneath hers to lift her onto her feet. Her knees nearly buckle, so I hug her to me—strictly to prevent her from falling. Mayhap her body does feel warm and supple pressed against me, but that has no bearing on the situation. When she gazes up at me with tear-filled eyes, I feel as if I'm the worst bastard on earth. I am that, aren't I? Alyssa arrived here against her will, thanks to my aunts. She did not choose to be sent here any more than I chose to bring her to this place. I instinctively brush hair away from her face. She gazes up at me with bleary red eyes. I swallow hard, but the tightness in my throat refuses to abate.

I clear my throat. "I, ah, apologize for my behavior."

"Which time? You've been a jerk since the moment we met."

"Aye. But I have my reasons for that."

"I'm listening." She almost smiles. "That means I want you to explain."

"Whatever my aunts might believe, I do not wish to marry. They should not have summoned you here, but I should never have treated you so...discourteously."

"That's putting it mildly."

"However, that does not negate the fact that you are under my aegis now, which means that you, in essence, belong to me."

She rolls her eyes. "Will you ever get over the ownership bullshit? I don't belong to anyone."

"In my world, you do."

Alyssa tips her head to the side, staring intently at me. "What year is this?"

"Fifteen hundred and ninety-eight."

Her eyes widen. "Oh. Well, that does explain a few things."

"From what time do you come?"

"The twenty-first century."

Now it's my turn to gape at her. "That is more than four hundred years into the future."

"Yeah, no kidding. Don't women in this time know how to do math? Maybe all men are like you, and they don't want women to think. We're just supposed to spread our legs and let you jerks use our bodies."

"Nay, I do not behave in such a manner."

"But you keep saying I'm your property. That means you believe my body belongs to you, which means you'll fuck me whether I want it or not."

I clench my fists tightly enough to cause pain. "Believe what you like. The fact remains that you cannot leave this place. Simidh Gunn has seen you, and he will believe you are my betrothed or at least my whore. That which I have, he wishes to take away."

"I don't belong to either of you."

"*Daingead*. For once, might you cease harassing me?"

"I might, if you answer a few questions for me."

The woman has left me no choice. Snarling at Alyssa and treating her like my chattel has accomplished nothing. I exhale a long sigh. "Come, sit with me on the bed."

She makes no complaints but simply follows me to the foot of the bed. We both sit down on the uneven mattress.

"Ask your questions, Alyssa."

"Why do you live in this dilapidated old castle with only your three aunts? Shouldn't a laird have his entire clan with him?"

"A laird isn't the leader of the clan." I resist the impulse to bow my head in shame, though I deserve to have shame heaped upon me. "And I am longer wanted by the rest of the MacTaggarts. They have...banished me."

"Why would they do that?"

"Because they believe I stole from members of my own clan. My father didn't want to banish me. I know this, and I don't blame him for what happened. Simidh Gunn gathered evidence that supposedly proved my guilt. I wasn't able to refute the false evidence. My father had no choice but to banish me for the good of the clan."

"That's horrible. Did your father send you to this castle?"

"Nay. As the chief of our clan, he couldn't aid me in any manner. But I knew my aunts had been living in an old castle, and so I sought them out."

Alyssa no longer seems angry or hurt. She watches me with a neutral expression. "Were your aunts banished too?"

"They left of their own volition. Lachina could never marry because her gift is deemed to be a curse by most folk. Morna's husband died, and she never wished to wed again. Efrica's husband and son were both killed during a skirmish with a rival clan, and she preferred to live in solitude after that."

"How long have you lived here?"

"Ever since my banishment four years ago. My aunts were already living here at Dùndubhan." I glance at her, moving only my eyes. "Why do you not seem aggrieved? You have been torn away from your own life without warning."

"My life back home wasn't so great. I do worry about my parents, but hopefully, I can find a way home before they realize anything happened."

"What if there is no way home?"

She sets her hands on her thighs and rolls her shoulders back. "I'll survive, and so will my parents. Grief doesn't last forever, though the scars it leaves behind can."

"You speak as if you have experience with grief."

The lass clasps her hands on her lap, her head bowed. "Yeah, I've got experience."

"I have no desire to fash you any further. But I will do whatever I must to protect my aunts, this castle, and my clan—even though the other MacTaggarts don't want me."

She lifts her head to look at me. "Is your father still alive?"

"Aye, as far as I know."

"Don't you ever sneak back home to see what's going on there?"

I scratch the back of my neck, avoiding her gaze. "Mayhap I do, on occasion. But I cannot speak to my father, and he cannot speak to me. It would weaken his position as chief of the clan. Banishment requires a complete severing of all relationships."

"At least you have your aunts. They clearly love you." She bumps her shoulder into mine. "And they definitely keep you in line."

"Did you hear my altercation with them earlier?"

"Yep. That's how I fell down. I was standing on the chamber pot to get a better look because I heard the commotion down there."

"My aunts are headstrong, but I've been told that I am as well."

"Really? I never would have guessed."

She seems to be mocking me in a playful manner. Her attitude toward me couldn't have changed so swiftly. Could it? I was once quite skilled at seducing lasses, but I never did well at romancing them. I had no need of such skills, considering that few couples wed out of love. It's a practical arrangement, nothing more.

For reasons I cannot fathom, I confess the truth to her. "My father tried several times to arrange a marriage for me, but I rejected every attempt."

"Why? Don't you want to have children?"

"Aye. But clan marriages are not borne of love. They're arrangements designed to strengthen alliances. A man may set aside his wife if he desires a better alliance."

"What? That's disgusting. Scotsmen throw away their wives to get a better deal?"

"I agree it's distasteful. But this is the way it has been for as long as anyone can remember."

"Well, I'm glad you didn't go for a scummy arrangement like that."

But I intend to do precisely that. The fragile peace I seem to have brokered with her will shatter the moment I explain my plan. "We must wed, Alyssa. It's the only way to ensure Simidh Gunn cannot take you for his own. Once you belong to me, fully and completely, he will have no recourse, unless he murders me."

"We've had this talk already. I don't belong to you."

"But you need to do so. As my wife, you will be protected from other men who might try to claim you."

She leaps up. "I am not marrying you. Until five minutes ago, you were acting like a total caveman."

I leap up as well. "You are behaving in a childish and irrational manner."

"Me? You're the jackass who threw me over his shoulder and wanted to toss me out like garbage." She jabs a finger into my chest. "I made one horrible mistake, and I will never do that again."

What horrible mistake did she make? I can't ask her because I'm too incensed to think properly. My gaze drops to her chest and the tantalizing amount of cleavage exposed by her shirt. She wears braies like a man, and that has the bizarre effect of sending all the blood in my body down to my *slat*. I've begun to breathe harder, my chest heaving—just like hers. Those breasts… I've never wanted to devour a woman more than right now.

I pull her into my body and lash my arms around the lass. Then I kiss her.

The entire world seems to stop. We gaze into each other's eyes while our lips remain fused and time seems to come to a halt, awaiting the inevitable moment. My heart beats swiftly and powerfully. Then Alyssa closes her eyes, and I know we are both lost. I crush her to me and plunge my tongue between her lips.

By God's bones, the taste of her… It's like nothing I've ever experienced. A thrill ripples through me from head to toe while I slide my palms down to her erse and squeeze those cheeks. She moans into my mouth. I rock my hips into her, rubbing my stiffening cock against her belly.

Alyssa wriggles out of my grasp and stumbles away from me.

The loss of her body heat causes my eyes to open. I still can't quite catch my breath, and I stare at the lass with what must appear to be a blank expression. I have not kissed a woman since before my banishment, much less fucked one. As desperately as I want to take her body, I cannot do that.

Not unless she becomes my wife.

Alyssa straightens her clothing and pats her hair in what seems like a nervous gesture. Then she squares her shoulders and clears her throat. "Don't ever kiss me again."

"You enjoyed it, and you want me to fuck you."

"Like hell I do." She points toward the door. "Get out. Now."

"When I leave, you will be locked inside this room."

"Don't care. I'd rather be trapped in here alone than be free and stuck with you."

My cock wants me to sink it into her flesh, but instead, I turn and walk out the door, slamming it behind me. I haven't caught my breath yet. With my hands tightly fisted, I stand in the hallway while I wait for my pulse and my breathing to calm. The memory of Simidh Gunn finding Alyssa on the path, alone, flashes through my mind. He would force her to marry him. And therefore I should coerce Alyssa into a marriage with me? No, I refuse to become like my enemy.

I stalk down the steps, intending to go outside, but my aunts waylay me at the bottom of the stair.

Efrica gives me her sternest look, the one that terrified me when I was a wee laddie because it meant she was angry with me. But I am a man now, and no woman will ever order me about again.

"Out of my way, woman," I snarl.

She does not move. "I know you've been without a wife for your entire life, but that is no excuse for your behavior. We summoned Alyssa because you need her. She is the mate our ancestors have chosen for you. Treat her well, and she will save your soul."

"Aye," Morna agrees. "But if you hurt her, 'twill be your undoing."

Lachina hands me the necklace they had given to Alyssa, the one I tore from her neck. "Return this to the lass. 'Twill be a gesture of good faith."

I snatch the necklace from her. "If I choose to give this to Alyssa, it will be my decision and mine alone."

Before my aunts can chastise me further, I storm outside and into the courtyard, not stopping until I reach the old bakehouse. No one bakes breads or anything else in here, not anymore. They haven't done so at Dùndubhan for as long as I have lived and probably longer than that. Only my aunts had lived here until I joined them. Their decade of voluntarily isolation had ended once I was banished and had no choice but to find safe harbor with them. Aye, I'm grateful they took me in. But nay, I am not grateful for the woman they conspired to bring here.

With nothing else to do, I wander about the courtyard as if I intend to do something. What? I haven't a clue. Dùndubhan, in its heyday, had been a utilitarian fortress. It was never designed to become a home for wayward women. I shall never spare a thought for that. I cannot. Lasses who decide to live in an abandoned fortress have no right to complain about it.

My aunts have never complained. But Alyssa has.

Which does not bother me.

As I survey the castle, I notice areas that are in need of repairs. Whilst I effect those repairs, mayhap I could create something for the lasses. For my aunts, not that infernal woman who wears braies. One section of the courtyard looks as if it could be fertile ground for a garden. My aunts would enjoy that. But where would I acquire seeds? Mayhap in the areas outside of the compound, such as the mountain behind Dùndubhan. Beann Dealgach has a craggy peak, yet its lower portions offer much vegetation. I might find what I need to start a garden on those slopes.

For my aunts. No one else.

But I have no time for frivolities such as a garden. With Simidh Gunn out there, I must reinforce the castle first. I have long neglected it.

And now my enemy is at the gates.

Chapter Six

Alyssa

I need to get out of my lovely little cell. Since I don't have thirty feet of hair to unroll out the window, like Rapunzel, I'll need to get creative. Maybe I can attract the attention of Kieran's aunts somehow. They like me. One of them might break me out of this prison. I can't believe I let that jerk French kiss me. Damn, I should've kneed him in the groin and run out the door. Instead, I kissed him back. Okay, maybe I loved the way he slipped his tongue into my mouth and drove me wild with every languid swipe. Maybe I even kind of wanted him to rip my clothes off and fuck me on the crappy straw mattress.

No, I absolutely did not.

Yeah, okay, I did want that. But never again. If that jerk deigns to enter my prison cell, I will grab his balls and twist as hard as I can.

My breasts still feel achy and sensitive, and the wetness that had blossomed between my thighs while Kieran kissed me hasn't gone away either. I can't help that I want him. Doesn't mean I like the man. He's evil.

So, I'm back to plotting my escape.

The distinctive sound of a key opening a lock echoes through my high-ceilinged prison cell. Efrica MacTaggart walks in, leaving the door partway open.

She approaches my bed and holds out the necklace Kieran had ripped away from me. Efrica says something that must be Gaelic, then slaps the pendant onto my palm and closes my fingers around it. "You will need this, dearie. The triquetra will protect you from whatever might come, and 'twill let you understand Gaelic."

"Yeah, I remember that part. What do I need protecting from? Your nephew is the only one treating me like an enemy."

"Kieran is conflicted. His banishment involved more than Simidh's false claims of thievery, but 'tis not my place to share his story."

"I know he's your nephew, but that man makes me so angry. I want to punch him."

She smiles with motherly knowing. "The most powerful loves often arise from disagreements."

"Yeah, sure, whatever."

Efrica tips her head to the side as if she's studying me. "How old are you, dearie? You seem more mature than most young women."

"I'm not that young. I turned forty a week before I wound up here. So if you're expecting me to give Kieran a child, that's unlikely to happen." Even if I wanted to have sex with him, I won't do it because I will not bring a child into the world under these circumstances. But Efrica doesn't need to know that. "I'm too old. That means you picked the wrong woman to be your nephew's wife."

"Fiddlesticks. I've seen women of more advanced age than you give birth to healthy children."

"But did the mother survive?"

"Aye, most of the time.""

Oh yes, that's very comforting.

"Kieran is thirty-five years past his birth," Efrica says. "I adore the laddie, but he needs discipline. An older woman could provide that."

Medieval mothers in their forties have survived childbirth "most of the time." That's what she said. Life is much harsher in this century than in the one I came from. But that doesn't matter because I will never have sex with Kieran.

"Come outside with me, *gràidh*." Efrica squeezes my hand. "You need fresh air and sunshine."

"Is the sun actually out now? I thought Scotland was always cloudy."

"Aye, it can often be that way. But it's a bonnie land, and I know you will come to love it as we do."

"Maybe." I glance around my oh-so-cheerful accommodations. "I would love to go outside with you, Efrica."

"Wonderful." She clasps her hands under her chin and smiles, the expression carving out dimples in her cheeks. "I will show you the grounds while we chat about whatever we like. Kieran calls it 'wasteful nonsense,' but then, he isn't the sort who prattles."

"Yeah, he doesn't seem like the talkative type."

Efrica leads me downstairs and out the stairwell door. Clouds cover the sky, muting the daylight. Just as we step out into the courtyard, I notice Kieran standing near the rear wall of the compound, not far from the bakehouse. He kicks at the dirt with the toe of his boot, seemingly deep in contemplation. Though I try to veer us away from that area, Efrica hooks her arm around mine and urges me to go with her—toward Kieran. I really don't want to see him right now. Besides, he will undoubtedly be livid that Efrica released me from my jail cell.

As we approach Kieran, he finally notices us and straightens, maintaining a neutral expression even when we stop a few feet away from him.

"Ye can't keep the poor lass locked away," Efrica says. "She is not a criminal, *gràidh*."

"Thus, you freed her without my permission."

"Aye. And I'll do it again if you insist on imprisoning her. Morna and Lachina feel the same. So unless you mean to lock us all up, you will stop treating Alyssa like your enemy."

I love this woman so much.

Kieran squints at her, but she pays no attention to that. Then his gaze drops to my hand. To the pendant I'm still holding, and the chain attached to it that dangles from my fingers. He rips the necklace out of my hand, brandishing it at Efrica while shouting in what must be Gaelic. I can't understand it since he stole my translation device. His aunts gave it to me. The necklace does not belong to him any more than I do.

So I yank the necklace out of his hand. Before he can try to reclaim it, I have the chain draped around my neck with the pendant hanging down between my breasts.

He squints at my chest. His lips flatten. He reaches for the pendant and...

Efrica slaps him.

Holy shit, I love that woman even more now. Whoever said women in medieval times were meek and subservient never met a Scotswoman.

Kieran's eyes have gone wide, and he stays frozen for several seconds. Then the jerk pulls his hand away, clearly abandoning the idea of stealing my necklace.

Efrica plants her hands on her hips and gives him a look of stern, motherly disapproval.

"I need to effect repairs," he says. "With Simidh out there, I need to make certain our fortifications can withstand an assault."

"Do you really think there will be an assault?" I ask.

"Mayhap there will be. Or mayhap there will not."

"Thanks for the crystal-clear answer."

He stomps away.

"Give the lad time," Efrica says. "He has no idea how to deal with a strong lass."

"No shit. I think you might've picked the wrong woman to summon."

"Oh nay, you are the right one." She winks. "I trust Lachina's *da-shealladh*. It never leads us astray."

"Her da-what?"

"*Da-shealladh*. It means the Two Sights. Lachina has insight into this world and that of the spirits. Our ancestors guide her, and that's how you came to be here." She gives me a quick, firm hug. "We know you are the one who will save Kieran from himself."

What if I don't want to save him? I tried to save a man once before, and it ruined my life.

At least now I know what Kieran meant by "Lachina's gift."

Efrica starts talking again, telling me about the castle and what it was like living here with only her two sisters for ten years before Kieran came. I can tell she honestly loves him and believes he's a good man, but I've seen very little that suggests he will treat me any better than my husband did. Still, Efrica is a smart and honest woman. I can't believe she would tell me Kieran is good if he's actually a bastard at his core.

Should I cut him some slack? Not sure.

Our stroll around the compound gives me plenty of time to watch Kieran. I half-listen to what Efrica says, but not because her chatter is boring. I just can't stay focused on what she says because I keep getting glimpses of Kieran. He seems to be shoring up a corner of the wall, and the strip of his kilt that he used as a sash has fallen away from his chest. Sweat glistens on his upper body. His muscles flex as he works, and when he wipes his brow with the back of his hand, he also leans back to stretch his arms above his head.

Damn, he has an incredible body. And yes, he knows how to kiss. But he also knows how to scramble my brain so much that I might do something stupid like rip his kilt off to mount him right here in the courtyard. For all I know, he put a spell on me with his lips to make me want him.

"Did ye hear me, Alyssa?"

Efrica's voice yanks my attention back to her. She smiles knowingly. "Kieran is quite a fetching man, aye?"

"He's a Neanderthal. Don't get any ideas in your head about me and Kieran getting married."

"Would you rather become the bride of Simidh Gunn?"

"Of course not. He gives me the creeps. But I shouldn't have to choose between a satanic lech or a total jerk. I do not want to get married at all."

"Let's go into the solar. It has the best view of the courtyard."

If she's taking me to the "solar" because she knows I'll have a great view of half-naked Kieran and that will make me swoon for him, she had better prepare for a big disappointment. I might have casually admired his body a moment ago, but I do not want to screw him.

What the heck is a "solar," anyway?

Efrica and I head back into the castle, which she refers to as "the house." Though I had thought of the castle that way earlier, calling a giant stone structure a house still feels like a severe understatement. It's a fortress, for sure. But it's not what I could call a home. Bare stone floors. Bare stone walls. Straw for a mattress. Yeah, that's not homey. But I get that I'm now living in the sixteenth century where things aren't as plush and luxurious here as back at my apartment in the twenty-first century. I need to lower my expectations.

The solar turns out to be a rather cozy space of the type I would call a living room. Kieran's aunts must have decorated this room because it does not seem like the sort of decor he would choose. No, the rat bastard would want weapons hanging on every wall, plus a few bear skins with the heads attached and probably a rickety wooden chair to sit on. But the solar is nothing like that.

Flames flicker within the stone hearth, and a small pile of wood sits nearby. A bench with a padded seat stands against the wall while two chairs positioned near the tall windows seem to have padding too. A couple more chairs flank the hearth. I don't see any curtains, but there is a woven rug that covers a large area in the middle of the room. Candles in metal holders sit on the mantel, though the wicks aren't lit.

"This is nice," I say. "I love the rug."

"Kieran thought we were off our heads to weave a rug of that size. But once he saw it, he agreed it was just what the room needed."

"You ladies are true artisans."

"Nay. We simply enjoy making beautiful things."

When I move to sit on the bench, Efrica shoos me away from it. Instead, she guides me to one of the chairs by the window. She takes the one opposite mine. I've just settled in and started to relax when movement outside catches my eye.

Kieran is striding across the courtyard while carrying wooden poles, one on each shoulder. His kilt hangs so low over his hips that it seems like it's about to fall off.

I give Efrica my sternest look. "You did this on purpose."

"What, dearie?" she says with too much innocence.

"You know what I mean." I point out the window. "You told me to sit here because you knew I'd have a great view of your nephew."

"Is Kieran still out there?" She leans forward to peer out the window. "Oh aye, there he is. What a coincidence."

"Yeah, sure, it was purely by accident that you put me in this chair."

She pats my knee. "Dinnae be angry. We love our nephew, and we've come to love you too, even after knowing you for such a short time. If we try to guide you and Kieran toward each other, it's only because we want you both to be happy."

"Uh-huh. Can you dial back the matchmaking and let us decide for ourselves if we want to get married?" I absolutely do not want that, but I know Efrica and her sisters are honestly trying to do something good. They're misguided, that's all.

Kieran has no excuse for his behavior.

More movement spurs me to glance out the window. Now Kieran is carrying large chunks of stone on his shoulders. And that kilt has slid even lower. If it slipped a teeny bit further, I could get a glimpse of his dick. Not that I want to see it. Even if he has a big, thick rod, I still won't screw him. No, never.

I mean it. Never.

But then Kieran's kilt falls off, and I know I'm doomed.

Chapter Seven

Kieran

Magairlean. My kilt just came undone and slumped onto the ground. How did that happen? I haven't been concerned with my clothing because only my aunts ever see me. They pay no heed if my kilt falls out of place. I used to take great care that I secured my plaid with belt loops hidden inside it, but I'd grown rather lax in such matters. My aunts have ignored my behavior, except when Efrica called me a heathen a few times. She said that with a sigh and a slight smile, so I assumed she had no genuine objections.

Mayhap I should strive to be more careful now that Alyssa is here.

I gather up my kilt and attempt to reassemble it. That's when I finally discover the reason that my clothing fell to the ground. Two of the loops are torn, probably because I work hard and rarely examine my clothing. The one remaining loop could not hold the garment in place. I can't fix that here in the courtyard. I'll need to go inside and ask one of my aunts to mend the kilt.

Slinging the plaid over my shoulder, I walk into the castle and pause at the bottom of the stair. The kilt has fallen off my shoulder. While I attempt to gather it into a lump and tuck it under my arm, footfalls echo from elsewhere in the house.

"Oh, shit!"

I spin toward the lass who had spoken.

Alyssa covers her eyes with her hands. Most of her face is covered too, leaving only her mouth exposed. "Why are you naked?"

"Because I dropped my kilt. That's obvious, aye?"

"Uh, yes. But I meant why aren't you wearing your kilt?"

I grumble out a sigh. "The loops are worn and can't hold the fabric up any longer. My aunts will repair the kilt."

"And you're, um, going to walk around naked until then?"

Before this moment, I'd been too preoccupied with trying to rid myself of the lass to pay heed to her manner of speaking. But no longer. "You are French or German, aye?"

"What? No."

"Then from which nation do you hail?"

"No one has ever asked me where I 'hail' from before. I'm American."

I blow out a sigh. "Remove your hands from your face."

"Not if you're still naked."

My grumbling becomes a growl. "Lower your hands, woman, or I will do it for you."

Alyssa peels her palms away from her face but keeps her eyes squeezed tightly shut.

"*Iasg is feòil.*" I quickly wrap the kilt around my hips and use the long section to tie it around my waist. Then I stalk up to the daft woman. "I am no longer unclothed. Open your eyes."

The lass cracks one lid open. Her shoulders relax, and she blows out a breath. Then she opens both eyes. "Thank you."

"*S e ur beatha.*"

"What does that mean?"

"You are welcome."

She bites her lip. "And that other thing you said? *Isag is…*"

"*Iasg is feòil.* It means 'fish and flesh,' which is a curse."

"Must be a Gaelic one, huh?"

I grunt and ignore her statement. "Why did you call yourself ah-mere-ick-in?"

"That means I'm from the United States of America." She bites her lip again, and her forehead wrinkles. "But the USA doesn't exist yet. It's not even one of the British colonies in this time. It's barely been discovered."

The meaning of her statement doesn't sink in at first. But when I at last realize what she meant, I freeze. "You are a Sassenach."

"I'm a what? I told you, I'm American."

"And you said that suggests that you are a British citizen. That makes you a Sassenach, though you dinnae sound like the British folk I have met."

"You're not like the Scots I've met, so we're even."

The British are my enemy. My aunts might have summoned Alyssa here with their magics, but mayhap an English witch interfered with their spell. The Queen of England might have sent a bonnie spy into our midst. Aye, she went to the trouble of using witchcraft simply to insert a spy into Dùndubhan and…accomplish what? I haven't a clue, but I dinnae trust a Sassenach. Yet if I take Alyssa as my wife, that might thwart whatever plot Elizabeth wants to enact.

"What crazy bullshit are you dreaming up now?" Alyssa asks. "I can tell from your squinty eyes and flattened lips that you're up to something. How many times do I need to say it? I am not English. If you hate the Brits, you're barking up the wrong tree here."

Very little of what she says makes any sense at all.

"Mayhap you are French," I say, "and attempting to trick me into believing you're British."

"What would I gain from doing that? You hate the Brits. Do you hate French people too?"

"I have no particular quarrel with them."

"Great." She sets her hands on her hips. "Then I'm French."

Whatever ploy she believes she is engaging in, I don't understand it. Why will the woman not simply tell me the truth? Mayhap my behavior has not given her reason to believe I will accept anything she says. But I have no reason to believe she's not a spy or a demoness determined to destroy me. Aye, I've gone insane. She does this to me.

"*Je suis ravi de vous rencontrer*," I say. "*Comment ça va?*"

Alyssa stares at me. "That wasn't Gaelic. My necklace can translate that language."

"I spoke French. I said that I'm pleased to meet you and then asked how are you." I lean toward her and point a finger in her face. "If you were French, you would have known what I said."

"Wow, what a genius you are to figure that out." She spreads her arms and leans toward me. "I told you where I'm from, but you wouldn't believe me. So guess what? I lied to get you off my back. But nothing will satisfy a jackass like you."

"The truth will satisfy me." Our faces are so near each other that I could kiss her with only the slightest movement.

"Fine. Here's the truth." She raises onto the tips of her toes to level our gazes. "I'm from the United States of America, and until your aunts brought me here, I was living in California."

"Your words are gibberish."

"Open your mind, you dumb brute. Your aunts summoned me. You can believe that, but you can't accept that I come from the future where countries you've never dreamed of exist."

What if the lass is correct and I am misguided? A spell did transport her to this land. So mayhap… *Bod an Donais*. I shift uncomfortably, which has the unfortunate effect of loosening my plaid. I grip a handful of the kilt before it can slide off my hips. "I accept that I might have been wrong, and you might be correct."

Her expression goes blank. For a moment, she does not move or blink. Then the lass's mouth stretches into a smug smile. "The Scottish ass admitted he was wrong. Thank you, Kieran. I love being right and making you squirm."

"I did not 'squirm.' "

"Do you even know what the word means? You don't look like you have a clue."

Mhac na galla. I grow weary of needing to admit to things I do not know, especially when I must admit that to Alyssa. "What does the word squirm indicate?"

"It means you were uncomfortable and wriggling like a slippery little worm."

"Dinnae call me a worm." I sling my arms around the lass and pull her close. My erection forms an iron line between our bodies. "But if you prefer a Scottish caber, I'll gladly accommodate you."

I push my hips forward, rubbing my cock against her belly.

"Caber? You need to find a better innuendo. And if you try anything, I'll grab your balls and twist them hard."

"Whatever you might think of me, I would never force you to do anything. When I fuck you, the desire will be mutual."

"I hate you."

"Doesn't matter. We share the same need. The sensual tone of your voice proves I'm right."

"You sound the same way. But I still hate you."

"And I despise you. If you tell me to stop, I'll do it."

Her eyes appear darker now, but I know from past encounters with women that it means she wants me now as badly as I want her. "You'll stop what if I tell you to?"

"I shall cease fucking you."

"Oh, I get it." She gasps when I close my hand around her breast and flick my finger across the nipple, the stiff peak of which is visible through her clothing. "How many women have you slept with?"

"Why would I share my bed with them for the night? I want their bodies, not their hearts."

"No, I meant how many woman have you gotten naked with?"

"Why do you ask me such a question?" I push my hand inside her braies, where I feel some sort of undergarment. "Men fuck women. That's all anyone needs to know."

"No, that's not all. Tell me about your liaisons."

I massage her breast and her erse while nuzzling her neck. By God's bones, she smells and feels like no other lass on earth. "I will answer your question—after I've taken your body."

"No dice. Tell me first."

"You are not in command of me." I yank her shirt up, intending to remove it over her head, but she refuses to assist me. "Raise your arms. Now."

"No."

"As you wish." I grasp the front of her shirt with both hands and tear it in half. "You may keep your shirt on now."

She slaps my face.

I take hold of her hands, pressing her into the wall, and pin her hands there. "You haven't told me to stop."

Her breasts heave. "You are a spoiled brat."

With one hand, I cuff both her wrists to the wall above her head. Then I grasp her braies and rip away the button that holds them in place. While her cheeks turn a bonnie shade of pink, I grasp the strange second closure that still holds her braies up and tear that open as well. The lass drags her tongue over her lower lip, now breathing so roughly that her breasts quiver. I shove her braies down to her ankles, and with one swift tug, yank her undergarment off. Then I dispose of the bizarre device that restrains her breasts.

"Shall I remove your torn shirt and braies?" I ask. "Or would you rather I take you right here, the way you are?"

My cock has grown so rigid that it begins to throb. I discard my kilt, sending it flying through the air behind me. Dinnae care what happens to the plaid. I need to make this woman mine and satiate the lust she inspires in me.

She struggles against my hold. "Need to get these clothes off."

I release her hands and step back.

Alyssa strips off her ruined clothing and stalks toward me. Though I could stop her easily, I allow the lass to push me backward with each step, even while she smacks my chest to punctuate her words. "You are the most obnoxious, petulant, rude, self-centered, arrogant bastard I have ever met."

I grasp her wrists and tug her into me. "Aye, lass, I am all of those things. And ye still want me."

"Yes. And I hate that I do." She shakes my hands off, though only because I let her do it, and gives me a hard shove. "Get on your back, MacTaggart."

She shoves me again, and I allow her to push me backward, making me stumble and fall. While I lie here sprawled on the stair, she kneels to straddle my hips. "No talking. If you want to growl, go ahead. But I don't want to hear any actual words come out of your mouth until we're done. Got it?"

"Aye. You won't speak either."

I still have my boots on, but she doesn't seem to care about that. Alyssa grasps my cock at the base and lowers her body onto my length until I'm seated deeply inside her. I've taken other women, but feeling Alyssa's body cradling my cock gives me a sense of excitement I've never experienced before. When she sets her hands on the step above my head, I grasp her hips, about to thrust up into her, but she claims my hands to secure them to the step above my head. The lass begins to fuck me, rocking her hips wildly while her juices dribble onto my balls and the scent of it surrounds us.

Her breasts dangle over my face. I lunge upward to latch on to one peak and suckle it fiercely, making her cry out and ride me even harder. When her womb tightens around me, I know she will come at any moment—and I dinnae want her to do that yet. Dinnae want myself to do that either, not yet.

I cradle her erse in both hands as I surge to my feet and set the lass down on the cold stone floor. "Need a moment."

"To do what? The only thing you should be doing is fucking me. And besides, I ordered you not to speak."

"The rules have changed."

She smacks my chest. "Make me come, or I'll do it myself."

"No, ye won't." I spin her around and press her body to the wall, using mine to cage her there. "Because ye want me to give you pleasure. Tell me I'm wrong."

"I can't. So go on, Kieran, take control."

Chapter Eight

Alyssa

Why do I want to have sex with this man? I despise him, and he feels the same way about me. So what if he kind of opened up to me earlier when I was crying. He thinks I belong to him. I should never have let Kieran kiss me, much less demanded that he make me come. But damn, when he tore my clothes off, I got so turned on that I could've orgasmed just from listening to the rough growl of his voice. I'm too old to act like a sorority girl who drank too much and got it on with a bad boy.

But I can't stop myself. I want Kieran. The lust is too powerful to deny.

That doesn't mean I have to let him know how good he is at sex. I let out a feral growling noise. "You're not wrong, you bastard. So get the job done."

"I will. Eventually."

"Just do it now." My whole body is on fire with the kind of liquid heat that makes it impossible for me to think straight.

"Desperate to play at couch quail, eh?"

What on earth does that mean? Don't care. I need to come with his dick inside me, that's all I know.

He pushes his knee between my thighs to spread my legs, then thrusts his cock between my folds. A deep groan resonates in his chest. "Ye make me so *dàrail*, and yer *camas* feels so good I could spend all night teasing you and never let you come. We'd both balance on a razor's edge until dawn."

"I'd have a heart attack if you did that. So finish me off, please."

Kieran rocks his hips with such languid strokes of his cock that I can barely breathe and my ears begin to ring. I've never wanted any man the way I want him. Why does the most obnoxious cretin I've ever met have to be the only man who understands how to give me real pleasure? Weren't medieval people supposed to be pent-up and prudish?

Not Kieran, that's for damn sure.

The crown of his cock pokes out between my folds every time he lunges forward. I can't resist staring down at my mound so I can watch the rosy, glistening head of his erection peeking out, then disappearing, over and over. The slowness of his strokes has my pulse beating like a drum roll.

"Please, Kieran," I beg, sounding so desperate that it's embarrassing. "Please make me come."

"Nay." His voice is strained, as if he can barely stand it either.

He picks me up and cradles me in his arms. Then he stalks up the stairs—all the way up, mounting three flights that take us to the highest level in the castle, or so I think. But he doesn't stop there. The Laird of Dùn-dubhan stomps over to the far end of the hall, to a doorway that blends into the stone wall unlike the wooden door I see a few yards away.

"Where are we going?" I ask, though I rather doubt he'll respond.

Kieran slings me over his shoulder.

Yep, I was right. Can't see what he's doing. All I can see is his ass, which is quite a sight, but it doesn't give me any information.

A metallic chunk suggests he unlocked the camouflaged door. A creaking sound follows. With a grunt, Kieran kicks the door open and goes inside whatever room he's taken me to, but I still can't see much. A blade of light cuts across the stone floor, and I get a glimpse of some kind of furniture.

Kieran tosses me onto…a bed.

This is not a crummy straw mattress like the one he had so graciously provided in my lovely little cell. No, I'm pretty sure this is feather bedding.

"You rat bastard," I hiss. "When you want to fuck me, you bring me to your secret hideaway that has a nice soft mattress. But when I annoy you, I get dumped in a prison cell."

"Haud yer wheesht, woman." He crawls onto the bed and halts with his body directly above mine. His hands bracket my shoulders. "Are ye wanting me to make ye come or not?"

"Yes, dammit, do it already."

"As my lady commands." He lifts my knees onto his shoulders and plants his palms on the mattress at either side of my head. "Scream all ye like. I give lasses so much pleasure that their eyes roll back in their heads. I hope you have a strong heart."

"Shut up and do it. Christ, you're driving me crazy. I had no idea the gruff, sullen, overgrown baby would yammer so much during sex."

He punches into me with such ferocity that I yelp. "I am a grown man. No bairn could make you feel the way I do. Women love the way I fuck them."

Is he trying to impress me? No, of course not.

"Just do it," I say, sounding breathless though I don't want to sound that way. His cock feels too damn good inside me, and I need to climax right now. "Show me how fantastic you are, Kieran."

I only said that so he would do something. He won't rock my world.

Kieran thrusts into me deeply, starting off at a measure pace that won't make the bed creak, though it feels incredible. In, out. In, out. My breathing grows labored, and I bite down on my bottom lip while clenching the sheets. Oh God, it won't take long at all. The pleasure is already ramping up inside me, tingling through my sex, heating me up from the inside out.

The wet sound of our bodies merging echoes through the room.

With Kieran's head directly above mine, I have no choice but to gaze into his beautiful, whiskey-brown eyes. This man intoxicated me with one kiss, and I haven't gotten that out of my system yet. How will I feel after I come with him buried deep inside me? I can't look at him anymore. So I squeeze my eyes shut and revel in the sensations.

"Open your eyes, lass."

I shake my head.

"Do it now," he growls. "Open your eyes and watch me taking your body."

Though I don't want to do it, I can't stop myself. I pry my lids open and gaze down at our joined bodies, where his cock keeps pumping in and out. My cream glistens on his dick, and drops of it glisten on the hairs on my mound too. I can't tear my focus away from the place where our bodies merge, and the sucking sound our flesh makes is the most erotic thing I've ever heard.

"Faster," I say. "Please, Kieran, go faster. Take me harder."

He obeys my command, pumping his hips with brutal force and thrusting so fast that the bed starts to creak and thump. Wild cries erupt out of me while he shouts and snarls words that must be Gaelic. My inner muscles begin to pulsate around him, and my whole body curls in on itself while I unleash a series of strangled cries.

Kieran throws his head back and roars as he blows apart inside me.

He falls onto his back on the mattress beside me. "Still think I'm not that good?"

I could lie. I want to lie. But I promised myself I would never do that. "Maybe you are incredible in bed, but you're still a jerk."

He chuckles. "Thank you for admitting I am incredible."

Damn, I wish his throaty chuckle didn't turn me on. But it does. Right now, I'm too high on post-coital hormones to argue with him.

I push up on my elbows and study the room. "Why did you bring me here? We could've had sex on the staircase."

"The stone is too hard. You might've been bruised."

Kieran cared if I got bruised? I can't understand this man. He calls me his property and snarls nasty things at me. But then he carries me all the way up here to the top of the castle to give me a soft bed to lie on while we screw.

I sit up and wriggle around to face him. "Why do you treat me like dirt most of the time but then do nice things too?"

"Nice things?"

"Yes. Like bringing me here where there's a soft mattress, or trying to comfort me when I was upset."

He rubs his eyes with his thumb and forefinger. "Dinnae know."

"You 'dinnae' know what?"

"Why I behave the way I do. Mayhap I have a demon inside me."

"You can't blame demons. Take responsibility for your actions. Then maybe you'll figure out why you are the way you are."

He squints at me. "What about you? I'm not the only one who behaves badly."

I want to tell him that's crap, but it would be a lie. "Point taken. We both have issues to deal with."

"Issue? I have no bairns."

"What is a 'bairn'?"

"A child."

"Oh." I consider what he said and suddenly realize the problem. "An issue is something that's bothering you. I guess medieval Scots have a different term for it."

He clasps his hands under his head, staring up at the ceiling high above us. His features are pinched, but he seems unlikely to speak anytime soon.

I can't help poring my gaze over his body, exploring every inch of him without touching his skin. I want to touch him. Want to taste him. Want to kiss and lick and fondle and tease him. No man should look so good, not unless he's a god come down from the heavens to give women pure, unadulterated ecstasy. Since his aunts have magical powers, I wonder if Kieran does too.

As much as I loved having sex with him, I will never do that again.

He sits up and drops one leg off the side of the bed. The other he keeps bent in front of him, like a half cross-legged position. "I needed to do this once, but now I no longer have any need for your body."

Kieran slides off the bed and saunters toward the door.

"Oh, no, you don't get to just walk away." I leap off the bed and hurry after him, catching up halfway down the staircase. I seize his arm. "Stop, Kieran. I know we will never do that again, but we are stuck with each other. We need to figure out how to get along."

"No, we do not."

He takes the remainder of the steps three at a time, reaching the huge empty room on this floor faster than I can. The third level of the castle bears no resemblance to the top floor of the modern version. The Dùndubhan of the twenty-first century features a third level that houses bedroom suites. As I struggle to catch up to Kieran again, I notice a brown smudge on his back, just above the crease of his buttocks. I can't get close enough to figure out what it might be. Dirt from the stone floor? We did get started on banging each other on the floor, so maybe that really is a smudge of dirt.

Enough of this. I sprint across the room and veer in front of Kieran before he can start down another flight of stairs. Spreading both arms across the doorway, I blockade the way.

"Move, woman," he growls. "Or I will do it for you."

"Shut up and listen."

He lifts one brow but reveals no other reaction to my statement.

I try to maintain my resolute composure while buck naked and faced with the big, hot body of one rude Scot. "You do not get to treat me like a blow-up sex doll."

His brows cinch up.

Right, they don't have things like that in this time. "A sex doll is something creepy men use to get their rocks off alone. And getting your rocks off means having an orgasm."

"I see. But I was not alone. We enjoyed each other's bodies together."

"Yeah, I know. I'm trying to make a point, but my metaphors all come from a century you know nothing about. That makes it harder to explain why I'm mad at you, which means I can't reasonably yell at you."

His confusion softens his expression, and he suddenly looks much younger, like a teenage boy who has no idea how to deal with a girl.

"We need to have a serious conversation," I say. "No more wriggling out of it or shouting your way out of it. After what we just did together, you owe me that much. Please."

He winces and grasps the back of his neck. "Aye, we should do that. But I will only tell you what I want you to know, nothing more."

"I can live with that. For now."

"Will you tell me about your past?"

"Yes."

He glances at my body and smirks. "You need clothing, else you'll die of the cold. Spring is coming but not yet nigh."

I rub my arms. "It is a bit chilly in this castle."

Kieran sweeps me up in his arms and makes his way down the stone steps to the second floor. There, he turns left toward a closed doorway, kicking it open and then shut again once we've entered the room. I can't believe what I'm seeing. As Kieran sets me down on a high-back chair, I survey the decor with a growing sense of wonder. This bedroom features a gorgeous tapestry that hangs above the fireplace, which seems to be composed of river stones. A sword lies on the mantel, and I'd swear that's the blade I'd seen in the modern version of Dùndubhan, in the hall of antiquities. Though I desperately want to get a closer look, I have more urgent matters to discuss with Kieran.

"It's time to tell me the truth," I say. "About everything."

Chapter Nine

Kieran

Alyssa will not give up her quest to unearth all my secrets, though she has no conception of what she might learn if I do as she asked. I did vow to answer her questions. She doesn't understand what my life has been like since my banishment, and I'm not at all certain I want her to understand. My aunts have never demanded that I share the details with them, so I haven't offered to share any.

Simidh Gunn is out there plotting, I'm certain. I'd seen the look in his eyes when he spoke to Alyssa. He wants her, but for what, I cannot yet say.

I drag another chair over to where Alyssa sits, settling in beside her. "I shall answer your questions now. Even if the room catches fire, I won't leave."

"Good."

"Ask your questions." The way she keeps admiring my body causes me to admire hers, and that reminds me of what I have neglected to do for her. "I destroyed your clothing. Let me find you garments to wear for now, so you will not grow chilled."

"I would appreciate that." She eyes me with suspicion. "Unless that's an excuse to get away from me."

"You have my word it is not. If you're chilled now, I will give you the quilt from the bed."

"That's okay. I can wait."

As I turn to leave, I suddenly halt and look back at her. Alyssa is rubbing her arms again. That will not do. I march up to her, lift both the chair and the lass, and deposit them both on the floor as near to the hearth as possible.

While she gapes at me, I walk out the door and head down to the ground floor where I know my aunts will be in the kitchen cooking our supper. Along the way, I retrieve my kilt from the floor at the bottom of the stair. By the time I step into the kitchen, I have my plaid in order. I never removed my boots, so I have no need to concern myself with that now.

My aunts turn toward me and smile.

"There you are, *gràidh*," Efrica says. "We wondered what became of Alyssa's clothing. It was strewn about on the stair and seemed to have been torn."

"Aye. She, ah, had a wee bit of trouble with the strange clasps on her garments. I had no conception of how to assist her with that, since I know nothing of twenty-first-century clothing."

My aunts don't seem reassured by what I told them.

Lachina eyes me with suspicion. "Where is the lass? We haven't seen her since we heard you two having a barnie in the entrance room."

"Aye, that was quite the barnie," Morna agrees, her tone dripping with sarcasm. "I've ne'er before heard a shouting match that didn't involve words."

Efrica clucks her tongue. "Oh, Kieran, you naughty, naughty boy. What have ye done with the lass?"

I fist my hands and squeeze words out between my clenched teeth. "I have done nothing to Alyssa. She's in my bedroom, warming herself by the fire. I came down here to find new clothing for the lass. Will you help me? Or would ye rather make rude jokes?"

Their insinuations might be accurate, but I dinnae care to discuss sex with them.

My aunts begin chattering, and their discussion of what garments Alyssa might like becomes an excuse for making more jokes about what the lass and I did on the stair. We've all been speaking. Now that the translation pendant has been returned to Alyssa, I must be careful of what I say in her presence. She wouldn't want to hear the literal version of *bod an Donais*. It means "the devil's penis." As for *bod an Ciaran*, I would gladly translate that for her. She can discuss my cock as often as she likes.

Once my aunts have gathered some clothing that should fit Alyssa, they bundle it up and secure the lot with a length of cord like the ones used to pull curtains back from windows. Efrica commands me to "take good care of the lass" because Alyssa is the one to set me right. Whatever that means.

I return to the bedroom, where Alyssa still sits huddled in her chair by the hearth. Her head pops up when I shut the door.

"Did you bring me clothes?" she asks. "That looks like quite a bundle you've got there."

"Aye. My aunts chose these items for you. I know nothing about how to clothe a woman." I can't help smirking. "Well, I know how to undress a lass."

"If you 'undress' every woman the way did for me, there must be a lot of naked Scottish lasses running around out there."

As I set the bundle on the floor beside her chair, I experience a twinge of discomfort. "You believe I've bedded hordes of women."

"I don't know how many you've 'bedded.' You won't tell me anything about yourself."

"Get dressed, then I will explain."

While Alyssa unties the bundle of clothing my aunts had provided and sorts through it all, I move her chair back to its original position. That places it beside my chair. She will be able to glower and roll her eyes at me well enough from this distance. Aye, I deserve her scorn. But she knows nothing of why.

"How do you like this?"

Alyssa's question draws my focus away from the floor and back to her. I get a strange pang in my chest when I look at the lass. She wears a long plaid skirt in the MacTaggart clan tartan as well as a long-sleeve white shirt and a dark-blue vest that's strung tightly to her form, accentuating her breasts. Her auburn hair hangs loose over her shoulders.

I sit up straighter in my chair. "Ye look bonnie, lass. Very bonnie."

"Thank you," she says as she curtsies. "I'm glad my laird is well pleased."

"No man could be more pleased. You are an angel come down to earth."

Her cheeks dimple. "After what we did downstairs earlier, I don't think I qualify as an angel."

"Ah, but you do." I pat the empty chair beside me, and Alyssa settles onto the seat. "Angels mated with mortals. It says so in the Bible."

"Yeah, but I'm not one of those. You 'mated' with a plain old American woman."

"Those words do not describe you. Plain? Old? Nay, never."

She sets her elbows on her chair's arms and clasps her hands over her lap. "I'm five years older than you, Kieran. Doesn't that make me old in medieval terms?"

"What is 'medieval'?"

"That's what people in my century call people in your century."

"Ah, I see." As I skim my gaze over her one more time, I find myself licking my lips while my cock thickens. Aye, I want the lass again. But first, I need to do as I promised. "You asked how many women I've bedded. The answer is eight."

"That's all? I would've thought a thirty-five-year-old man in this century would have gotten more action than that."

"How do you know my age?"

She smiles. "How do you think?"

I groan and sink back in my chair. "My aunts told you."

"Efrica told me, actually."

"Of course she did." I lean my head back against the chair, staring at the ceiling while I confess. "You want to know why I've bedded only eight women. The first was a French whore I met when I was in Edinburgh. I'd gone with my father to make an alliance with another clan leader. My mother had long since died, and my father needed to take a new wife. Whilst we were there, the French whore offered to show me how to please a woman—for a price."

"Did you enjoy having sex with her?"

"It was…strange. Over the course of a single night, she taught me many things about how to pleasure a woman." I cannot force myself to look at Alyssa. Do men of her century bed many women? Or fewer women than the lads in my time? I have no conception of what is normal in her eyes. "The other women I've been with were trying to earn a place as the wife of the chief's son. The last lass I bedded I had intended to marry, strictly to form an alliance with a neighboring clan. But she ran away with a laddie from a different clan. It was quite a scandal."

"Ooh, juicy gossip. Tell me more."

"Gossip?"

"Unfounded claims about other people. Don't medieval folks gossip?"

"Aye, we do. Unfortunately. Do you enjoy hearing rumors?"

She shrugs. "Not particularly. I was joking, anyway. Who was the last woman you were with?"

"You know the answer. The last woman was you."

"Oh. I didn't think you would include me in your list." She turns slightly toward me. "So, you'd only been with seven women before I showed up."

I nod.

She lays her hand over mine, where it rests on the arm of my chair. "That's nothing to be ashamed of."

"Most men of my age have already married. I'm considered to be too chaste, essentially a virgin, because I fucked each of those women only once and never took one as my wife."

Alyssa laughs. "That's crazy. Nobody who's as good at sex as you are could ever be called chaste."

"I learned my skills from a French whore. I am not 'good' at sex."

"Yes, you are. You're amazing, in fact. I've been with five men in my entire life, and none of them could hold a candle to you."

"I appreciate the compliment. But aren't you curious about why I have abstained for most of my life?"

Alyssa turns toward me even more, bending one knee to get closer. "I am curious about that. You clearly love sex."

"I love fucking *you*." I scrub my hands over my face and sigh. "I did not want to marry for political reasons. In fact, I was relieved when that silly lass ran off with someone else. I've remained unmarried since because I wish to wed for…less acceptable reasons."

"You want to marry someone you love."

"Aye. And that is why I was an outcast even before my banishment."

She splays a hand over my cheek and exerts gentle pressure to encourage me to turn my face toward her. "You're a good man. That's nothing to be ashamed of."

I grunt. But the warmth of her palm feels good on my cheek. I want to kiss her again, fuck her again, but she deserves better than an outcast. Yet I've already taken her body, which means I might have seeded a bairn inside her womb too.

"Tell me about Simidh Gunn," she says. "The whole story."

"My banishment was the culmination of several factors. The lies Simidh told, claiming I was a thief, were only the beginning. He spread rumors that I assaulted women and men alike, forcing my depravity on anyone who annoyed me."

She studies me for a moment with no discernible expression. "Are you a witch, Kieran?"

"Why do you ask?"

"Because your aunts used magic to summon me here."

"I forgot about that."

She leans closer, her gaze locked on mine. "So tell me the truth, Kieran. Are you witch?"

"Aye. But not the sort you might think. I have on occasion created potions and salves to treat illnesses, and I've also cast spells to ward off evil."

"That's it?"

I nod. "You might call it white magic, as opposed to the black sort."

"Did you expect me to be shocked and horrified by what you've told me? I'm not."

"But I've treated you with disrespect at best, and loathing at worst. You should not care to know more about me."

She gazes at me for a moment, giving away nothing in her eyes or on her face. Then the lass climbs onto my lap and links her arms behind my neck. "Yes, you have been a jerk to me. But I'm beginning to understand why. Your father sent you away to live in this lonely, abandoned castle with your aunts. That must have been painful for you to deal with."

"My aunts chose to live here, but my father did not send me to this place. I chose it myself. I won't complain about the conditions of my banishment since they have chosen to live in the same manner." I gingerly curl my arms around her. "Mayhap now you will tell me your story."

"Yes. It's time." She closes her eyes briefly, then aims her shimmering gaze straight into mine. "My husband destroyed my life."

Chapter Ten

Alyssa

I watch Kieran, waiting for his expression to change into... I don't know. Disgust? Shock? Maybe a combination of the two? But he doesn't do either of those things. Instead, Kieran pulls me a touch closer and rubs his nose against mine. The sweet little smile curling his lips portrays nothing close to revulsion, but instead, seems compassionate. The man who looked like a wild beast when we first met now intends to comfort me.

"You can tell me anything," he says. "Or tell me only what you feel safe sharing with me."

"I want to explain everything. I need to do it. This weight I've been carrying around for years has dragged me down more than I realized—until I met you."

"That could not have helped. *Cuiridh cu e fhein air thoiseach.*"

"What did you just say? I put my translation necklace in my pocket."

"*Cuiridh cu e fhein air thoiseach,* that's what I said. Literally, it means 'a dog puts himself forward.' A reference to bad manners. It's a way of saying I'm a rude bastard."

"Sometimes you can be. But I've gotten to know you better, and I like this version of you best."

He slides one hand down to my thigh, but that doesn't feel like a sexual move. "You said your husband destroyed your life."

"Right. It's time to explain." I focus on his kilt, toying with the sash that drapes over his chest. "I married Tony Schneider six years ago. He was charming and hard-working, and I thought we had a good marriage. Until

I got a job that paid more than he was earning. Tony showed his true face then, and it wasn't an attractive sight."

"The *bod ceann* didn't approve of your success." He gives my thigh a light squeeze. "A *bod ceann* is a dickhead."

"Oh, I get it. Yes, Tony turned into a *bod ceann*. He apparently decided that the way to deal with his envy was to ruin our lives, but I only found out what he was doing two years ago."

"I assume he had been doing something terrible."

"You could say that." I force myself to lift my head and gaze directly into his eyes. "He had been embezzling money from his employer just so he would appear to have more money than I did."

"But husbands and wives share the marital coffers."

"Not in my century. Not always, at least. Tony and I did have a shared bank account, but he kept track of everything he deposited into our account so he would know when he had more money than I did." What he'd said a moment ago finally surfaces in my brain. "Do men in this century let their wives have jobs if they want?"

"Aye. My mother wove rugs and kilts, among other things. My aunts trade their wares, selling potions and salves and whatever else they brew up."

"They practice witchcraft openly?"

He shakes his head. "The potions and salves they sell are not magical. They're simple remedies derived from plants. They have also been known to weave and sell those items as well. Lachina made my kilt."

"Your aunts are wonderful. A little strange, but still wonderful."

"Aye, they are. I might want to strangle them with my kilt on occasion, but that's only a passing thought when they annoy me."

The way his mouth kinks up on one side assures me that he's kidding. Probably.

"If you wish to earn money," he says, "I have no objection to that."

"Gee, thanks. You don't object? I'm not your wife. The job I used to have wouldn't work in this century."

"What sort of wares did you peddle?"

Yeah, this is going to be damn hard to explain to a man who has no idea what technology looks like in the twenty-first century. "You wouldn't understand."

He scowls. "I am not an illiterate heathen."

"I know that." Oh, what the hell. Might as well go for it. "I was a social media manager at a tech startup in Silicon Valley."

His face goes blank. Though his gaze is still aimed at mine, he doesn't seem to be looking into my eyes. His eyes have glazed over. "I do not understand. Where is this Silicon Valley? Not in Scotland, of that I'm certain."

"No, it's in California. But you wouldn't know where that is either. I don't think that region has been discovered yet. Let's just say it's in the New World."

"Oh, aye. Cristoforo Colombo traveled there, and other explorers have followed suit."

"You know about Christopher Columbus? That's what Americans call him, but you used the Italian version of his name."

Kieran lifts his brows. "You believe I'm uneducated. My father fought the English and was imprisoned there for two years. He learned the heathen language and taught it to me. My father also told me about England and the lands beyond. When I was seventeen, I told my father I wanted to join the crew of a French ship that often sailed to Edinburgh. I wished to see more of the world."

"Did your father let you go?"

"He did. I have seen France, Portugal, Spain, and even Egypt."

"Wow. I'd never traveled outside the United States of America until I came to Scotland."

He sweeps a hand up my cheek, pushing his fingers into my hair. "I would take you wherever you wish to go."

"I think getting thrown back in time to medieval Scotland is enough excitement for me right now."

"You haven't explained what a 'social mee-dee-uh man-ij-er is."

"It means I, um, disseminated information kind of the way a newspaper does. But without the actual newspaper. I suppose a town crier would be the closest comparison." Considering the way his forehead has wrinkled, I think I'd better change the subject. "Never mind about that. Getting back to my jerk of a husband, because we shared a bank account, I wound up being liable for the money he embezzled from his employer. We got wiped out financially."

"He deserves to be skelped. If I could locate the *bod ceann*, I would do that for certain."

I can't help smiling. "You're surprisingly sweet, in a cutthroat way."

"A man should defend his woman and protect her from all threats."

"How many times do I have to say it before you grasp the concept? I am not *your* woman. I don't belong to anyone."

Kieran bows his head. "I understand. Mayhap I wish for you to be mine, but you have no desire to be so."

Does he have hurt feelings? Because I don't want to be his chattel? Maybe we're experiencing another round of miscommunication. Trying to mesh my world with his has turned out to be incredibly complicated. On the previous occasions when I informed him that I'm not *his* woman, he had gotten angry. Now, he seems depressed.

"What's wrong?" I ask. "You should be snarling at me about how I belong to you."

"I realize you don't want that." He raises his head. "Tell me the rest of your story."

"Okay." A change of subject sounds good right now. "My husband was never convicted of embezzlement because of a hung jury. Then he got sick, and I wound up taking care of him until he passed away."

"Why in the world would you care for the man who mistreated you?"

"I felt sorry for him. He was in a lot of pain. Cancer is a vicious disease, and he had ignored the warning signs for a long time. That meant there was nothing left to do but watch him wither away."

Kieran touches his lips to mine. "You are a kindhearted and forgiving lass. He was fortunate to have you in his life."

I hunch my shoulders, having no clue what to say in response.

"This man, this Toh-nee, he used you terribly. Then he had the temerity to ask you to care for him during his illness. I watched my mother die slowly from an incurable disease, and I understand the toll that takes on the family." He grasps my face in both hands while his expression hardens and his voice grows fierce. "If that man were not already dead, I would hunt him down and rip the heart from his chest."

His bald statement stuns me for a moment, and I can't speak or look away. The fire in his eyes matches the ferocity of his voice. This man would kill for me. I believe that with every fiber of my being. But do I want to live with someone that vicious? Maybe I needed a deadly protector for all those years when I stayed with Tony, though I knew I should have left him. To have a man like Kieran MacTaggart defending me… A hot shiver ripples through me. Maybe I like the idea a little too much.

"I don't want to talk about Tony anymore," I say. "I'm exhausted. Sleep is all I can think about right now."

Before I can climb off his lap, Kieran picks me up and strides over to the bed. He pulls the covers back, then lays me down on the mattress. Just when I'm about to point out that I'm still fully clothed, he begins to undo the laces on my vest.

I shoo his hands away. "I'd rather undress myself."

"You are exhausted. Allow me to do this for you."

"If you undress me, I'll be too horny to fall asleep."

His brows crinkle in the most adorable way. "What is 'horny'?"

A laugh bubbles out of me. "It means I'll be too sexually aroused to sleep."

Kieran smirks and leans over to trace his fingertip over my bottom lip. "Mayhap I want you too aroused to sleep."

"Maybe I should go back to my prison room. That's the only way you'll keep your naughty hands off me."

"I intend to spend the night in the solar." He resumes unlacing my vest, accomplishing the task with deftness and precision as if he's done this a thousand times before. "You deserve to sleep in a soft bed with a warm fire to chase away any chill. And you deserve to remain unmolested for the entire night. I can't promise not to make love to you if I wake in the dead of night. The desire to touch you again might prove too powerful to resist."

He wants me that much? No other man has ever expressed his lust for me with such eloquent sincerity. So I shut my mouth and observe while he carefully removes my vest, then does the same with the rest of my clothes. Once I'm lying here naked, he tugs the covers up to my neck.

Kieran bends over me to kiss my forehead. "Sleep well, *mo leannan*."

The most unusual man I've ever met walks out the door, gently shutting it behind him. I listen as his footfalls recede and eventually fade into silence. The only sounds in the room are the faint crackling of the fire, the ticking of a clock on the mantel, and the whispering of my own breaths. As I settle in and gradually sink into slumber, my thoughts rewind to the moment when I had crawled onto his lap and he had looped his arms around me.

What do I dream of? Kieran MacTaggart, of course.

I wake in the morning just as the sun crests the castle walls. Its light beams through the large window in my room—Kieran's room, technically—and sprays its warmth over my face and shoulders, the only parts of me not covered by the down-filled quilt. For several minutes, I let myself soak up the sunshine while a satisfied smile curves my lips. I would love for Kieran to kiss me again, but I don't think that's a good idea. His kisses feel like the heat of sunshine, and they melt me like butter left outside on a sunny day.

Finally, I rise and get dressed. Well, I try to do that. But I can't remember how to do up all the laces and buttons that hold my getup together. I'll need help dressing. The sexy Scot had carefully set my clothing on the big chair he'd sat in last night. Since this is not the twenty-first century, which means I can't call those ladies on my cell phone, I'll have to resort to the old-fashioned means of communication.

I open the door a few inches and holler, "Efrica! Lachina! Morna! I need some help. Can you hear me?"

Silence.

"Hey, ladies! Future girl needs some assistance in dressing. Please."

They can't hear me. *Damn.* That means I'll need to fight with my gorgeous outfit all by myself. I pick up the plaid skirt, but it's thick and hard to work with, at least for someone like me who hasn't done this all my life. My fingers slip, and the skirt falls out of my hands.

Footfalls pound in the hall outside my room. Large, powerful footfalls.

Oh no, I don't want *him* touching me. The dreams I had about him last night have left me turned on.

The door swings open, and Kieran stalks into the room. He studies me for a moment. His lips tick up at the corners as he roves his gaze over my entire naked body. Then he kicks the door shut and saunters up to me. "You requested help."

Oh, I am going to get my revenge on him somehow, some way.

Chapter Eleven

Kieran

As I had been striding into the castle moments ago, my aunts had waylaid me at the bottom of the stair, all three of them breathless as if they had been running. I waited patiently, or mayhap not so patiently, while they caught their breath. Efrica recovered first and informed me that Alyssa urgently needs help. Before they had the chance to explain why the lass needs assistance, I was already thundering up the steps. Now, I stand inside my bedchamber, staring at the goddess whose glorious nakedness is spread before me.

"Go away," Alyssa commands as she scrambles to pick up her white shirt but fumbles it. She tries again with no better result. "I need your aunts, not you."

"I am here. Thus, I will help you with your clothing."

"No, no, no." She gives my chest a shove, but I remain unmoved by her attempt. "Go away, Kieran. Tell your aunts to come instead."

"They're busy cooking the morning meal." I snatch up her tartan skirt. "Either let me help you, or attend the meal without clothing." I can't resist skimming my gaze over the lass's body again, this time licking my lips because I would love to devour her rather than food. "I wouldn't mind if you prefer to remain nude."

"No thank you." She crosses her legs while still standing and holds her arms over those lush breasts, as if that will prevent me from spying her figure. "Oh, I don't care how cute and sexy you are. I will never forgive you for tricking me this way."

Cute and sexy? I have an idea of what she means, but I find it odd that she labels me thus.

"I did not trick you," I say, unable to stop myself from smirking again. I need to taste this woman immediately, but I doubt she would permit it. "Mayhap you would prefer to remain in this room until my aunts are available. I can keep you warm until then."

"No way." Alyssa lowers her arms and sighs, her posture sagging. "Fine, go on and help me. But you are forbidden from copping a feel."

"What does that mean?"

"Don't touch me unless it's necessary to get my clothes done up."

I continue to smirk, admiring her form without "copping a feel" while I do up her clothes faster than even I imagined I could. I slip her shoes onto her feet as well and button them up. I've acquired a great deal of experience with dressing women, though I shan't explain that to Alyssa. Once I've finished my task, I step back and nod. "You are ready for the morning meal."

She curtsies. "Thank you, my laird."

Bod an Donais. The lass should not have done that. When she knelt before me, I could see down her shirt. The vision of her bosom has stolen my breath, but only for a moment. Then my lust takes control, and I drag her in for a quick, firm kiss that gives me the barest taste of her. "Dinnae say that again unless you want me to fuck you. Dinnae curtsy either."

The lass shakes her head while one side of her mouth ticks upward. "Well, it figures that my chaste maiden act would turn you on. You love to be in control—of everything, but especially me. I let you take command only when we're having sex. Which we will never do again."

"Aye, never again." I wink. "What is the twenty-first century definition of 'never'? In my world, it means 'whenever the laird likes.' "

She punches my arm, though with little vigor. "You are so full of yourself."

"When I'm inside you again, you will be full of myself."

Alyssa gives me an exasperated look as we head downstairs and into the dining hall where my aunts have already set the meal on the table. I take the chair at the head of the table, naturally, as Laird of Dùndubhan—a title I gave myself. Alyssa and Efrica sit at either side of me while Morna takes the seat next to Alyssa, leaving Lachina beside Efrica.

The woman whose bosom I can still see in my mind leans forward to sniff the air above her plate. "What kind of food is this?"

"Venison from a stag I killed yesterday."

"Hasn't the meat gone bad by now? I mean, there's no refrigeration. The food isn't kept cold."

"We preserve the meat with salt." I stab my knife into my venison steak and raise it to my mouth, then gnaw off a chunk and speak while chewing. "Eat, lass. You need nourishment."

Efrica smiles knowingly at me.

I scowl at her. "What are you smiling about?"

"The way you take such care in ensuring Alyssa eats."

"You should eat too, Efrica, so I won't need to listen to you prattling."

My aunt keeps smiling in that irritating manner even while she begins to consume her food. Morna and Lachina dig into their meals as well, but Alyssa pokes at the food on her plate with her fork.

"What's fashing you now?" I demand. "The rest of us are eating, but you sit there staring at your plate."

"Venison is from a dead deer, right?"

"Aye. Killed it myself yesterday."

"I've been a vegan for five years."

She's been a what? Her statement sounds like nonsense. Mayhap she means that her astrological sign is Vegan, but that would hardly clear up the matter. I clap my fork down on my plate and squint at the lass. "What do you mean you are 'vegan'? Dinnae understand."

"It means I only eat vegetables."

"Still dinnae understand."

Alyssa rolls her eyes. "What don't you get? I prefer to eat only vegetables. No fruit, no meat, just carrots and peas and other veggies."

"Veggies? I've ne'er heard anyone call them that."

"Because you're from the wrong century. If you lived in my time, you'd understand."

I grunt and resume eating. "If you only consume vegetables, ye won't last long in my world. De ye eat grass and weeds too, then? They're vegetative matter."

Efrica smacks my hand. "Behave yourself, Kieran. Of course Alyssa doesn't want to eat weeds. You don't eat the hooves of the deer you kill, so dinnae be harassing the poor lass about her food habits."

I hack off a piece of meat and shove it into my mouth.

Lachina clucks her tongue. "Are ye wanting a spanking? You're acting like a wee bairn, which does not suit the Laird of Dùndubhan."

Morna pats Alyssa's hand. "Do try to eat something, dearie. You need more nourishment than vegetables can provide. Efrica, Lachina, and I cooked and seasoned the meat ourselves."

"It does smell good," Alyssa says. "I'll give it a try. After all, you guys spent a lot of time preparing the food. It would be rude to refuse to eat it." The lass daintily slices off a piece of meat and slips it between her lips. As she begins to chew, her face lights up. "Mm, this is delicious."

I cross my arms and smirk at her. "Not a vegan after all, eh?"

"To be honest, I only became a vegan to make my husband happy. After he died, I kept it up out of habit." She devours another bite of meat and moans with deep satisfaction, her eyes half-closed. "This is unbelievably yummy."

Her erse of a husband forced her to live on what is essentially weeds and grass. I enjoy eating vegetables, but not as my only source of nourishment. If I'd known she only ever ate that sort of food, I wouldn't have fucked her like a mad demon yesterday. But now that she is eating real food, she will have all the energy she needs for another round of hochmagandy.

No, I shouldn't touch the lass again. What if I've already seeded her womb? Some idiots believe that if a woman and man both achieve pleasure during intercourse, it means they've made a bairn. But I dinnae believe that nonsense. When a woman comes, it means she enjoyed the way I fucked her. If a bairn results from that pleasure, so be it.

"How did you become the Laird of Dùndubhan?" Alyssa asks. "You were banished, so I'm confused."

I've just finished my meal, so I decide to explain it to her. "Being a laird simply means a body owns the land."

"By 'a body,' you mean a person."

"Aye."

She spears a carrot with her fork and chews it while studying me. "Do you own this property?"

"Not in the strict sense."

"In what looser way do you own it?"

"My aunts told me it's mine."

Alyssa puckers her lips. Her body begins to quiver. Then she erupts into laughter.

"Why are you laughing?" I squeeze the words out between my clenched teeth. "It is not amusing."

"Oh, it absolutely is." She clears her throat and wipes her eyes with her fingers. "Sorry. But it is hilarious that you claim to own Dùndubhan simply because your aunts told you it's yours."

"They lived here long before I did. So, when they invited me to live with them, they gifted Dùndubhan to me since I am the only man on the premises."

"If they were here first, you shouldn't have stolen the property away from them."

"Stolen? I did no such thing."

"Dùndubhan was not ours to own," Effrica says. "We kept watch over the castle and its lands until the true laird could claim his place. This is more than simply a castle, *gràidh*. It is the heart and soul of the MacTaggart clan."

"But only you guys live here. How can it be the soul of a clan that doesn't want to take up residence at the castle?"

Lachina leans forward to gaze directly at Alyssa. She speaks in a voice of power that I've heard many times before, though never quite as determinedly as this morn. "I have *da-shealladh*, the two sights. That means I can connect with the spirits of this earthly world and of the netherworld. My ancestors guided me toward the necessary path and warned me that it would take patience and perseverance to convince you and Kieran of the truth."

A strange sensation tingles over my skin as Lachina turns her gaze to me. I shift uncomfortably in my chair. "Mayhap you do have *da-shealladh*. But I know nothing of whatever truth you believe I need to accept."

"Of course you know nothing of it. I haven't tried to convince you yet."

"Um, excuse me," Alyssa says. "What does any of this have to do with how Kieran owns the castle?"

"Because he and Dùndubhan are inextricably bound," Lachina says, "just you are bound to it, and both of you are bound to each other."

"That's nonsense," I say. "You three are mad."

Lachina sighs. "One day you will believe. The spirits have told me that the fortunes of the MacTaggarts lie in the hands of the Laird of Dùndubhan. Do with it what you may, but take care in how you treat the castle. It has a heart and a soul, just like you."

"I dinnae believe that nonsense." I push my chair back and rise. "Enough of this foolishness. I have work to do."

Before anyone can accost me with more foolish ideas, I storm out of the dining hall and out of the house. In the courtyard, I turn to head toward the bakehouse where I have stored some items that might be of use in the repairs I mean to effect. Mayhap I hadn't considered making such repairs until recently, but that matters not one whit. Aye, "recently" means in the past few days. It has nothing to do with Alyssa or what Lachina said at breakfast.

I sort through the items I have at hand, but as I examine them, I realize I don't have nearly enough supplies to do what needs to be done. Dùndubhan is an ancient castle that had lain in disrepair for many years before my aunts took up residence here. They lacked the experience and physical strength to accomplish the sort of widespread repairs that were needed. I should have been working on the castle since the day I moved in here. Instead, I behaved like a *cacan*. Aye, only a wee shit would treat women the way I've done.

Mayhap I can't renovate the castle inside and out, but I can at least shore up the outer walls. I have enough stones to accomplish that task as well as the proper ingredients to create mortar. As I begin my work, I feel the tension that has lived inside me ever since my banishment begin to sift out of me. There's nothing like hard labor to remind a man that he is a man and not a ghost of who he once was.

While I'm toiling to repair a section of the wall near the gatehouse, out of the corner of my eye, I catch sight of a figure behind me. When I swivel my head to glance that way, my heart beats faster.

Alyssa leans against the corner of the house, head tipped to the side, observing me with keen interest.

"What are ye doing, lass?"

She approaches me, laying her palms on my chest. "I love a half-naked, sweaty man."

I can't speak, which is nonsense. Of course I know how to speak, but the tone of her voice stole away my breath.

"You must need a break," she says. "So let's fuck."

Chapter Twelve

Alyssa

I can't believe I suggested we should have sex again. But I didn't lie. The sight of a sweaty, muscular man always gets me hot and bothered, especially when that man is wearing only pants and boots. I can see the bulge of his dick getting bigger. He's as turned on as I am. I swore to myself that I would never have sex with him again, but I need to renege on that vow. Right now.

"Have you been drinking?" Kieran asks.

"I'm not drunk." I splay both palms over his chest and skate them up and down his skin. "I want you, Kieran. Are you going to say no to that?"

He wraps an arm around my waist and pulls me close. "Nay, lass. I won't say no. What would you say if I suggested we do it right here in the courtyard?"

"Won't your aunts be scandalized?"

He chuckles. "That's highly unlikely. They plotted to bring you here, and they want us to marry. They'll be shrieking with delight if they catch us fucking out here."

"Your family is bizarre."

"Aye. It's the MacTaggart way." He moves his hand down to my thigh and starts hiking up my skirt slowly. "I want my woman to be wet as a rainstorm for me."

I just stifle a gasp when he pushes his hand under my skirt and cups my groin. "Already there. You make me so damn wet that I can't think straight."

"And you make me as hard as a block of granite."

Can't resist rocking my hips into his touch. "What shall we do about that, hmm?"

He groans, his eyes hooded. "I need to feel your body wrapped around my cock so badly that I can hardly breathe."

Oh God, hearing him say those words makes me desperate for him too. As if I hadn't been desperate already. How can I feel this way for a man who annoys the hell out of me most of the time? Yet he has shown me his softer side too, and I think that's why I need to get naked with him again. There's nothing sexier than a man who will bare his heart and soul to a woman. The fact that he still snarls at me sometimes doesn't erase the good things.

Kieran scoops me up and carries me away from where he'd been working with stones—to repair the wall, I'm sure—and sets me down on an area of bare, smooth earth. He unbuttons his pants. "Lie down, Alyssa."

"Shouldn't I undress too?"

"Not yet."

I obey his command for two reasons. I want him inside me now, and the rough tone of his voice got me even more aroused. Once I'm lying on the ground on my back, he kneels at my feet. After roving his gaze over my body, he rubs his cheek and then bends forward to plant his hands at either side of me. I've already begun to breathe more heavily, which makes my tits heave. Kieran's focus becomes bound to my chest as he drags his tongue over his bottom lip. When he reaches for the laces on my vest, my heavy breathing turns into panting.

"Hurry, please, I need you inside me, Kieran."

A deep groan resonates in his chest. He undoes the laces as quickly as he can, fumbling twice, a sure sign that he's as hot for me as I am for him. I feel like a teenager again, like I'm about to lose my virginity. I hit that milestone a long time ago. But something about this man makes me feel like I've done more than travel back in time. I've rewound my life too, that's how it feels.

Kieran has just spread my vest open when Efrica rushes out of the house while shouting, "The devil has come! Hurry! The devil has come!"

We both race over to Efrica, who has stopped halfway across the courtyard. Bent over from the waist, she struggles to catch her breath. My open vest flaps, but I'm not in any danger of flashing my tits at Efrica. I still have my white undershirt on.

Kieran grips his aunt's shoulders. "What is it, Efrica? What devil has come?"

"The fire-haired fiend."

"Dinnae understand."

She sucks in a big breath and exhales it slowly. "The red-haired man who Alyssa met on the path. He has returned."

Kieran grits his teeth, his eyes narrowing, and curls his lip. "Simidh Gunn."

"Aye, the red-haired fiend."

Simidh Gunn does have red hair. When I'd met him on the path to wherever that trail goes, a shiver of unease had rippled through me. I'd never believed someone could sense another person's character simply from talking to them, but Simidh Gunn changed my mind about that.

"How do you know he's here?" Kieran asks his aunt.

"I saw him out the window."

Whistling starts up outside the walls of the castle compound. It seems to originate from a distance, but soon, the lyrical whistling grows louder until it sounds as if it's right outside the walls.

Lachina and Morna sprint out of the house and halt beside Efrica.

"We saw the red-haired devil too," Lachina says. "He even whistles like a demon from Hell."

Kieran nods once, with resolute determination. "Remain here. I will deal with the *bod ceann*."

"Shouldn't you take a weapon with you?" I ask. "Who knows what Simidh Gunn plans to do."

"Dinnae care about his plans. I will strangle him with my bare hands if he tries anything."

"Please be careful. That guy gives me the creeps."

Kieran scrunches his brows briefly, undoubtedly because he didn't understand what I said, then he marches up to the gatehouse entrance. While Gunn keeps whistling out there, Kieran opens a hidden hatch in one of the doors that I hadn't noticed before. It's a little window that lets him peek out at whoever is waiting on the other side.

"Haud yer wheesht, Simidh," Kieran snarls. "Dinnae care to listen to your off-key whistling."

"I request entry into your fortress," Gunn says. "The laird cannot deny a traveler safe passage."

"Of course I can. Away with you."

"But I have come to pay my respects to the lady who has taken refuge in your castle. Would you deny me that pleasure?"

Kieran slams the window shut.

Will Simidh go away? It's doubtful, in my opinion. Not that anyone has asked what I think. Both men assume they know what I want. While I appreciate that Kieran wants to protect me, I have an idea of my own.

"Let me talk to him," I tell Kieran. "Through that little window thingy."

"No."

"He can't grab me through that hole. It isn't big enough."

Kieran grinds his teeth, which I can tell because his jaw muscles twitch. While he glares at me and I fold my arms over my chest, more whistling starts up outside the walls.

I lay a hand on his arm. "Let me do this. Trust me, please."

He blows out a breath through his nostrils. "If you insist."

"Yes, I do." I kiss his cheek. "Thank you for trusting me."

Kieran opens the window and backs away, allowing me to approach the hatch and peer out at Simidh. He stands there with a relaxed posture, his expression neutral except for the slight smile on his lips. That smile broadens when he notices me.

"Good day, *bòidheach*," he says, then bends his knees and spreads his arms in some kind of weird attempt to appear gentlemanly. He wears a kilt and a white shirt, but that's not what grabs my attention. The red-headed visitor also has a sword strapped to his hip. "May I approach, my lady?"

"I'm not a titled lady, so you can cut the crap." I gesture for him to come closer but hold up my hand to stop him once he's gotten close enough. "What do you want?"

"To court you, *bòidheach*."

"Whatever you just said is not my name." Why didn't my necklace translate? Maybe it's because he's lying about...something.

"It means 'beautiful' in Gaelic," the man says. "You are a vision of perfection, and I wish to pay my respects as well as court you, if you agree."

"No thanks."

He leans toward me, though several yards still separate us. "May I at least know your Christian name?"

Kieran pushes me away from the hatch. "Nay, you may not know anything about the lass. Leave now before I decide to insist you depart."

The way he said "insist" suggested he means "kick your ass." Not that medieval people would use that phrase. They'd say something eloquently insulting. Of course, they do say "fuck," so maybe medieval Scots aren't so different from people in my century.

Kieran growls words in Gaelic that my necklace doesn't seem able to interpret.

Simidh Gunn chuckles. "Dinnae fash, lass. We will meet again."

He saunters off down the path. I know that because I lean sideways to peek out the hatch—until Kieran shuts it.

Whistling starts up again outside the walls, gradually fading away as Simidh, presumably, heads off down the path.

I raise my brows at Kieran. "What did you say to him? My necklace refused to translate."

One corner of Kieran's mouth kicks up. "I told him to go fuck a donkey."

"Well, I guess my pendant is programmed not to use bad language."

Efrica comes up beside me. "It's more likely that Kieran's anger and fear interfered with the spell."

"What fear?" her nephew says. "Ahmno afraid of Simidh."

"But you worry about losing Alyssa. Simidh is the greatest threat to your relationship with her since he is willing to do anything to achieve his goals."

"What do you know about Simidh Gunn's goals? He's a *tolla-thon*."

"An ersehole he might be, but he wants Alyssa." Efrica picks up his hand, then mine, and sandwiches them between her own palms. "And you wish for her to become your woman, which means you and Simidh are enemies in more ways than one."

"Of what do you speak? I know he falsely accused me of thievery and seduction. He is my enemy in only that respect."

"Tosh." She lets go of our hands. "Lachina's *da-shealladh* has shown her signs that must be interpreted before we share everything. But please believe me, Kieran, much more is at stake than Simidh's desire to harass you."

She turns and walks away. Her sisters follow her into the castle.

Kieran releases my hand. "You will stay away from Simidh Gunn."

"I will do what I believe is best."

He fists his hands, and his biceps flex. "Woman, you—"

"Don't ever call me 'woman' again. My name is Alyssa. You know that, and I know you only call me 'woman' when you think I'm behaving like a silly female."

"I should never have allowed you to speak to Simidh. You belong to me."

"Like hell I do." I march up to the big wooden bar that blockades the gates and struggle to lift it. When Kieran chuckles, I flash him a scowl. "Let me out of here."

"Nay, I will not."

"I need to get out of this damn castle. Feel like I'm being dragged down into a deep, dark hole." My hand slips, and my knuckles get whacked by the big bar. "Goddammit!"

Kieran gently takes my hand and examines my knuckles. "These are scrapes, nothing more. They will heal."

Despite his rough palms, his touch feels delicate and tender.

"What fashes you?" he asks gently. "It must be more than the fact I would not allow you to step outside. That was for your protection."

"I know. But I feel like the walls are closing in around me, and I have no way out. I'm trapped—in a strange time, in a strange place, with strange people."

"Ah, lass." He draws me into his arms. "You are not a stranger any longer. We have welcomed you into our home. What can I do to ease your burden?"

"I'd love to go for a walk—outside the castle walls. But I know that's not safe."

He combs his fingers through my hair and murmurs soothing sounds. For a long moment, I shut my eyes and let myself sink into the intimacy of being held by Kieran MacTaggart. I don't understand how he can be sweet one minute and angry the next, but I suppose that's the result of his banishment and the knowledge that Simidh Gunn wants to torment him.

"We will go for a walk," Kieran says. "Outside the walls."

I pop my head up. "Really? Are you sure?"

"Aye, I'm sure." He urges me to back away, then swings one half of the huge gateway open just enough that we can walk through the gap. And he shouts through the opening, "Efrica! Lachina! Morna! I'm taking Alyssa for a walk, but we won't go far. Do not leave the castle."

I hear a chorus of ayes from his aunts. It sounds like they're shouting from somewhere above the ground floor. As Kieran leads me away from the castle, I spy three pale faces in a window on the highest floor.

"There is a river," he tells me. "Would you like to see it?"

"Yes, I'd love that. Is it really safe to leave your aunts behind?"

He gives me a wry smile. "They know every way to hide in Dùndubhan. Believe me, not even Simidh Gunn could find them if they dinnae want to be found."

"Oh, good. If you say it's true, I believe it."

And strangely, I *do* believe it.

Chapter Thirteen

Kieran

I retrieve my sword and then lead Alyssa around the castle walls, but I still can't understand why the lass believes what I said about my aunts simply because I told her it's true. She seems to vacillate between suspicion and trust when it comes to me. I can't blame her for that, but it does leave me rather confused. Mayhap we can discuss that later. For now, I want to give Alyssa what she craves—freedom, at least from the confines of Dùndubhan.

We cross through the forest, leaving the castle behind as we make our way to the river. Alyssa grows a wee bit excited when she hears the first trickles of water in the distance. I love the look on her face, full of sweet innocence that I wouldn't have expected from a forty-year-old woman. She doesn't seem older than I am. Mayhap I have grown older than my years because of my banishment.

I stop us partway to our destination so I can pluck a handful of flowers. When I offer them to Alyssa, she seems rather surprised. But then she smiles with such bonnie sweetness that I forget about everything else. Mayhap I did surprise her, but she clearly likes it. I snatch a small flower from her hand so I can tuck it behind her ear. Aye, she looks even bonnier this way.

"Thank you, Kieran," she says. "I love the flowers, and I'd love to see the river. Is it far from here?"

"Nay, it's close."

As I guide her deeper into the forest, I begin to wonder if I've been reckless in taking her outside the fortress walls while Simidh Gunn is out here somewhere. Twice, he has attempted to engage Alyssa in conversation. I should not have allowed her to speak to him at the gatehouse. But she was unhappy, and I could not stand to see her in that state. At least I had the wherewithal to bring my sword. That means I can defend her, if necessary.

Alyssa keeps bowing her head to look at the flowers in her hand. Every time she does that, her gaze flicks up to mine and she smiles sweetly.

If I'd realized that all I needed to do to make her happy was to pick flowers for her, I would have done that yesterday.

The sounds of rushing water grow louder as we approach the river, but we still can't see it yet. Then we crest a small rise, and the river comes into view a few yards away. As we reach the bank, Alyssa kneels to comb her fingers through the water and gaze down into the depths. I crouch beside her, but I watch her face, not the river. She seems relaxed, her expression more serene and beautiful than I've seen her since the moment she arrived.

"We should return to the castle," I say. "Remaining outside the walls is dangerous."

"Because of Simidh Gunn. Yeah, I know." She rises, then turns her head left and right to take in the scenery one last time. "I'm ready to go."

We wander back to the castle while holding hands. Alyssa seems no more anxious than she had been before our journey to the river, despite knowing that she must remain within the walls of Dùndubhan henceforth. As we approach the gates, I perform one final survey of the vicinity to assure myself no one has followed us. Even if Simidh has managed to track us without being seen, he will not breach the walls.

The rogue does not have an army.

Just as I'm lowering the crossbar to seal the gates, Morna emerges from the house. She informs us it's time for the midday meal. Though I turn to head for the dining hall, Morna stops me with a hand on my arm.

"No, dearie," she says. "We are not having the midday meal inside. Alyssa wants to be outdoors. Therefore, we have arranged to eat here in the courtyard."

I glance at Alyssa. "Is this what you want?"

"Yes, it sounds perfect."

"Then we shall eat out here. But we should have a quilt or some such thing for all of you to sit on."

"Already taken care of," Morna says. "Follow me."

My aunt leads us around the rear of the house, though I've begun to wonder if Dùndubhan qualifies as a home. It was designed to serve as a fortress, not a place where a family might live and raise their children. Besides, I'm living with four women—and lasses deserve to have all the womanly things. I allowed my aunts to decorate my bedchamber, yet I have not helped them gather materials to decorate their own rooms.

In the area directly across from the main door to the castle, my aunts have set up a small feast. A quilt lies spread out on the ground with bowls and plates full of food lying atop the quilt. My aunts have managed to create a full-fledged meal outdoors, complete with wine and dessert. When I compliment their handiwork, each of my aunts kisses my cheek and calls me "a sweet laddie." Efrica goes further, claiming I have become the wee laddie she knew years ago. She also claims I have found the woman whose heart beats in time with mine.

It's romantic nonsense.

While we enjoy our meal, I notice the wildflowers that have grown up naturally on this section of earth. I'd once visited a castle that had a flower garden outside the walls, and I wonder if Alyssa might like that. But since it's not safe to go outside, mayhap I could create a garden inside the walls. I could even erect a wall around the garden itself to create a private space where the lass could enjoy whatever bushes and vines I plant here. I know it won't be as good as strolling through the forest, but at least she would be able to enjoy a small bit of the wilderness here inside the safety of the castle.

My aunts finish their meals first and return to the house. They did that on purpose, I'm fair certain, to give me and Alyssa time alone.

As much as I would love to share my garden idea with her, I decide to keep it a secret for now. I would love to surprise her with this gift. How will I prevent her from realizing what I'm doing? I'll need to invent an excuse for keeping her away from this corner of the courtyard. Or I could somehow conceal the project itself. Mayhap I'll need to use both techniques. How long will I need to complete my surprise? As I glance about the grounds, I think I might have enough materials already.

Alyssa waves a hand in front of my face. "Are you sleeping sitting up with your eyes open?"

"Pardon?"

"You're not paying attention to me."

"I apologize. My thoughts took control, and I was not paying enough attention to the bonnie lass in front of me."

She picks up a piece of bread and studies me while she breaks off a small piece. "What thoughts had you so distracted? Is it Simidh Gunn?"

"No. I would prefer not to share my idea yet."

"Fair enough." She consumes that bite of bread while still studying me. "You know, I haven't properly thanked you for taking me on a nature hike."

"What is a nature hike?"

"That's when people walk in the woods to enjoy the scenery."

"Of course. I understand now. But there's no need to thank me again."

She slants toward me until our mouths hover inches apart. "I said I need to thank you *properly*."

"What does that mean?"

"Get naked, Kieran."

I glance about, but I see no sign of my aunts. They had mentioned they wanted to weave a rug, or mayhap it was a quilt. That means Alyssa and I are alone, essentially. "What did you have in mind, *mo leannan*?"

"That sounds like Gaelic, but my necklace won't translate it."

"Aye, it is Gaelic. I'll tell you what it means after we fuck. I assume that's your intent."

"Yes, that's exactly what I want. But this time, you're going to let me take charge."

"Do what you will, *mo leannan*. I am yours to command."

No, I won't tell her that phrase means "my sweetheart." Not yet. I also won't point out that she might already be with child, or if she is not, she will be soon. I intend to make love to her as often as possible, and I will take her as my wife soon too. She belongs to me. Simidh Gunn will never claim her for his own because she is already taken.

I obey her wishes and "get naked," as she phrased it. Then she commands me to lie on my back on the ground. While I clasp my hands under my head, the lass removes her clothing piece by piece. She begins by removing her boots, then unties the laces on her vest ever so slowly, biting her lip and releasing it little by little while her gaze remains on me. My cock thickens, and I fight the urge to stroke myself. Nay, I dinnae want to spill my seed yet because I need to watch the lass undressing. No other woman has ordered me to observe while she does this, but Alyssa clearly feels no shame in disrobing before me.

Once she has freed the laces, she shrugs out of the vest, taking her time with that task as well. Then the lass pulls her shirt off over her head, lifting it inch by inch while shimmying her hips. By the time she tosses the garment away, my cock is throbbing and I can't stop myself from stroking my length lazily.

"I want to lick your *boicionn* and suck on your *bodach beag a' bhàta*."

"Guess my necklace doesn't translate dirty Gaelic," she says. "I could tell from your tone of voice alone that what you said was filthy."

"Aye, I said I want to lick you folds and suck on your clitoris."

"Mm, yes, please do that." Her mouth curls into a sly smile. "By the time I'm done getting naked, you'll be as warm and pliable as clay in my hands."

"Mold me however ye like, lass."

She pushes her skirt down over her hips, letting it crumple to the ground. The bonnie lass now wears only her long chemise. She pushes it off one shoulder, then the other, but the chemise still covers her figure. Alyssa turns away from me to gaze at me over her shoulder. Then she eases that strap down her arm whilst the garment gradually exposes her shoulder. I cup my cock, fighting against the compulsion to relieve the pressure, as she lowers the other strap so that her back is fully exposed. I can just make out the upper curves of her erse cheeks.

I release a long, guttural groan.

Alyssa lets the chemise tumble to the ground.

Bod an Donais, that woman has the perfect body. I need to bury myself inside her right now. But when I lift my head, she wags a finger at me.

"Uh-uh-uh," she says in a sultry tone. "You follow my orders, remember? I know it's hard for a strapping laird to let a woman take control, but I can tell you love being under my thumb."

"Aye. But hurry, lass. I might not last much longer."

She drops to her knees and crawls up my body. When her lips meet mine, I can't restrain myself. I grasp her face with both hands, plunge my tongue between her lips, and devour her like a man who hasn't eaten in months, so starved for the taste of her that I groan and grasp her erse.

Alyssa breaks the kiss. But rather than mounting me, she turns around and positions her face over my cock. Her mound hovers above my face.

"What are you about?" I ask. "This is nothing I've seen any lass do before."

"We're going to eat each other up, Kieran." She glances back at me. "While I feast on your dick, you'll feast on my cream."

Though I've not heard the word dick before, I understand what she means. And I want to do it. Need to do it.

"Is the Laird of Dùndubhan ready?"

"Aye."

She lowers her body onto mine and takes me into her mouth little by little, teasing my flesh with her tongue, until her lips meet my balls. At the same moment, her *boicionn* descends on my lips. I open wide and take her flesh into my mouth, suckling her rigid nub and lapping up the juices that flow from her folds. Instinctively, I grasp her hips to hold her *boicionn* in position so I can devour her *brillean* even more fiercely, nipping at her clitoris too, which makes her moan. She pumps me by raising her head and plunging it downward, over and over, while I thrust my tongue inside her opening.

Every time her hair brushes my balls, my pulse beats faster and I know I won't last much longer.

The lass massages my inner thighs.

Fuck, she's trying to drive me insane.

I latch on to her nub again and devour it as if I'll die without her flesh in my mouth. The pressure to come builds inside me, and it feels like I'm running up a steep hill toward a cliff. I know once I jump off that precipice,

I will erupt inside her mouth, and I want that more than I've ever wanted anything. But I need her to plunge off that cliff with me. When I pull her nub into my mouth and suckle it hard, her entire body goes rigid.

She throws her head back and cries out.

The lass isn't done yet. So I torment that stiff nub and slide my fingers between her erse cheeks to tease her there, and her cries echo off the castle walls. Just as her pleasure seems to be waning, she takes me fully into her mouth again and tugs my balls while pumping my cock in and out, in and out. Now I can sense that precipice though I can't see it, and I'm barreling toward the edge with my pulse thundering in my ears and the need to come clenching my entire body.

With a hoarse yell, I spill everything I have between her waiting lips. She keeps fucking me with her mouth until I have nothing left to give. Then the lass wriggles about until she's lying on top of me with her chin on my chest. She drags her tongue over her lips and moans with satisfaction.

Mhac na galla. We need to do that again.

Chapter Fourteen

Alyssa

Holy shit. I've done the sixty-nine thing twice before with other men, but doing that with Kieran… I can't even describe how incredible it was. I expected him to balk when I told him I should be in control of him this time. But he didn't complain. He essentially told me to go for it. The more I learn about Kieran, the more I like him. Well, that might not be the most appropriate way to describe how I feel. It's much stronger than liking him. I've never experienced a connection as deep and unfathomable as the one I have with him.

A medieval Scot has shown me the meaning of real intimacy. Who knew that could happen? Men in this century are supposed to be raging assholes, according to modern definitions. Kieran MacTaggart can be overbearing at times, but he also has a good heart. Screw those modern ideas. People are complicated, no matter what century they live in.

I thread my fingers through his hair and gaze up at the face of the man who made me come like the world was ending. "Have you ever tried that position before?"

"You wanted to be in control. Was that not the position you wanted?"

"I meant the sexual position. You know, when my groin was mashed to your face, and your dick was in my mouth."

"Oh, aye, that position." He grins. "I had never known such a thing existed, but I enjoyed it immensely."

"Me too. But I had tried that before. It's called the sixty-nine position."

"Does that mean we must do it sixty-nine times? That might prove exhausting."

I laugh. "No, silly. That's a description of the position."

"Dinnae understand."

"Well, you know what the numbers nine and six look like, right?"

He rolls his eyes. "Of course I do. I'm not illiterate."

"What we did is called sixty-nine because we're not facing each other. We're inverted like the numbers six and nine. Understand?"

Kieran scrunches his face as if he's struggling to picture how we had been lying together a moment ago. Then his face lights up. "Aye, I do understand. That's a clever name you invented for that position."

"I didn't invent the name. Not sure who did. Doesn't really matter, though."

"Nay, it does not." He grasps my ass. "I enjoyed having your erse in my face. Lapping up your juices was the best dessert I've ever had. I might need to feast on you every evening before I sleep."

"That might be the strangest compliment I've ever received." And the weird compliment reminds me of something. "Where did you sleep last night? I was in your room, alone."

"I slept in the solar. On the floor."

"Aren't there any other bedrooms in this big castle?"

He shrugs one shoulder. "None that are furnished."

"You can sleep with me tonight. The bed in that room is plenty big enough for the two of us."

"If we share a bed, I might end up fucking you."

"That's a risk I'll take."

He hugs me to his body and surges to his feet, setting me down. "I have some, ah, repairs to undertake out here. You should go inside and blether with my aunts."

"I'd rather watch you work."

"Not this time. These repairs are… I dinnae want you watching, that's all."

He can't possibly be embarrassed to have me see him making repairs. That would make no sense. Whatever his reasons for not wanting an audience, I will abide by his wishes. So I kiss him goodbye and head into the house. This big, drafty castle has begun to feel like home instead of a fortress.

I find Kieran's aunts in the solar. Lachina is knitting while Morna and Efrica sit at a table playing chess. Okay, I hadn't expected to find them doing that. I don't think they're too dumb to understand chess. I'm just surprised they would play any kind of game. So far, I've only seen them cooking. But now I know they have interests beyond food.

"Sit down, *gràidh*," Efrica says, patting the chair beside hers. Morna sits across from Efrica.

I accept her invitation and settle onto the chair.

"Do ye play chess, *gràidh*?" Efrica asks. "We love the game. It's challenging and requires a great deal of skill and strategy."

"Sorry, I've never played. It always sounded boring."

"Oh, no." She winks. "Not the way we play."

"Would ye like to learn?" Morna asks. "Chess is a good way to pass the time."

"Sure, I'd like to learn."

For the next two hours, Morna and Efrica attempt to teach me how to play chess. It is kind of interesting, but it's also damn confusing. I think I'll need years to figure out how this game works, thanks to all the intricacies and strategies involved. I'm not a dummy, but chess is complicated. Maybe I don't have enough desire to play the game.

All my desires revolve around Kieran.

Lachina seems to notice that I'm not totally invested in chess, and she waves for me to approach her chair. "Morna and Efrica are cutthroats at chess. Would you like to learn to knit instead? It's much more relaxing."

"Sure, that sounds good."

I drag my chair over to the fireside, next to Lachina, and absorb her knitting wisdom. Soon, I'm learning how to cast on and how to purl, giving me the basics I need to start knitting right away. The result isn't beautiful, but I made it with own hands. Lachina assures me I will get better at knitting the more I practice. I'd spent years working as a social media manager, dealing with data and images and everything else involved with helping companies craft a cohesive brand online. All of that means nothing now. I'd felt adrift ever since I got thrown back in time, but now I realize I can develop new skills.

Not totally useless after all.

"Checkmate!" Efrica shouts. She leaps out of her chair and claps her hands while grinning. "Morna is defeated!"

Lachina shakes her head, smiling at her sister's antics.

Morna stows the chessboard and playing pieces in their wooden box. "Gloat all ye like, Efrica. I won the five previous matches and cleaned the floor with you."

Lachina glances at the clock on the mantel. "Where is Kieran? It's nearly time for the evening meal."

Efrica trots over to the windows and peers out, holding her hand above her eyes like a visor. "Oh! There he is. What on earth is he doing? The laddie seems to be hauling stones across the courtyard with a wheelbarrow. Dinnae know what he thinks that will accomplish. That section doesn't need mending."

I hurry over to the window and peer out there too. "But Kieran told me he'd be doing some repairs."

"Can't see enough from here." Efrica seizes my arm and tugs. "Let's go outside and see for ourselves."

"Sure. I'd like some fresh air, anyway."

Efrica glances at her sisters. "Are you two coming with us? Morna might be so devastated by her chess loss that she'd rather hide under her bed."

"*Pòg mo thòin*," Morna says. Then she thumbs her nose at her sister.

I look at Efrica. "My necklace didn't want to translate that."

"Morna told me to kiss her erse. I'm sure she intentionally kept you from understanding. She's devious that way."

Lachina sets her knitting on the floor and rises, tugging her vest down. "Would you two please behave like grown women? You're giving poor Alyssa the wrong impression of us."

"You once called Hamish Fraser a stupid piece of shite."

"Well, he deserved that. The man asked to see my bosom."

Once the ladies have finished insulting each other, they begin to chatter away about the MacTaggart clan, though none of them have had much contact with their own family since they moved to Dùndubhan, especially since Kieran was banished and came to live here. But I enjoy listening to their stories as we lazily make our way downstairs. They don't seem to be in any hurry to figure out what Kieran is doing out there.

The four of us traipse across the courtyard to the area where Kieran is hefting stones out of the wheelbarrow one by one. I think he's making a wall. But why would he do that?

"Kieran, dearie," Efrica says. "We were wondering what you might be about with those stones."

He straightens and turns toward us. Since he's not wearing a shirt, I can see the sweat glistening on his chest and arms. "I'm working. That's what I'm about."

"But why? What are the stones for?"

"I'll tell you when I'm ready."

I tear my focus away from his slick, suntanned flesh and meet his gaze. "Are you building a wall?"

He freezes. "Why would you ask that?"

"Because you're collecting large rocks and placing them in rows with what looks like mortar between them." I lean sideways to see what's behind him. "And that looks like a pail of mortar you've mixed up."

"Aye, it is. You might have deduced what I'm doing, but you have no idea why I'm doing it." He leans toward me. "And I won't tell you."

"Not even if I beg?"

He stares at me for several seconds, then glances at his aunts before veering his attention back to me. "Leave. I have work to do."

"If ye want to roll about with Alyssa," Morna says, "we'll go back inside to give you two privacy."

"Roll about? You're off your head."

"It's time for the evening meal," Efrica announces. "That means no more work for today, *gràidh*."

Kieran stares down at his rocks and mortar. "I need to finish this section, then I will meet you in the dining hall."

"Dinnae be long."

Efrica leads the rest of us back into the house. I offer to help make dinner, but the ladies urge me to go into the solar for a "wee rest." I do head into the solar, but I have no intention of napping. I'd rather practice my knitting, so I sit in Lachina's chair and get out the thingy I'd knitted earlier. Even Lachina didn't know what I'd made. She called it "a bonnie piece of art." So yes, I will knit instead of napping.

You know what they say about best-laid plans.

A strong hand gives me a rough shake. "Wake up, Alyssa. 'Tis time for the evening meal."

I mumble things that aren't quite words. My eyes don't want to open yet.

The hand shakes me again, but the accompanying voice has become annoyed. "Wake up now."

"Huh?" I rouse myself and push up straighter in my chair. I'd slumped down pretty far. "Kieran? Why are you glaring at me?"

"Because it's time for the evening meal. Did you drink an entire bottle of Scotch? I've only seen drunkards sleep as soundly as you."

"I am not drunk." I jump out of my chair and stumble, falling into Kieran. Yeah, that probably didn't convince him I'm sober. "You didn't have to shake me so hard."

"Aye, I did. A gentle shake had no effect on you."

Wow, I must have been a lot more wiped out than I realized. Knitting must use quite a bit of energy. Or maybe it was that sixty-nine interlude in the courtyard that drained me. I also went for a nature hike with Kieran, so it's almost impossible to pin down the source of my tiredness. But I feel awake and energized now.

I stretch and yawn. "That little nap really refreshed me. And now I'm starving."

"Did you not eat enough at breakfast? Mayhap I should carry you if you are weak from hunger."

"No, Kieran, you will not do that. I ate plenty. When I said I was starving, that was hyperbole meant to point out the fact that I'm definitely ready for dinner."

He stares at me with an adorably baffled expression.

I lay a hand on his chest. "I'm not about to keel over. Promise."

"But ye said—"

"Hyperbole, remember?"

"Oh, aye."

He glances down at my knitting, which had fallen on the floor when I slipped into a semi-comatose state. That's more hyperbole, so I won't say the words out loud. Kieran might take it the wrong way. Instead of sweeping me off my feet again, literally, the way he loves to do, he clasps my hand to lead me out of the solar.

The moment we step into the dining hall, Kieran's aunts break into wide grins. Jeez, it's not like we've been gone for a month. They saw me an hour ago and Kieran a few minutes ago. I get that they're happy to see their nephew with a woman, but if they're hoping I'll announce I'm going to marry him, they need to take a deep breath and calm down. No wedding. I might've discovered that Kieran isn't a total jerk, but I do not want to tie the knot with him—or anyone. I tried marriage once, and it ruined me.

Even if I wanted to marry Kieran, I can't spend my life in this drafty, abandoned castle with a banished Highlander. What kind of life would that be? Maybe I'll ask him about that later so I can at least understand what living with him would mean.

No, I don't need to ask him. I will not marry Kieran.

He pulls out a chair for me, the one kitty-corner to his, and smiles sweetly as I sit down. When he kisses my forehead, I get a pang in my chest. No, no, no, I will not fall for him. Time travel plus banishment is not a good way to start a relationship.

Kieran takes his seat and gazes at me with that same sweetness as a moment ago.

Why won't he stop looking at me that way? I really, really need him to growl and snarl at me right now so I can get rid of this warm and fuzzy feeling that seems to have taken root in my chest. I barely know him. That means I cannot have developed an emotional attachment.

Efrica pushes her chair back and rises.

"What are ye doing?" Kieran asks. "It's time to eat."

"Aye, but I need to record this moment in my book. I've been remiss of late, what with our guest arriving so suddenly. 'Twill only take a moment to get my book and write down my observations."

"Sit down, Efrica. You can do that later."

I glance at Kieran, then Efrica. "You're writing a book?"

"Aye. It's a history of my life and experiences. And you will be in it."

Chapter Fifteen

Kieran

"Mhac na galla, Efrica," I say, and to my ear, it does not sound as if I'm growling. The women will most likely claim I am doing that. "Ye dinnae need to write down every moment of your life. Only monks do that, but they record the history of a nation or the world, not the everyday affairs of people whose lives will mean nothing once we die."

"Our lives will mean something," Efrica says. "I know your banishment has changed you and made you feel as if you don't matter to the world. But you matter to us and to your father." She casts a sly glance toward the lass who sits beside me. "And to Alyssa, I'm fair certain."

The lass's eyes widen, though only for a brief moment.

My aunt has embarrassed Alyssa. All I can do to alleviate her discomfort is to change the topic of discussion. "Has Lachina been teaching you to knit, Alyssa?"

"Yes, she has. I never thought I'd enjoy knitting, but I've found that I love it. There's something tranquil about it."

"Oh, aye," Lachina agrees. "I learned to knit out of necessity, but I quickly came to love it. God is in the stitches, that's what I like to say. You've taken to the art of knitting so quickly too."

"Thanks." Alyssa seems almost bashful after hearing Lachina's praise for her knitting skill. "It's definitely more my style than chess."

"What about checkers?" Morna asks. "You might enjoy that one. Oh, but you could also try fox and geese."

"Aye, that would be an excellent choice for Alyssa," Efrica says. "She could play that game with Kieran. He would be the fox, naturally, and would try to catch all of Alyssa's geese. She could overwhelm him with her flock and hem the laddie in so he would be at her mercy."

My aunt manages to make a meaningless game sound like a wanton act of debauchery simply because of the tone of her voice.

"It's a gaggle of geese, Efrica," Morna declares. "Flocks are for sheep."

"Enough!" I shout as I pound my fist down on the table, causing it to tremble. "Let's eat. We are in the dining hall, after all, which is meant to be a place where we consume our food in silence."

Lachina laughs. "When have we ever eaten in silence? This isn't a monastery, Kieran."

Since I have no chance of convincing them to stay silent, I give up and begin to devour my meal. The women somehow can eat while chattering away like squirrels. Mayhap I grew a wee bit annoyed when my aunts insisted on discussing games at the dinner table, but only because Efrica tried to harass me with her insinuations. It's unseemly for a woman to discuss sex as frankly as Efrica had done. I wouldn't mind Alyssa speaking to me that way when we're alone and naked.

Eventually, the conversation returns to normal yet no less irritating subjects. The way women blether has always been a mystery to me. But I'm glad to see Alyssa smiling and laughing again despite Efrica's behavior. Mayhap my aunt is not at fault. It might be I who should temper my behavior.

No, it's Efrica who should do that.

Fox and geese. What a ridiculous sexual metaphor.

We retire to the solar after dinner, and my aunts insist on serving us Atholl Brose. I love whisky, but drowning it in oatmeal and honey has never appealed to me. Alyssa wants to try the drink, though, and I don't want to disappoint the lass by refusing to partake. I might not love Atholl Brose, but I do relish watching her experience it for the first time. At first, the lass appears uncertain as she raises the glass to her lips and inhales the aroma. But then she takes a sip, and her expression brightens.

"Mm, this is good," she says. "Can't believe you don't like this stuff, Kieran. It's got whisky in it, after all."

"I never said I don't like it. It isn't my favorite beverage, that's all. But I'm glad you're enjoying it."

"Never tried whisky before. But honestly, I didn't enjoy alcoholic drinks that much overall." She takes another sip. "I could get used to this, though."

"Dinnae drink too much. You might lose your balance going up the stair."

"Aw, it's so sweet of you to worry about me. But I'll be fine." She leans over to reach my chair and pat my arm. "You can always carry me up the stairs if you're worried about my balance."

"I thought you disapproved of me carrying you."

"Not anymore. I kind of like it now."

My aunts begin to make ridiculous noises that imply they think my desire to carry Alyssa is sweet or adorable or whatever nonsense they have in their heads. Soon, the conversation turns to other subjects that also hold little interest for me but at least don't involve me. They talk about knitting and games and what my "secret plan" in the courtyard might be. Nay, I will not tell them. It wouldn't be a surprise for Alyssa if I confessed my intentions now.

Finally, my aunts announce it's time for bed. Aye, of course they all wink and smile deviously as they tell us that. Then the three of them leave the room.

I rise and stretch. "Time to carry you up the stair."

"You mean the stairs, plural. Right?"

"No. I said what I meant. We're going up the stair. Why would that be plural? There is only one set of steps that lead to the upper floors."

She raises her hands. "Okay, fine, I give. It's a stair, singular in construction but plural in fact."

"You are harassing me again."

"What if I am?"

"Oh, lass, you know what that means." I pluck her out of her chair and throw her over my shoulder. "I'm carrying you up the *stair.*"

While I march down the corridor and to the stair, Alyssa grasps my erse with both hands, one for each cheek. "Damn, you've got incredible glutes."

"You are speaking gibberish again."

"No, I'm not. But I guess medieval people don't know about the gluteus maximus muscles, huh? Those are muscles in your posterior."

"My erse, you mean. Speak English, *mo leannan.*"

"I should learn Gaelic. Then you'd understand me."

She keeps her hands on my "posterior" while I mount the steps on our way up to the bedchamber. Once I've shut the door behind us, I set the lass down on her feet.

Alyssa bends from the waist to peer behind me. She slaps my erse, then straightens. "You definitely have the best glutes in Scotland, maybe in the whole world."

"I admire your erse too, but that is not my favorite part of you." I clasp her breasts. "These are."

She presses her body to mine, tipping her head back to meet my gaze. "Let's fuck."

"Now? You drank quite a bit of Atholl Brose."

"Not too drunk for sex." She wriggles against me, which rouses my cock. "Come on, Kieran. You know you can't keep your hands off me."

That might be true, but I have never taken advantage of a woman who was in this state. Mayhap she isn't drunk. But she might regret asking me to seduce her when she wakes in the morning. I want her to beg me to fuck her while her mind is clear.

I turn toward the door.

She wraps her arms around my midsection from behind, nuzzling her cheek against my back. "Please don't go. I want to sleep with you, even if we don't have orgasms."

"What are 'orgasms'?"

Alyssa squeezes me gently as her sweet laughter tickles my senses. "An orgasm is what happens when we both experience the ultimate pleasure at the end of sexual intercourse."

"I see." I peel her arms away from my torso and face her. "I would also like to sleep with you without orgasms."

She grins, though her state of mild inebriation makes the expression rather aslant. Then the lass tries to unlace her vest, but her fingers can't quite manage the task.

I push her hands away from the vest and loosen it swiftly, then remove the garment altogether and drop it onto a chair. She chews on her bottom lip while I get rid of her shirt, shoes, and tartan skirt, leaving her clad in only her chemise. I slap her erse. "Get in bed, lass."

She takes hold of her chemise and lifts it as if she means to remove that too.

I stay her hand. "Keep the chemise on. That is an order."

"Yes, Your Majesty, the Laird of Dun-not-doin' me."

Her drunkenness is charming in a strange and entirely inappropriate manner. I carry her to the bed and lay her down. Then I remove my braies and boots but leave my shirt on. It's long enough to conceal my cock even if I grow stiff from lying in bed with the drunken woman beside me. The fact that she is mildly inebriated does not arouse me. But her behavior while in that state arouses me without my permission. My body cares nothing for what I would prefer.

I crawl onto the bed and lie down on my back.

Alyssa rolls onto her side, slinging an arm across my chest. "Mm, you smell so good. I could just eat you up."

The husky tone of her voice spurs my cock to rouse. But when she wriggles against me, I know I'll be doomed if I remain in this bed with her. A man only has so much willpower.

She slides her hand down to my groin.

Mhac na galla. I shan't get any sleep if I remain in this bed. While the lass begins to snore softly, I sneak out of bed and steal her tartan skirt, using it as a quilt when I lay down on the floor near the hearth. My dreams all involve Alyssa, naked and doing things no proper lady would do, but I dinnae care if she doesn't meet the expectations of courtiers. This is Scotland, not England. I revel in my dreams of her, of the filthy things I'd love to do with the lass and the way she looks when she reaches her ultimate pleasure.

Aye, I wake up with my cock as hard as the stones that make up the castle walls. At least I didn't fuck the lass while she was drunk. My aunts would have chastised me for that, and aye, they would have known what I did. Not because they have *da-shealladh*. Nay, they simply have common sense and functioning eyes. I can't hide my lust for Alyssa from anyone, but especially not my aunts.

I rise and start hunting for my braies, leaning over to check under and behind various pieces of furniture, but I can't recall where I left them last night.

"Now that's what I like to see when I wake up."

"Good morning, *mo leannan*." I straighten and saunter over to the foot of the bed. "What do you like to see? Dinnae understand."

She slides off the foot of the bed and slaps my erse. "You were mooning me."

"That must be another twenty-first-century term."

"Yep. It means you were giving me a great view of your bare ass."

"Was I? That was purely accidental." I throw an arm around her, tugging the lass into my side. "But if it aroused you, mayhap we should fuck right now."

"Afraid I need to use the, um, chamber pot first."

I stare at her for a moment, baffled by her statement. "What chamber pot? The only one in the castle is broken."

"Yeah, but I found a similar-size pot in the kitchen and took it. I have to relieve my needs somehow."

My mind can't seem to comprehend her statements. Then it dawns on me like the sun on a summer morning. "Alyssa, have you been relieving yourself in a chamber pot ever since I released you from that wee room in the tower?"

She hugs herself. "Yes."

"Why would ye do that?"

The lass throws her arms wide. "What, was I supposed to relieve myself on the floor?"

"You're supposed to use the garderobe like the rest of us."

"The what robe? You want me to squat on a piece of clothing?"

"No, Alyssa." I cover my face with my hands and groan as the truth finally penetrates my ironclad mind. Then I look at her. "The garderobe is a wee room where you can do whatever you need to do in private."

"It's a toilet?"

"Mayhap it is, but you must be using a word from your century."

"Sorry. A garderobe is a privy, right?"

"Aye."

Her shoulders flag. "Well, at least I understand now. A toilet is a privy too, by the way."

"Ah, I see." I grasp her shoulders and bend my knees so I can look her in the eye, but she refuses to meet my gaze. "You should have asked me how you should relieve your needs."

"I figured you'd snarl at me, and besides, I was embarrassed to ask you about that again. Couldn't convince myself to ask your aunts either." She still won't meet my gaze, and she keeps her head bowed slightly. "I'm a stranger here. Excuse me for not feeling a hundred percent comfortable asking those kinds of questions."

What a fucking idiot I am.

Chapter Sixteen

Alyssa

Kieran studies me for a moment, and his proximity is starting to make me feel less than comfortable in a different way, one that is not helpful right now. "I understand you won't be comfortable coming to me for help, but you can always talk to my aunts. They never snarl or stomp about like demons."

"You aren't a demon. But I would feel better talking to your aunts about this kind of thing, if you're really okay with that."

"I am."

"Thank you, Kieran."

"Dinnae thank me." He steps back and sighs. "It's my fault you feel this way. I should never have locked you in the tower room. Why on earth would you let me fuck you if I make you so uncomfortable?"

"You don't make me feel that way, not most of the time." I wrap my arms around myself again. "But you are a man. Women don't usually like to talk to the man they're sleeping with about where and how to relieve their needs."

"I will apologize as many times as need be. I'll get down on my knees to beg your forgiveness too."

"Don't do that. You haven't done anything wrong. I shouldn't have been so squeamish about talking to you."

He raises his brows. "Don't you need to use the garderobe anymore?"

"Yes, absolutely. Where is it?"

"Come, I'll show you." He glances at my body. "I assume you'll want to dress first. But I'll have no complaints if you prefer to wear only your chemise."

"Uh, no. I think I'd freeze to death before I get to the garderobe."

I find my shirt and vest quickly, because they're hanging over the back of a chair. Kieran must have done that. I have only vague memories of him undressing me in the most chaste and respectful way. But I was wearing that plaid skirt too, and I don't see it anywhere. So I rotate in a circle to make a visual search for that garment. There it is. But locating the skirt only brings up another question.

"Why is my skirt on the floor by the hearth?" I ask. "Can't believe I would've left it there."

"Ye didn't." He winces and rubs a hand over his mouth. "I, ah, slept on your skirt last night. My braies wouldn't work for that purpose."

"I don't get it. You slept in the bed with me."

"Nay." He averts his gaze to the window. "You were still rather, ah, lustful after drinking Atholl Brose in the solar. Dinnae ye remember when I carried you into the bedchamber?"

"Yeah, I remember that. I know you undressed me. But once you set me down on the bed, things got fuzzy."

Kieran snatches the skirt off the floor and hands it to me. "I shall wait in the corridor for you."

"Oh, come on. You've seen me naked twice. Might as well stay in here while I get dressed."

"If you wish me to do so, I will."

"Yes, I wish it."

He turns toward the hearth, giving me his backside.

I try not to do it, but I can't squelch my snorting laugh. "Um, Kieran? Your shirt rode up when you were bending over a minute ago, and it's still stuck to your ass. Not that I mind…"

He spins around and grabs his pants and shirt off the floor. "We should both dress for breakfast."

"Don't think your aunts want to see us half-naked? They seem like liberated women."

While he struggles to pull his pants on, he flashes me a scowl. "Of course they are liberated. I did not hold them prisoner."

"Ohhh, so it's only me you lock up in the tower."

He straightens and buttons up his pants. "Are you done harassing me?"

"No, not really. I plan on harassing you as often as I feel like it."

Once we're both fully clothed, Kieran leads me out of the bedroom but not down to the first floor. Not sure why I expected that's where we would go. I haven't seen any evidence of a septic system or plumbing, so I don't understand how the medieval toilet will work. Kieran takes me upstairs to the third and highest floor, not counting the tower and turrets. He shows me a door that lies at the end of the hall, then turns the knob to ease it open a smidgen.

"Here it is," he declares. "The garderobe."

I push the door open further and tiptoe into the tiny room. It's no bigger than a stall in a modern restaurant bathroom, but at least this cramped space has a window that lets in fresh air.

"I'll wait for you in the corridor," he says. "Take care not to lift the seat, else you'll fall down the shaft."

"Shaft? How deep is it?"

"The garderobe goes down to just below ground level, where a subterranean shaft channels everything into the river."

"Remind me never to swim in the river."

"As long as you swim upstream from the garderobe shaft, you'll be fine."

Yeah, that makes me feel so much better.

At least this medieval toilet has a wooden seat. But I notice something that makes no sense. Kieran is just shutting the door, so I holler, "Wait! Why is there a pile of hay in the corner?"

He peeks his head through the gap where the door is still open. "I assume you'll want to clean your erse afterward."

"Oh. Thanks for explaining. You can shut the door now."

The latch clicks shut, and I do my business ye old-fashioned way. The draft on my bottom feels weird, but I manage to get it done. When I emerge from the garderobe, Kieran is leaning back against the wall a few yards away.

"I'm done," I tell him. "And now I'm even hungrier than I was earlier."

He pushes away from the wall and offers me his arm. "May I escort you to the dining hall?"

"Yes, you may." I hook my arm around his. "Thank you, my lord."

"I am not a lord."

"Should I say 'thank you, my laird' instead?"

"Just call me Kieran."

We've just reached the entryway that Kieran calls the stair when pounding erupts outside. His aunts race out of the dining hall and into the stair.

"Is that Simidh again?" Efrica asks.

"How could I know the answer to your question?" Kieran asks. "I do not have the power of *da-shealladh*. Don't you know the answer, Lachina?"

"You know very well that I can't see everything. The spirits guide me when they feel it's necessary."

He grunts.

Another round of pounding erupts, and a voice shouts, "Kieran! Are ye going to make your weary old father stand out here all day?"

Kieran freezes.

"That's Uilleam," Efrica says. She shoves Kieran toward the door to the outside. "Dinnae leave him standing out there."

He glances at me sideways.

"Go on," I say. "I'll stay here with your aunts."

"Oh, tosh," Morna says. "We will all go out there together. It's Uilleam, not a demon who crawled out of a hellmouth."

Kieran throws her a scowl, but then grabs my hand and leads the procession out to the gatehouse. We ladies move aside while the laird hauls one half of the giant wooden doors open and raises the portcullis enough that the man on the other side can sidle through the gap. Kieran's father looks a lot like him, aside from the gray hair and wrinkles. I wouldn't mistake Uilleam for Kieran, but anyone who saw them together would know they're closely related.

Uilleam gives his son a quick, firm hug. "Good to see you, *mo mhac*. It's been too long."

"You banished me. Did ye think I would walk into the village and ask for a dinner invitation? I would have been run through with a sword before I could pose the question."

"That's not what I meant." He hugs Kieran again, more fiercely this time, and he gets choked up. "I miss ye, laddie. *Do mhàthair* would be heartbroken if she knew we'd given up on each other."

"Mother would understand. But I'm relieved she isn't here to see what I've become."

Uilleam claps a hand on Kieran's shoulder. "Your banishment won't last forever. Will it, Lachina?"

Kieran seems less than convinced by his father's statement.

But Lachina nods vigorously, unshed tears shimmering in her eyes, as she pulls her brother into a hug. "Kieran doesn't believe in my *da-shealladh*, but he will soon enough."

"Aye, he will." Uilleam greets Morna and Efrica too with an equal amount of enthusiasm. To Efrica, he says, "Are ye still writing in your book?"

"Of course. Someone needs to document what the MacTaggart clan does."

"You keep doing that, *gràidh*. It's an important task." His gaze shifts to me, and Uilleam's brows lift. "Kieran, why didn't you tell me you had taken a wife?"

"We are not married," his son says. "This is Alyssa, and she is our, ah, guest for the time being."

"Guest?" Uilleam approaches me and clasps one of my hands between both of his palms. "You are a bonnie lass, for certain. It's no surprise Kieran would rather keep you hidden away in this ghost of a fortress. I've ne'er seen such beautiful blue eyes, or auburn hair that glimmers in the sunlight. Aye, you are a rare beauty and an angel, for certain. Only a divine creature could tame my wild son."

"I haven't tamed him. Kieran is as stubborn as a mule."

Uilleam chuckles. "You know him well, don't you? Aye, my son needs a good woman to stop him from becoming a wild boar who ruts on any lass he meets."

"Haud yer wheesht," Kieran snarls at his father. "Dinnae need to hear you insult me while trying to charm Alyssa into sharing your bed."

The elder MacTaggart gives his son a long-suffering look. "By God's bones, Kieran, do ye honestly think I want to bed your lass? She's far too young for me." Uilleam winks at his son. "But she's just right for you."

"Kieran has already bedded the lass," Morna announces. "They seem quite keen on each other."

Uilleam grins. "When will the wedding be?"

Kieran snarls something I don't understand, which probably means it was so vulgar that my necklace blushed and wouldn't translate it.

The elder MacTaggart throws his head back and laughs heartily. "At least ye haven't lost your sense of humor, laddie."

"Let us all go inside," Efrica says. "A wee nip of mead wouldn't go amiss, aye?"

Uilleam slings an arm around her shoulders. "You always were the best of my sisters. No one else offered me mead."

He aims a look of mock disapproval at Lachina and Morna.

We all amble into the house and straight to the solar. Efrica bustles off to get mugs of mead, and though her sisters offer to help, she shoos them away. A few minutes later, she returns carrying a wooden tray laden with six mugs that nearly overflow with the beverage. We each accept a mug.

And I take my first sip of a medieval drink. Mead tastes like a combination of a semi-sweet wine and sherry, yet with a hint of honey too. "I like mead. What is it made of?"

"Honey and water," Kieran tells me. "It's fermented with yeast."

"Do you make it yourself?"

"No, my aunts do. I tried to help, but they insist on making the drink themselves."

Efrica shakes her head at him. "You had never made mead in your life. Of course we didn't want you to interfere with our finely honed method for fermenting our favorite drink."

"Where do you do that?" I ask. "I haven't seen any barrels of, well, anything here at Dùndubhan."

"That's because we have our meadery in the far corner of the old bakehouse. Kieran didn't want us fermenting spirits in the house."

"You ladies are very industrious. Do you sell your mead?"

"Oh, aye." Efrica leans toward me and speaks in a fake whisper. "Dinnae tell Kieran, but we sell a variety of wares whenever we attend a market day."

"You do what?" Kieran says, and I swear his nostrils are flaring. "You told me you three were attending to elderly people. Were all those outings when you actually sold wares at a market?"

"No, dearie, we never lied to you." Efrica gives her nephew a patient smile. "Dinnae take this the wrong way, but the truth is that you are banished. We are not. That means we're free to go to whatever market we like to sell whatever we like. How do you think we can keep this castle from falling down around us? We earn money to buy materials for repairs."

His face goes blank. "You sell mead and whatever else to pay for fixing Dùndubhan? Why didn't you tell me?"

"Because you're a man, *gràidh*. We didn't want to injure your masculine pride."

Kieran continues to stare blankly at Efrica until, after a minute or more, he shakes off his shock. "I owe you a great debt, Efrica. And you too, Lachina and Morna. I had no conception of how much you've sacrificed for me. Thank you."

"We love you, dearie. No need to thank us."

All three of his aunts swarm him to kiss and hug their nephew, which clearly makes him uncomfortable—but in a good way. I think he needs a lot more of that kind of treatment. Maybe I haven't known Kieran for long, but even I can tell his banishment has affected him deeply, more than he would ever admit.

Lachina comes over to my chair and leans in close to whisper in my ear, "You are the one who can save him. Open your heart and let it happen."

She returns to her chair beside the hearth.

Could I save Kieran? The more important question is, would he let me save him?

Chapter Seventeen

Kieran

Alyssa is watching me as if she has never seen me before while my aunts and my father talk incessantly. I cannot keep track of their conversation. The only thing I can focus on is Alyssa. What did Lachina whisper to her? I saw my aunt approach the lass, and Alyssa's eyes widened so briefly that I almost thought I hadn't seen that. But she seemed quite surprised by what Lachina said, and the way she wrings her hands suggests she still has not recovered from the shock. I need to draw her away from the others to find out what's bothering her.

How can I take her away without my family noticing? The solution occurs to me suddenly, but I'll need to take care in how I implement my plan.

So I rise and stretch as if I simply need to iron out a kink in my back. When I glance around the room, no one seems to be paying any heed to me. That's just what I need. Now that I've assessed the environment, I casually amble over to the hearth. Alyssa's chair is only an arm's length away. Another quick perusal of the room assures me the others remain engaged in conversation.

I inch closer to Alyssa but keep my gaze on the hearth as if I do not even notice the lass. Then I pretend to examine the mantel, running my fingers over the edge.

"What are you doing?" Alyssa hisses under her breath.

Out of the side of my mouth, I reply, "Be quiet. I have a plan." I continue to sidle toward her until my calf meets her chair's leg. "I'm moving toward the door. Once I'm in the hall, make your way out there, but do not let anyone else see that."

When I cast her a sidelong glance, she seems a wee bit annoyed. Mayhap she dislikes the way I'm whispering.

"Please," I murmur. "Heed my instructions."

She compresses her lips but then hisses, "Fine."

I assume that means she agrees to my plan. A few moments later, I reach the door and close my fingers around the knob.

"You would make a terrible spy," my father says. "We've all been watching you sneak over to the door. If ye want a bit of hochmagandy with Alyssa, go on and do it, laddie. No need for subterfuge."

"I don't want any hochmagandy." But aye, fucking sounds like a good idea. That's not my intention at the moment, however. "I want to talk to the lass alone."

"Then take her out of the room. Dinnae creep about like a mouse hunting for cheese."

"Melted cheese, aye?" Efrica says. "He was creeping about so close to the hearth that it must have singed him."

I pull the door open. But I cannot look at Alyssa when I say, "Would you please come with me? I need to speak to you alone."

Alyssa rises and walks up to me. "All you had to do was ask. I'll happily go anywhere with you."

She can't mean that. It's nothing more than something a body says, not anything a body actually does.

But the lass takes my hand, and we shut the door behind us as we head up the stair to the bedchamber in which we both slept last night. Alyssa does not complain or ask questions. She simply goes with me. That does not suggest she meant it literally when she said she'd go anywhere with me.

Why do I keep thinking about that?

Once I kick the door shut behind us, Alyssa wraps her arms around my waist. "Do you want to have sex on the bed? Or on the floor? We could try chair sex if you're feeling adventurous."

Chair sex? Dinnae know how that would work.

"I did not bring you here to fuck, *mo leannan*. I need to discuss something with you."

She feigns pouting. I know it's nonsense because a woman like Alyssa would never stick her lip out so egregiously.

I smile a wee bit and give her erse a squeeze. "We can fuck later, *mo leannan*. Right now I'd like to know what had you so upset in the solar."

"You're asking what was bothering me. Right?"

"Aye."

She gazes at my chest while she speaks, but then, she can't see my face without tipping her head back quite far. "Lachina told me—She must be wrong. I mean, I can't do what she said."

"What did Lachina want you to do?"

The lass lowers her head and mumbles.

"I didn't understand that."

She winces. "Lachina thinks I can save you, but she didn't know from what or how I would do that."

"Lachina means well, but her *da-shealladh* is not infallible. I have no idea why she believes I need to be saved, much less from what."

"Maybe I should ask her."

The nearness of her body has begun to rouse my desire for her. She hovers a hair's breadth away with her arms about my waist, yet she barely touches me otherwise. I do want her. I always want her. Since the moment I first saw the lass, I've needed to feel her *baltan* enveloping my cock. I've never experienced this intensity of lust with any other woman. But it's more than a hunger for her body. I crave the woman herself too, for more than *bualadh craigeann*.

I fold my arms around her and tug the lass into my body. "Ask my aunt later. I want to try chair sex with you right now."

"There are a few ways we can do that. I've seen it in magazines." She reaches up to touch my brow. "You've got a crinkle over your nose. I'm guessing you don't know what a magazine is."

"Aye, it's a storage room. But you must have a different sort of magazine in mind."

"In my century, a magazine can also be a publication. You know, something you read."

"Ah, I see. What did your magazines tell you about sex?"

She raises onto her toes and feathers her lips over mine. "I know all kinds of ways that we can fuck in a chair. Wanna try it?"

"With you, I'll try anything."

A fist raps on the door. "Kieran, you'll need to wait on 'talking' with Alyssa. I nearly forgot what I needed to tell you."

The sound of my father's voice makes me groan and sag my shoulders. "We will meet you in the solar."

His footfalls recede.

I rest my forehead on Alyssa's. "Chair sex will need to wait for another time."

"No problem. Sounds like Uilleam has something important to say."

Once we reach the solar, Alyssa and I take the two empty chairs that await us. My father sits opposite us, while my aunts have taken the chairs furthest away so my father can sit across from us.

He leans forward, resting his elbows on his knees. "I was so glad to see you and my sisters, Kieran, that the main reason for the visit slipped my mind. I should have visited you sooner, and I apologize for that. But we need to set that aside for now. A grave matter needs discussing."

"What grave matter?" I ask.

"Simidh Gunn."

A cold pit forms in my gut. But I am not afraid. I despise Simidh, and hearing his name always infuses me with a chilling anger. "What has he done now?"

"Nothing dangerous, yet. But Simidh has begun to disseminate lies about you." He sits back, suddenly seeming weary. "He has been saying that you're a black witch allied with demons and that you will manifest in the beds of MacTaggart lasses to force your affections on them."

"I would never touch a lass from my own clan, and I certainly would never force myself on a woman."

"Everyone in this room knows that. The clan knows it too, but Simidh is quite skilled at convincing people that the sky is a blue kilt."

"Aye, he is good at that. If anyone is a demon incarnate, it's Simidh."

The lass beside me grasps my hand. "This is a big deal, isn't it? That creep wants to ruin your reputation and who knows what else."

I have no idea what to tell the lass. Simidh's hatred of me has been long-standing, but I still know nothing of why he despises me. What have I ever done to earn his ire? Nothing. The fact that he has begun his campaign to destroy me now, since Alyssa arrived, cannot be a coincidence.

"What would you have me do?" I ask my father. "Simidh has twice attempted to speak to Alyssa, and I believe his vendetta involves her, at least in part. But I can see no way to stop him from spreading lies."

"You must protect Alyssa. Whatever Simidh's plans are, he will try to make the lass his pawn. That man is capable of anything."

"Aye. But I have no weapons other than a sword. If he gathers an army to assault Dùndubhan, I won't be able to fend him off."

"He wants me," Alyssa says. "Maybe I should talk to him."

"You will do no such thing."

"Not alone. You would go with me."

"Where do you suggest we meet with Simidh?"

Her gaze goes distant as she seems to be considering the question. Then she straightens in her chair and looks at me. "We meet him somewhere away from Dùndubhan, a neutral place where it will be harder for him to do anything sneaky. You know the area better than I do. Can't you think of a place like that?"

"Mayhap I can." I turn to my father. "All of us together can surely choose such a location."

For the next half hour, according to the mantel clock, we have a group discussion about which location might prove the most appropriate. I would rather that Alyssa remained here at Dùndubhan, but I know she's right that Simidh will want to see her. If only I show up for the meeting, he will become suspicious of my motivations. He will be suspicious either way, but with Alyssa there, he might be less inclined to do anything overt.

We cannot simply wait for Simidh to return to Dùndubhan. He has a scheme in mind, of that I'm certain.

"When should we do this?" Alyssa asks. "And how will we let Simidh know that we want to see him?"

"Let me handle that," my father says. "I've met Simidh several times over the years, and I believe he will listen to our proposal if I deliver the information to him."

Lachina clasps her hands under chin and begins to rock slightly in her chair. "Dinnae like this. The spirits have become agitated, and I'm afeard of what might happen."

My father rubs his sister's back, clearly attempting to soothe her. "The spirits might be agitated for a different reason."

She shakes her head vigorously. "Nay, they do not like this idea. Darkness is gathering around Simidh, and he will not stop until he has everything he wants."

"Easy, *gràidh*," my father says while he continues rubbing Lachina's back. "We won't let anyone harm Alyssa."

"A terrible storm is coming. Darkness will fall upon the Highlands, and the most precious gift might be lost."

I jump up and ball my fists. "No one will lose anything. I will protect what belongs to me at any cost."

Alyssa rises too, facing me. "What property are you protecting?"

"You."

"We've been through this before, Kieran. I don't belong to you or anyone. I'm not your property."

"You are." I seize her wrists and drag her into me. "I will do whatever is necessary to stop Simidh Gunn from getting his way. If he claims I have dark magics on my side, then I'll give him exactly that."

"No, Kieran. You can't do that."

"I will do what I must." I tug her even closer, and despite my family watching, I crush my mouth to hers in a bruising kiss. I'm branding her as mine, though I have no idea what I hope to accomplish this way. When I release her, she stumbles backward a few steps. "If your idea to meet with Simidh doesn't turn out well, I will go to any lengths to ensure he fails in his quest to destroy me and claim you."

Efrica and Morna huddle around Lachina, whose rocking has become more furious.

My father approaches me, shaking his head. "This is wrong, *mo mhac*. You are my only son, and I cannot let you go down this path."

"Ye can't stop me."

We glare at each other in silence, though we both know we aren't angry with each other. He worries for me, but I worry more for Alyssa. We've reached a stalemate. It doesn't matter what anyone else thinks, though. Defending Alyssa matters more to me than my own life.

The lass moves between me and my father. "Before you two start pummeling each other, we should wait to find out if my plan will work. We *will* wait. Understand?"

My father and I exchange glances, and I know without either of us speaking that he agrees with what I'm about to say.

"Aye, lass, we will wait. But not forever."

Chapter Eighteen

Alyssa

Twice today, Kieran and I have gotten sidetracked when we were about to have sex. Maybe that's why he suddenly turned into an alpha male on the hunt, ready to tear to shreds any competitor who tries to steal away his woman. I'm not his, not in the way he means. I care about him, I love being with him, and I know he has a good heart underneath all the caveman bullshit.

Yet he still claims I'm his property.

Should I chalk that up to anxiety? I need to know more about Kieran, and I need to know it now.

We all tromp out to the gatehouse, and Uilleam says goodbye to his sisters. Lachina still seems severely disturbed by whatever vision or insight she thinks her ancestors gave her. Uilleam kisses her forehead and whispers something I can't quite hear. His words relax Lachina somewhat, but she still has silent tears trickling down her cheeks. As Uilleam walks toward Kieran, his sisters comfort Lachina.

Uilleam clasps his son's shoulders. "Take care, Kieran. Lachina rarely receives messages from the other side as powerful as this one. Mayhap the terrible event won't happen today, tomorrow, or even next month. But sooner than we would like, it will occur."

Kieran says nothing, just staring at his father without expression. "I shall defend the women at any cost."

Uilleam hugs his son, then thumps him on the back. "I know you will, *mo mhac*. You are a good man, and I'm glad I had the chance to meet the lass who captured your heart."

Kieran drags one door open and heaves the portcullis up and out of the way. His father passes through it. Soon, his figure recedes and vanishes completely, consumed by the shadows of the forest.

Why do I feel like we will never see him again? That's dumb. Of course we'll see him again—at the meeting with Simidh, for sure. But I can't shake this feeling that something dark and evil is slithering all around us.

Kieran's aunts hurry back into the house.

He pulls me into his arms and buries his face in my hair. "*Tha gaol agam ort, mo chridhe.*"

My necklace didn't translate that, but I know exactly why it failed. The depth of emotion in his voice is the answer. Efrica had told me that the enchantment spell might not work properly if enough emotion was involved. I can guess what he said, though. Should I say it back? If he'd wanted me to know what he said, he would have told me in English instead of Gaelic. Though it makes no sense at all, I can't deny the truth.

I'm in love with Kieran, and he is in love with me.

"Now we just wait, right?" I say. "Uilleam will arrange the meeting with Simidh."

"My father will need to find Simidh first. That could take weeks or months depending on where he has wandered to now. Simidh likes to travel far and wide."

"And in the meantime…"

"We live our lives."

And that's exactly what we do. Every day, Kieran works on his secret project in between dealing with more immediate needs to keep the castle in good shape. We all participate in cleaning the interior of the house to make it seem more like a home than an abandoned prison. Kieran's aunts had done a lot to improve conditions inside the castle, but now we expand on those efforts. Kieran, being a tough guy, balks at the little touches we add to make the place pretty and welcoming.

It's not like we hung pink lace curtains in every room.

Morna and Efrica begin teaching me how to weave, something I had asked to learn. I haven't given up on knitting, though. I'm learning two new skills simultaneously because I want to become as industrious as the aunts are. Kieran is plenty industrious himself, but as a medieval man, he prefers to focus on manual labor rather than handicrafts. I doubt any of us ladies could lift the big stones needed to repair the walls.

Every time he goes up to the walkway atop the outer walls of the castle, I stand in the courtyard to watch and pray he doesn't fall. I know repairs are necessary, but I can't stop myself from getting anxious. That wall is very high.

For three weeks, we go about our daily lives as if we aren't counting down the minutes until doomsday. Simidh might be only a man, but something about him gives me the shivers. I can't shake the thought that he might use some type of black magic to destroy Kieran. Keeping up our routines and staying busy seem like the best options to avert anxiety. So, I start helping the aunts with the cooking too, and I help Kieran as much as he'll let me. That means I mostly stand around and observe while he keeps throwing me slightly annoyed looks. Well, at least he doesn't glower at me the way he used to do. I'll take "slightly annoyed" over "snarling beast" any day.

Every night, Kieran and I share the bed in his room, though he insists the "bedchamber" belongs to both of us. He hasn't even tried to seduce me. Does that bother me? I wish I could say no, but the truth is that I loved being with Kieran both times we got it on. I want more of that.

But I can't risk having sex with Kieran ever again.

I didn't have my birth control pills on me when I got swept back in time, and the effects of the last one I took have probably waned by now. Not sure how long the drug will stay in my system. Shortly after the visit from Kieran's father, I had my period. So at least I haven't gotten knocked up yet. That means I need to stick to my resolution never to screw him again. But I love Kieran. That means if he wants to make love to me, I don't know if I can resist his seduction.

All I can do is pray he doesn't get horny.

One day, I'm helping Morna make lunch while her sisters are outside watching Kieran work on his mystery project. We've all become kind of obsessed with puzzling out his intentions. He's building a shorter wall that juts out from the side of the castle's outer wall. That's all we can figure out. But as I'm chatting with Morna while we cook, I develop a need that will not be ignored.

"Um, sorry," I say, making a sheepish face. "I need to use the garderobe."

"Go on, lass. I can manage on my own until you return."

I hurry upstairs to do my business, then scurry back to the kitchen. By the time I get there, I'm breathing hard. "Wow, that's a workout. How do you guys handle rushing upstairs to use the garderobe?"

"We simply do. You'll get used to it, *gràidh*."

My gaze lands on the table in the middle of the kitchen. "Looks like you finished up without me."

"Aye. But you can help me later if ye like, when I wash our clothes."

"Sure, I'm happy to lend a hand. Do you wash everything here in the kitchen?"

Morna laughs softly. "No, *gràidh*. We wash everything in the river."

I must be gaping like a cartoon character. "The river that the garderobe stuff flows into?"

She laughs even more this time. "No, dearie. Well, yes, actually. But we cast a spell to cleanse the water before it ever leaves the garderobe channel."

"But Kieran said all the dirty water goes into the river. He suggested that if I want to bathe in the river, I should do it upstream from the garderobe channel."

Morna shakes her head while smiling. "Kieran believes that, aye. But only because we never told him about the water cleansing spell. He wouldn't have approved. Believe me, everything that flows from Dùndubhan into the river is as clean as water blessed by the Lord himself."

I can believe Kieran wouldn't approve of what his aunts did. But their little magical sanitation project makes me feel a whole lot better. Maybe one day I will swim in the river. But not while Simidh Gunn is out there prowling around, plotting who knows what.

On the night that marks my third week in medieval Scotland, Kieran and I head for our bedchamber as usual. We both undress, though I keep my chemise on while he wears a long nightshirt. I miss seeing his naked body, and I've started to wonder if he feels uncomfortable with nudity unless we're having sex. It's time to ask him about that.

Kieran has just finished getting naked and is climbing onto the bed. I'm sitting up, leaning back against the wall, trying to work up the nerve to broach the subject. When did I become a coward? *Suck it up, woman.*

I clear my throat. "Are you ever going to make love to me again? Or are you tired of me?"

He veers his gaze to me. "Dinnae be daft, lass."

"You haven't answered my question."

"I assumed you would want to abstain since you declared that you don't wish to marry me."

"That's what you think? If I don't want to marry you, that means I never want you to touch me again. That's 'daft,' Kieran."

He lies down on his back, hands clasped over his belly, and stares up at the ceiling. "You might already be with child."

"I'm not. I had my period a few days after I came to Dùndubhan." I suddenly realize he will have no idea what that means. Medieval women must've had a different term for it. "I meant that I, um, had my monthly bleeding?"

"Oh, aye, that."

Thank goodness he understood that. Not sure I want to try to explain the menstrual cycle to him.

Kieran shuts his eyes and sighs heavily. "You are untethered to me."

"Did you want me to be with child? So I'd have to stay with you?"

"Nay, but—Pay no heed to what I said."

I lean toward him to brush my fingers through his hair. "I want to 'pay heed' to everything you say. Please talk to me."

"About what?"

"Us."

He opens his eyes, rotating his head to aim those gorgeous brown eyes at me. "In what manner do you employ the word *us*?"

"We need to talk about our relationship. If you want us to have one, or if we're sharing this bed strictly so neither of us has to sleep on the floor."

Kieran wriggles and grimaces as if he can't quite get comfortable. "Mayhap we should discuss this in the morning."

"No more avoiding the issue. We need to talk about it now."

"I am not trying to avoid anything. But your persistence arouses me, and if we continue discussing our association, I will need to fuck you."

A laugh bubbles out of me. "That's what you're worried about? Relax, Kieran. That's exactly what I wanted to talk about. I miss having sex with you."

His brows wrinkle in the cute way that always makes me want to kiss him. "You wish for me to fuck you?"

"Yes, I do."

"But we might create a bairn if we lie with each other in that manner."

I've been on the fence about whether I want to have a baby with him. Honestly, I don't even know if I could get pregnant. I'm forty, after all, and that's not the prime age for conceiving a child. But as I lie here with him, gazing into his eyes, a sweet warmth blossoms in my chest, right over my heart, and spreads outward. I'd already realized I love him. Do I want a baby with him? Yeah, I think I do. But I want to be with Kieran even if I can't conceive.

"I want you, with or without a baby." And it's time I told him the whole truth. "I love you, Kieran."

He stares at me for a moment without moving or even blinking. Then he pushes up into a sitting position and grasps my hand, kissing the knuckles. "*Tha gaol agamsa ort fhèin.* That means I love you too, Alyssa."

"My necklace can't translate what you said. Efrica told me that could happen if there's a strong emotion involved."

"What I feel for you is stronger than anything I've experienced before."

"The same for me. Sometime, I'd really like to learn Gaelic."

He slides a hand into my hair, splaying his fingers over my scalp. "I'll teach you. But not tonight."

That sweet warmth is spreading throughout my body, setting off a tingling in my sex and heaviness in my lower belly. When he touches his lips to mine, my clit throbs. But I know this time we won't screw each other like sex-starved wantons. No, we both want something more. So I clasp his free hand to my breast and whisper to him.

"Make love to me, Kieran. Please."

Chapter Nineteen

Kieran

Nothing in the world could make me leave this bedchamber, not even if the castle began to crumble around us. Alyssa asked me to make love to her. I understand what she meant even if I have never heard the phrase before. Her tone of voice and the look in her eyes makes her desire clear. With her breast cradled in my palm, I can do nothing but gaze into her eyes while my *slat* begins to swell and I struggle to catch my breath.

Alyssa always steals my breath, my mind, my heart, and my soul. Now I want to show her what that means.

"*Tha mo ghion ort,*" I murmur. "That means I love you with all my heart. My *crann* is as hard as the stone walls of this castle, but I dinnae want to rush this time. When I push my *slat* inside your *baltan*, we will become one."

"No more talking, please. Just make love to me."

"Aye. Whatever you wish, *mo chridhe*. I will do anything for you."

I take hold of her chemise's hem with both hands, dragging it up her thigh, over her hip, until I've exposed the auburn hairs at the apex of her thighs. Her breaths have grown heavier, and her breasts rise and fall, a clear sign that she is as aroused as I am. As I continue lifting her chemise, she raises her arms to help me pull the garment off over her head. I toss it away. Just as the chemise flutters down onto the foot of the bed, I strip off my shirt and fling it away as well. I pull back the bedsheet.

"Lie on your back, *mo chridhe*."

Alyssa shimmies into position, now stretched out along the length of the bed with her head on the pillow and her hair fanned out over it. Her eyes shimmer in the flickering light from the hearth. Their blue color seems more intense, darkened by the dilation of her pupils. I straddle her body and allow myself a moment to simply admire the beauty of her body, from the dusky rose of her nipples to the creamy shade of her skin and the pale brown of the freckles that dapple her flesh. I have seen her naked before, yet I had never taken the time to appreciate how bonnie she looks with nothing hiding her figure.

"*Tha thu bòidheach*, Alyssa. That means you are beautiful."

My cock hangs down between our bodies, almost brushing her skin. When I bend my arms just enough to feather my lips over hers, the moisture from my crown transfers onto her skin. I shudder from the arousing sensation. But I can't concentrate on that. The look on her face has stolen my senses and erased the rest of the world. If the earth exploded, I would pay no heed.

So I kiss her slowly, exploring every inch of her mouth while she glides her hands up my arms to settle them on my shoulders. The aroma of her desire wafts in the air, exciting me even more, but I shan't rush to take her body, not this time. When I give up her mouth and crawl backward little by little, she catches her lip between her teeth and follows my movements. I pause above her breasts to pull one nipple into my mouth and lave it with my tongue until she gasps and clutches the bedsheet beneath her. As her back arches upward, I flick my thumb over the other nipple.

"Oh, Kieran," she breathes.

I lift my gaze to her, and the sheer lust on her face steals my breath away. No other woman has ever looked at me the way she does, whether we're fucking or simply talking. She makes me feel as if I could lift the whole world onto my shoulders.

While she follows my every movement, I lower myself onto her body and crawl backward until my face hovers above the auburn hairs between her thighs. Their silky softness teases my cheeks. The lass spreads her legs for me without the need for me to ask, and I use two fingers to separate her outer folds so I can press my lips to her slick inner folds. The aroma of her juices surrounds me and infiltrates my senses so thoroughly that I can't hold back. I devour her flesh, licking with great fervor while I massage her nub with my thumb. She thrashes her head and cries out.

Her body goes rigid, and she seems not even to breathe for a brief moment. Then her mouth falls open, but she makes no sound. Still, I know she has reached her pinnacle of pleasure. Lasses always behave this way in that moment, but she looks even more beautiful in the throes.

As her pleasure subsides, I rise onto my hands and knees to thrust into her hot sheath. The sensation of her slick, soft flesh enveloping me feels wonderful, but I try to keep a measured pace because I vowed to make love to her, not ravish her like a wild beast. The look on her face grows softer, even while she still seems highly aroused, and the lass clasps my face in her hands as if she means to never let go. The merging of our bodies makes the bed creak softly while the scent of her juices fills the air. I bend my arms just enough that I can touch my lips to hers.

She grips my upper arms, her eyes half-closed and her lips parted. "Oh, Kieran, yes."

My cock has grown so stiff that I know I won't last much longer, but I experience a desperate need for her to come with me. If I reach down to massage her nub, mayhap she will come. But the way she grips my arms prevents me from doing that, and I dinnae want to break contact—with our eyes or her hands. As our gazes remain bound, I fervently wish for us to climax together. She comes with such languor that I only know it's happening because her fingers dig into my flesh, the spasms of her inner muscles rolling through her like a flower blooming ever so slowly.

I suck in a breath and struggle to hold on until she finishes. When her neck arches and a wee cry tumbles from her lips, I let go and come. It rolls through me as sensually as her climax had done, urging me to thrust into her with a leisure that makes my heart pound, and when I spill my seed inside her, that flows out of me just as casually.

The lass wraps her arms around me as I settle my entire body on top of hers. My head rests between her breasts.

What happened? I've never experienced anything like the way we both came tonight. It felt like…magic. But that's ridiculous. I have no supernatural powers like my aunts do.

Alyssa skims her hands up and down my back. "What's wrong?"

"How do you know to ask that question?"

"Because I know you. Will you tell me what's wrong?"

'Twill make me sound like an idiot if I tell her. But if I want to be with Alyssa, I must tell her everything. "While we were in the throes, I wished for us to come together, and my wish was granted. Did you not feel the difference between this time and the others?"

"Yeah, I noticed. It felt almost…magical."

I lift my head to stare at her. "You felt that too? Does it not bother you?"

"Why would it bother me? I love you."

" 'Twas magic. But I do not have such powers."

"Stop worrying, Kieran. Obviously, you do have powers. Think of that as a gift rather than something to panic about."

I slide off her body. "After a lifetime of denying what my aunts claim—that I possess powers like theirs—I can't believe it might be true. Of course, you might be the one with such talents."

"Nope. It's definitely you."

"Despite my desire to refute that suggestion, I cannot do it. Mayhap you are correct."

She rolls over onto her side, facing me. "The way you made love to me has left me feeling warm and liquid, like I might melt onto the floor. Let's cuddle up and go to sleep."

"Aye, that sounds like a good idea."

The lass drapes her arms and legs over my body and nestles her face against my neck. I listen to her breaths as they grow shallow and quieter, and I know she has fallen asleep. Alyssa always looks bonnier and sweeter in sleep, as if she has shed all the worries that harassed her in the daylight. The rhythmic sounds of her breathing lull me into slumber too.

I wake in the morning feeling better than I ever have before, as if I could lift the whole castle and reposition it precisely where Alyssa wants it. If I do possess magical powers, then mayhap I could do that. But I've only just begun to accept those powers, and I did not make us come together last night on purpose. I cannot replicate that event.

But I can give Alyssa a different sort of magic.

So I pull on my clothes and slip out of the bedchamber, leaving the bonnie lass asleep under the bedsheet. Even my aunts haven't risen yet, which means I have all the time I'll need to craft my surprise. As I return to the bedchamber, I see my aunts emerging from their quarters. They all cast me knowing smiles, but I have no wish to chastise them for their impudence this morning. I'm too well-pleased to care.

Alyssa is still sleeping when I walk into the room, and I carefully push the door shut behind me so as not to disturb the lass. I shall disturb her shortly, but first, I will lay out our meal. Once I've finished my task, I sit on the bed's edge near her hip and lean over to rest my arm on the pillow above her head. Then I feather a kiss over her lips.

She stirs but does not rouse.

I press my lips to hers. "No more sleeping, *mo leannan*. 'Tis time to rise and enjoy another day."

She moans, the sound infused with a touch of irritation.

"Rise, lass, or I'll tickle your belly until you laugh so vigorously that your eyes water."

"Mm, one more minute."

I sigh with sarcasm. "You leave me no choice."

She mumbles and covers her eyes with one hand.

"As you wish." I pull back the bedsheet and lay my mouth on her belly and blow, keeping up the torture until she does as I predicted. The lass laughs so vigorously that her eyes water. "Will you arise now? Or should I do the same thing down here."

I move my hand to cover her mound.

She wipes at her eyes while still grinning from the way I had teased her with my mouth. "Good morning, Kieran."

"Good morn, lass." I straighten and wave toward the area behind me. "I have prepared a bath for you."

"Bath?" Her look of surprised excitement makes me want to kiss her, but I restrain the impulse. "How did you do that?"

"My aunts have a special room for bathing, though they prefer to wash themselves in the river. I created that room after I found an old tub in the bakehouse and cleaned it up."

"They didn't mention that to me."

"Your arrival upset our routines, but none of us would complain about that." I slide off the bed, then pick her up and carry the lass to the tub. As I move to lower her into the water, she winces as if in anticipation of diving into cold water—until she feels the warm liquid surrounding her. "I heated the water over the hearth for you."

"Thank you." She grins as she swishes the water with her hands. "Never thought I'd get a warm bath in the medieval era."

"You seem to have the idea that men and women of this time are heathens who know naught about hygiene."

"How often do you bathe?"

"My aunts do so once a week. I, ah, wait a bit longer."

She lifts her leg out of the water to nudge my knee with her big toe. "You seem pretty clean to me."

"I bathed in the river yesterday. Upriver from the garderobe channel."

Alyssa bites her lip, a mannerism I've come to know means she wants to tell me something but fears how I might react.

"You can tell me, *gràidh*. I shan't bark at you."

"I guess you really don't know." She pushes herself up to sit straighter in the tub. "Your aunts cast a spell that cleanses the water before it even leaves the garderobe channel."

"They did what?"

Aye, I might be digging three graves today.

Chapter Twenty

Alyssa

Don't be mad at them," I say. "Your aunts meant well. They wanted to make sure the water was clean, for drinking and bathing. I shouldn't have told you about that since they didn't tell you themselves. But I don't want you to feel like you have to worry about my health if I decide to go swim in the river. Promise me you won't snarl at them. Your aunts only wanted to help, but they know how you feel about magic."

"I am not angry."

"Good." I draw my knees toward my chest. "Then climb in, and we can get clean together."

He shakes his head slowly. "If I do that, I'll be fucking you within a matter of seconds."

"I have more faith in your willpower than you do. Give it a try. You might surprise yourself."

Kieran eyes the tub with suspicion, then steps in and gingerly lowers himself into the water, bending his knees once he's settled. He picks up a sponge that had been lying on the floor and dips it into the water, squeezing out the excess. "Shall I bathe you first?"

"Sure, I'd love that."

While he runs the wet sponge over my body, I let my eyes drift shut and simply enjoy the sensations. I do get mildly aroused, but mostly, I let my other senses take over and treat myself to the best massage I've ever had, thanks to the Laird of Dùndubhan. Kieran constantly surprises me with his tenderness, even while he also annoys me sometimes with his bossiness and his insistence that I belong to him. I need to understand more about his past, so I'll know for sure whether we can make a future together.

Yes, I love him. But we are literally from different worlds.

When he stops washing me, I open my eyes and take the sponge from him. "Your turn."

"No one has bathed me since I was a wee laddie."

"Then it's about time you had that experience again." I dip the sponge in the water to get it nice and wet. "And while I get you clean, I'd like to hear more about your life."

"My life? It's nothing of interest."

"Baloney. You were banished from your own clan. Please tell me about that."

"No."

I drag the sponge down his chest, swirling it to wash off his skin. "That's not good enough anymore, Kieran. You need to talk to me. Or would you rather I asked your aunts? Come to think of it, your father would probably be happy to share that information."

"Are you extorting the truth out of me?"

"Of course not. I want to know you better, that's all."

He grunts. "Knowing who I was in the past has no bearing on the present."

My goodness is he stubborn. I'd known that already, but I hadn't counted on him staying this pigheaded even after we both said the L-word. I'll need to come up with an alternative solution to crack him open.

"I'll let you keep your secrets," I say. "For now."

"But you expect me to confess eventually."

"Expect? No. I hope you will want to willingly share your past with me. I want to understand you, that's all. There's no nefarious reason for me wishing I could understand you." I slide the sponge below the water, gliding it down his lower belly until it bumps into his cock. "I could seduce the truth out of you. That might be fun."

"What does 'fun' mean?"

"Something that's enjoyable." I toss the sponge onto the floor and wrap my legs around him. Since his legs are spread, his dick now nestles against my groin. "Let's try, hey? Couldn't hurt. At the worst, you'll get a nice orgasm out of the deal."

"I have made no bargain with you."

"Not yet. But if you'll just—"

He springs up out of the water, sending me flailing, and steps out of the tub. Water pours off him, from his hair down to his toes and his dick too. He snatches his kilt off a chair and uses that to dry himself off. Then he drapes the plaid over the chair again.

And he stalks out the door, slamming it shut.

In about ten seconds, I bet he'll realize that he stomped out in the nude. Nine, eight, seven, six, five, four, three—

The door bursts inward, and Kieran stomps back into the room.

Didn't take him as long as I expected to notice he had no clothes on.

Still lying in the tub, I observe his actions with a combination of bewilderment and admiration. I love admiring his hot body, but I cannot understand his dogged determination never to share his past with me. While Kieran finds his clothes and gets them on, I begin to wonder if I can ever break through to him. I know, without a shred of evidence, that cracking him open will reveal everything.

As he stalks to the door and tears it open, I call out to him, "Forgot your boots, oh great lord of the dark and dusty castle."

He freezes with his hand on the knob. After a moment, he gusts out a sigh and spins around to search for his boots.

My fingers have started to prune, so I leave the tub and do what he seems incapable of handling. I find his boots. When I come up beside Kieran and dangle the boots in front of him, he makes a pained face. Without so much as thanking me, he yanks the boots on and leaves. The door slams shut behind him—again.

I borrow his damp kilt to dry myself off, then get dressed. I wish I had more than one outfit, but I can't be finicky when I'm living in the past. Which has become my present. Which sounds completely insane. Only a few times since I've been here have I wondered if I'm in a coma, lying in a hospital somewhere. All of those passing thoughts happened in the first three days of my tenure here at Dùndubhan.

Does that mean I've accepted that this is my home now?

No, it's worse than that. I've accepted that Kieran is my home now. And that doesn't bother me at all. It does, however, make me even more determined to root out Kieran's secrets, whether he cooperates or not.

By the time I reach the dining hall, Kieran's aunts are already seated and politely waiting for me. Their nephew is nowhere in sight.

As I sit down beside Efrica, I ask, "Where is Kieran?"

Morna huffs. "The *cacan* stole food from the table and ran away without so much as a by-your-leave."

"He is not a wee shit," Efrica says. "Kieran is confused and struggling with his emotions. Give him time."

"Hah. The laddie would carve his feelings out of his head with a knife if he could."

I pick up a piece of sausage but halt with it hovering an inch from my lips. Then I drop the fork.

"What's the bother, dearie?" Efrica asks.

"My pendant. I forgot to wear it, but I can still understand what you're saying."

Lachina smiles. "Of course you do, *gràidh*. We are speaking English."

"But you gave me the pendant because none of you speak English, and I didn't understand Gaelic."

"Nay. The pendant was meant to make it easier for you to learn our language. But then we realized you do speak English. We are most comfortable with Gaelic."

"Uh-huh." Yeah, that explanation makes perfect sense. We're dealing with magic here, so I shouldn't expect everything to make sense.

After breakfast, I ask the aunts where they think their nephew might have gone. But they have no idea. Kieran apparently stormed out so quickly that none of them had the chance to say "good morning," much less to ask him questions. If I can't interrogate Kieran, maybe I can find answers in a different way. I can investigate Dùndubhan and the clan that banished him. And I'll start with his aunts.

I help with the breakfast cleanup, then follow the aunts out into the courtyard where a much larger tub of water awaits us. It's time to wash the clothes. The kitchen has a pump for bringing water into the sink, but there are no washing machines in this century. Cleaning up after breakfast had been easy compared with washing the clothes. But I learn skills I'd never thought about before. Nobody in the twenty-first century worries about manually cleaning their clothes.

Kieran appears now and then, carrying a wheelbarrow full of rocks every time he enters the courtyard. He leaves the gatehouse portcullis up and the doors ajar just enough that he can maneuver the wheelbarrow through the gap. Though I try to watch what he's doing, I also have to assist in the clothes washing, so I only get brief glimpses of the manner in which he carefully spreads mortar and sets each stone on top of the layers he'd already created over the past three weeks.

"What do you think he's doing?" I finally ask Lachina, who stands closest to me.

"Kieran? I haven't a clue."

On the other side of the trough, Morna shakes her head. "He's making a wall, of course."

"Aye. But Alyssa and I have no conception of why he's doing that. If he wanted to fortify the walls of the castle, he's doing it the wrong way round. His wall will be inside the fortress."

"Perhaps he's building a nursery," Efrica suggests. "He and Alyssa have grown much closer of late."

Morna rolls her eyes. "Why would he build a nursery over there? Inside the house would be the obvious choice."

Oh jeez, I wish I'd never posed the question. "Could we stop talking about Kieran? He'll tell us what he's doing when he's ready."

"You brought up the subject," Lachina says. "You must be dying to know the answer."

"Sure. But I tried to get Kieran to talk to me, and he won't do it. I should never have brought up the subject."

Luckily, we've just finished washing the clothes. The aunts have other things on their minds now, like what to make for the midday meal. Kieran shows up for lunch, but he doesn't speak to any of us, not even when Efrica tries to cheer him up with a silly joke. If I'd known how much asking about his past would upset him, I wouldn't have brought it up. Well, that's not true. I probably would have done it anyway.

After lunch, Kieran announces he's going hunting.

"You're going out by yourself?" I say. "That doesn't seem smart given that Simidh Gunn is still out there."

"I went beyond the walls all morning. How do ye think I collected those rocks? Ye saw me bringing them into the courtyard."

"I know. But I assumed you got them from down by the river. That's not very far away. Hunting must require you to travel to where the game is."

"Aye. And there's plenty of game close to Dùndubhan."

"Can I go with you?"

He stares at me like I've suggested I want to become his human sacrifice and he should eat me for dinner.

"Don't look at me like that," I say. "If it's safe enough for you, it's safe enough for me. Besides, you can give me a weapon."

"A weapon? Ye dinnae even know how to clean a carcass."

"You can do that part. Or, you could teach me."

He looks only slightly less horrified by that suggestion. Luck is on his side, though, because someone bangs on the castle doors. That means he has a get-out-of-jail-free card.

"Kieran, *mo mhac*! Let me in."

Uilleam shouts so loudly that it almost sounds as if he's here inside the fortress rather than outside. Kieran jogs over to the gates and hefts the massive wooden crossbar out of the way so he can push the left side of the gate open.

His father marches into the courtyard, heading for us ladies, and waves for his son to follow him. Uilleam's expression tells me everything I need to know. He looks as fierce and determined as a warrior about to confront his mortal enemy. When he halts near me and the aunts, he turns sideways to watch his son approaching. Kieran seems equal parts confused and angry, probably because he knows his father must have dire news to share. I've gotten to know most of his expressions and what they indicate, but I have never seen the look he's wearing now.

Once we're all gathered in one spot, Uilleam glances at each of us in turn before he speaks, then he focuses on his son. "Simidh Gunn has agreed to meet with you and Alyssa."

Chapter Twenty-One

Kieran

I do not trust Simidh Gunn, and I never will. But I need to know what the *bod ceann* is after, because I'm dead certain it's more than a chat with Alyssa. I'd gone along with the notion of meeting with Simidh, but I knew from the start that it would be a trick of some sort on his part. My gaze shifts from my father to Alyssa and back again. "Aye, and a meeting is what we agreed should happen. It was your idea to negotiate with Simidh and come to an agreement about where to meet. Why do you seem ill at ease?"

"Because this is Simidh Gunn we're talking about. I do not trust him, and something about the way he smiled when he agreed to the meeting made me feel as if I'd made a pact with a demon."

"Any negotiation with Simidh involves risk. But this meeting was what Alyssa wanted, and you agreed it was the right decision."

"Simidh cannot be trusted." My father rubs the back of his neck. "But that is not the reason for my discomfort."

"What is your concern, then?"

"He wants to meet at the top of the trail where you like to hunt. That means he must have followed you up there at some time in the past, else how would he know of that place." My father looks directly at me, his gaze filled with what I can only describe as fear. But Uilleam MacTaggart does not give in to such things. "He wants to meet on Beann Dealgach."

Alyssa raises her hand. "Um, what is Beann Dealgach?"

"The mountain behind Dùndubhan."

"Oh. Well, at least that means we don't have to go far to meet Simidh."

"It is further than it appears from down here," I say. "But the distance hardly matters because you will not go up the mountain."

"He wants to meet with us both."

"Why should I give him everything he wants? I need only pretend to agree to his terms. By the time he realizes you are not coming, 'twill be too late."

Mayhap the worry in her eyes should give me pause, but I care naught for anything but her safety.

"You can't go alone," she says. "And he's expecting to see me. If you show up alone, he'll be very angry."

"Dinnae care about his feelings."

"You damn well better care about your own life."

"Stopping Simidh matters more than anything else. It is how I'll protect you."

Alyssa marches up to me and slaps my chest with both hands, hitting me with enough force that I stumble slightly, though not enough to move me from the spot on which I stand. Tears shimmer in her eyes. "You arrogant, selfish asshole. Did you ever stop to think about how I'll feel if Simidh murders you?"

No, I hadn't thought of that. My only goal has been to protect her. But the look in her eyes tells me I've made a grave miscalculation. When she slaps my chest again, with less force, I grasp her wrists and pull her close. "*Tha mi duilich, mo chridhe.* I've been an arrogant, selfish asshole just as you said. But my reasons for wanting to meet Simidh alone have nothing to do with that. I love you, and if you died, I would not wish to live any longer."

Her anguish has softened into what seems like a cross between love and anxiety, and I release her wrists. She sags against me with her cheek on my chest. "I love you too, you pigheaded jerk."

"I know. You've already told me that."

She sniffles. "I hope that first thing you said was an apology."

"It was. I said I'm sorry, my heart."

The lass raises her head and wipes away the tears. "We go to the meeting together or not at all. Teach me how to use a sword or a dagger or whatever, if that will make you feel better. But I *am* going with you." She grasps my face, rising onto her toes. "I don't want to live without you either."

In what manner can I respond to her words and her expression? For once, I let my heart make the decision. "You will come with me to the meeting on Beann Dealgach." I look at my father. "And you will come with us."

He raises his brows. "Simidh was explicit in stating that only you and Alyssa should be there."

"You know how to hide yourself. And I dinnae trust Simidh to keep to his word and bring no one else with him."

My father nods once. "Aye, I'll be there."

Efrica lifts her chin. "Dinnae forget about us, Kieran. We will not let our brother hunker in the trees alone."

"*Mhac na galla.* For once, can ye do what I say and remain here?"

"We are witches, dearie. Our skills could come in handy."

Alyssa smiles up at me. "No point in arguing. Your family is full of people as stubborn as you are."

"Why dinnae we invite the whole clan? Might as well bring a feast and a barrel of whisky."

"Now you're just being contrary. Your aunts have magical powers, you know. Surely that could be useful."

I exhale a long sigh. "Useful and advisable are not always the same thing."

"The matter is settled," my father says. "As chief of the MacTaggart clan, I declare that all of us here at Dùndubhan will participate in the gathering on Beann Dealgach."

Though I would prefer not to bring my father and aunts with me, much less Alyssa, I'm beginning to realize they might be right. We need more than Alyssa and me. Mayhap I dislike it when my aunts employ their unique skills, but I do understand the value of witchcraft when it's employed for good reasons.

I kiss the top of Alyssa's head. "We will all attend the gathering."

My aunts swarm me and Alyssa, kissing my cheek and blubbering like silly old women, though none of them qualify as such. Even Efrica, with her gray hair and wrinkles, is no silly old woman.

Once they finally move away, I ask my father, "When are we expected on the mountain?"

"Tomorrow at midday."

I would have preferred to have more time, but I doubt Simidh would agree to that. "If that is the time we have, then I should instruct Alyssa in the use of some sort of weapon. Whichever you are comfortable with, *mo leannan.*"

"Show me what you've got." Alyssa smiles and taps my nose with her fingertip. "Weapons, that is. I already know what else you've got."

Humor seems inappropriate at the moment, but I suppose we all need a wee bit of humor under the circumstances.

"I will work with my sisters," my father says. "We can surely come up with a plan to protect you and the lass."

He leads my aunts into the house.

Once they've gone out of sight, I grasp Alyssa's shoulders. "Are you certain you want to do this? To use a weapon means you must have the will to take the life of another. If your opponent senses that you lack the will, he shall defeat you. That means death."

"I understand that. Do you think I can't kill someone? Because if Simidh tries to take you out, I will strangle him with my bare hands if necessary."

"Aye, I know. I believe you have all the strength inside you that the task requires. But having that strength and using it aren't always the same."

"Either you believe I'm strong enough or you don't." She nails her gaze to mine. "But you need to decide now, before you commit to training me. Isn't it important for the teacher to believe the student can do it?"

"I've ne'er taught anyone to fight. But I do believe you can master the necessary skills. I hesitate only because I worry for you."

She lays her hands on my chest. "I know, and I love you for that. But if you'll be worrying about me during our meeting with Simidh—"

"I could make a terrible mistake, I know." I take her hand. "Let's go inside and find out which weapons you're comfortable using. I'll feel much better about what's to come when I see how well you can handle a weapon."

Once we go inside the house, I don't see my aunts or my father. They aren't on the ground floor or in the cellar. As we climb up the steps to the first floor, I begin to hear voices echoing inside the great hall. When we walk into that space, I see my aunts and my father standing in the middle of the room, engaged in a spirited discussion in Gaelic.

"What are they saying?" Alyssa asks. "I took off my necklace so I could have my own immersion course in Gaelic."

"Put your necklace back on. You'll need to understand everything that's said when we meet Simidh."

"Oh, sure. I didn't think of that." She pulls the necklace out of a pocket in her vest and drapes it about her neck. "Oh, this is better. They're talking so fast I have trouble keeping up, though."

Keeping her hand in mine, I approach my family. "What are you four discussing? It almost sounded like an argument."

"No, dearie," Efrica says. "We were not arguing. But my brother thinks our idea is unworthy of discussion."

"At this moment, everything is worthy of discussion. What is your idea?"

"We want to cast a spell to hide us from sight. It would prevent Simidh from seeing us, but you and Alyssa would still know we're there. Uilleam would also be hidden."

I look at my father. "What's wrong with their plan? It seems reasonable to me."

His brows rise. "When did my son decide that magic is an acceptable option? You fought the notion of spells and enchantments, accepting only that potions and herbal remedies might have merit."

"I have never said that magic is nonsense. I simply prefer not to engage in that sort of endeavor." I glance at Alyssa and can't help smiling a wee bit. "After all, magic brought me the best gift I've ever received."

"Mayhap you do see the merits of employing magic," my father says, "but my sisters have another idea."

I turn to my aunt. "Tell me this other idea, Efrica."

"You and Alyssa must wed—before the gathering on Beann Dealgach."

A few weeks ago, mayhap even a few days ago, I would have balked at such a statement. But when I consider the implications, I realize I want to do this—even if Simidh, by some miracle, should cancel our meeting tomorrow. "How will that play into your plans? Marriage is not a bond borne of magic."

"No, not in and of itself," my father says. "Efrica, why don't you explain?"

"Marriage is a sacred bond," my aunt says, "beyond any church or pagan rite. It is a spiritual union borne of love and commitment. Those bonds can give you a power you've never known before, though not in the sense of granting you physical power. 'Twill be love that protects you. Even Simidh cannot break such a bond."

I face Alyssa and take both her hands in mine. "Do you wish to marry me? I have no desire to force you into this union."

"Of course I want to marry you."

"Even if 'twill be an irregular union? That means we will eventually be fined by the kirk."

"A kirk is a church, right?"

"It is."

She grips my hands firmly. "I want to do this, Kieran. I want to become your wife, whatever the circumstances."

I turn to my father. "When will we do this? And how shall we do it? We won't have a minister to perform the ceremony."

My father smiles and pats my shoulder. "Irregular marriage, remember? You and Alyssa need only declare your desire to wed before two witnesses. We have four."

"When should we do this?"

"Whenever ye like, *mo mhac*. But I'd rather ye didn't wait so long that I die of old age before ye take the lass as your wife."

Alyssa and I are still holding hands, but now we gaze into each other's eyes. Which one of us should make our vow first? I suppose I should since I'm the one who stated that I want to marry her.

"Use your full names," my father says. "That's the proper way."

"Haud yer wheesht." I lean in close to whisper to the lass, "What is your full name?"

"Alyssa Maria Vescovi."

"Mine is Kieran Aulay MacTaggart."

"We can hear you, Kieran," my father says. "Get on with it, would you?"

I pull in a deep breath and let it out slowly. "I declare my fervent desire to marry you, Alyssa Maria Vescovi, and to become your wedded husband. My love and respect for you are my only reasons for making this vow."

"I declare my fervent desire to marry you too, Kieran Aulay MacTaggart, and to become your wedded wife. My love and respect for you are the sole reason that I make this vow."

"We declare you husband and wife!" my aunts and my father shout. They throw their arms up and cheer.

Bod an Donais, I have a wife. For a moment, I remain frozen in body and mind, unable to comprehend that this has really happened. Then a joy like none I have ever before experienced rushes through me.

I hoist her off the floor and spin us round and round.

Chapter Twenty-Two

Alyssa

When Kieran finally sets me down, I feel a touch woozy from all that spinning. I never imagined he could be so happy. But I feel that way too, ecstatic and over the moon and every other cliche anyone has ever invented. I just got married. After the way my first husband treated me, and the way he left me with nothing to show for all those years when I stayed with him, I swore I would never walk down the aisle again. Well, I've kept to that vow, in essence. I didn't walk down the aisle. Kieran and I traipsed into the great hall and declared our desire to become man and wife.

Who knew getting married in medieval Scotland would be so easy? Say the words, and you're done. I'm still not completely clear on what "irregular marriage" means. But I can ask my husband about that later, after we've dealt with Simidh Gunn.

"Should we do something to celebrate?" Uilleam asks. "Feels like we should, but I can't think of how we would do that."

Kieran glances at me and smiles in the sweetest way. But when he meets his father's gaze again, he grows much more serious. "The best wedding gift would be to settle this feud Simidh has created between me and himself. Assuming my wife agrees."

"Absolutely," I say. "Once he's been dealt with, we can do all the celebrating we want."

"The clan will want to know about this," Uilleam says. "But not until after it's done, as Alyssa suggested. By then, we will have proved that Kieran never stole from his own clan and he is not a devil worshiper."

I suddenly recall that Uilleam and his sisters had intended to hone their magic today. "Have you guys already come up with a cloaking spell?"

"Not yet, *gràidh*," Lachina says. "We were debating where to practice our spell when you and Kieran arrived. Uilleam was concerned that we might accidentally burn the castle down if we practiced indoors, but Efrica reminded him that castles are made of stone. That doesn't burn."

Uilleam shakes his head. "Mayhap not, but everything inside the castle that isn't stone would be burnt to ashes. Unless you three can conjure more possessions for us."

Conjure. The word echoes in my mind and spurs a revelation. Whether anyone else will be impressed with my revelation remains to be seen. "Um, I was just wondering…if you three could conjure me from the future, couldn't you conjure Simidh away to somewhere he could never bother us again?"

The aunts exchange glances as if they're actually considering my suggestion.

Uilleam stares at them. "Surely ye didn't do that. No one can conjure another person."

"We didn't conjure Alyssa," Efrica says. "We summoned her. There is a difference, though you never bothered to learn it. Magic is in the MacTaggart blood, Uilleam. You could at least make an effort to understand it."

"Quiet!" Kieran's shout echoes in the great hall. "No more arguing. You four should go to wherever you plan on practicing. Alyssa and I will go upstairs to the long gallery where I've kept my weapons."

No one moves.

"I said *go*."

"We will be outside in the courtyard," Uilleam informs his son.

Then he and the ladies hurry out of the great hall and down the stairs. Once their footfalls have faded into silence, Kieran takes me up to the second floor where the long gallery takes up nearly the whole space, and he tells me to stand in the center of the room. He saunters over to the cabinets that line the shorter wall and begins rummaging through the contents. Once he finds what he wants, he carries everything over to me and drops the weapons on the floor.

"Time to enlighten you about weaponry, *mo leannan*." He studies my clothing, and his mouth kinks downward at one corner. "You can't learn to fight while wearing a skirt. Go upstairs and change into those braies you wore on the day we met."

"Uh, you shredded them."

"Then get my braies."

I scamper out of the long gallery and up to the top floor, which I've come to think of as our suite since no one else lives up there. The aunts prefer to have their quarters on the first floor. Once I've changed clothes, I rush back down to my husband. Yeah, I love thinking that word. I love saying it out loud even more.

Strictly to yank his chain, I curtsy deeply before him. "I'm ready, my lord and master."

"I am not a lord, ye saucy wench."

Rising, I give his belly a light punch. "And I am not a wench, you arrogant beast."

"You love it when I behave like a beast."

"Oh, boy, do I ever. Makes me want to fuck you right here on the floor."

"We can do that after your lesson." He squeezes my ass. "We need to consummate our marriage, after all."

Since we've already had sex three times, I think we've already consummated. But I guess we need to do that again because we weren't married before. I'm totally on board with doing the deed again for the sake of tradition.

Kieran picks up a sword and holds it in both palms. "This is a claymore."

My focus lands on the blade and travels up toward the hilt, where I can see a familiar inscription. "That's your sword. It has your name engraved on it."

He stares at me, clearly surprised. "How did you know that? Were you sneaking about in my weapons closets?"

"No. I, um, saw that claymore in my century." How much should I tell him about the future? Since I already admitted I've seen his claymore before, I guess there's no harm in sharing the rest. "It was an exhibit in a museum that's inside the twenty-first-century version of Dùndubhan."

"Exhibit? What is a museum?"

Oh, shit. How am I going to explain this? "Well, a museum is basically a building that houses old things that have historical importance. An exhibit is a collection of items that are usually housed in glass cases to protect the artifacts."

He sets the tip of his sword on the floor, keeping his hand loosely curled around the pommel. "I understood most of that. But 'artifact' is a word unfamiliar to me."

"An artifact is something that has intrinsic historical value. In my time, your sword is considered to be an artifact."

"In your time? You live here now."

Of course I do. I just married him, so that means I've committed to staying here with Kieran. "I meant in the time that I used to live in."

He lays the sword down on the floor and picks up another blade. "This is a basket-hilt sword, also known as a broadsword. Its blade is wider than the claymore, but its length is shorter." Kieran offers me both swords. "Take one and try it out, then test the other."

I pick up the claymore first and swish it in the air, which probably makes me look like a goofball. It's heavy, and I'm not sure I could pull off mastering the claymore in the short amount of time we have. So I trade the claymore for the broadsword and do my swishing thing again. This blade isn't quite as heavy as the claymore, but I still don't feel confident in my ability to learn to use it by tomorrow at midday.

"What else do you have?" I ask. "Swords are cool, but I think I'd better try something lighter weight."

"Cool? I assume that means you like the swords."

"Yes."

"Let me show you a few more weapons." He stashes the swords in a cabinet and brings out smaller options, laying all but one on the floor. "This is a dirk."

"That's one long knife."

"A dirk is more of a small sword than a knife or dagger." He flips it around to offer me the hilt. "Try this one."

I accept the "small sword" and play around with it, though I can't make the sweeping gestures I'd used when I tested the big swords. I don't need to do that with the dirk. It's longer than any knife I've seen and does indeed look and feel more like a small sword. The weight of it doesn't feel too awkward, and the more I use it, the more comfortable I feel with the blade.

"What do you think of the dirk?" Kieran asks. "It seems to fit well in your hand."

"Yeah, it does. I like it."

"Good. But are you prepared to gut your enemy with that blade?"

"Are you trying to scare me?"

"No." He grasps my wrist and pulls my arm toward his stomach, while my hand still grips the dirk. The blade nudges his belly. "I'm asking a pertinent and vital question. Do you believe you could gut your enemy if need be? Answer honestly but without hesitation."

"Yes, I could do it. If anyone hurt you, your father, or your aunts, I would do whatever is necessary."

"I believe you would." He releases my wrist. "Any woman who could put me in my place can handle anything."

"Do you want the dirk back?"

"No. You should keep it." He slides an arm around my waist to pull me close. "Watching you wield a sword makes me want to throw you over my shoulder and carry you upstairs to consummate our union immediately."

"Shouldn't we be focused on preparing for the big meeting with the red-haired creep?"

He chuckles. "Red-haired creep? I'm not entirely certain what a 'creep' is, but it sounds like a dire insult against Simidh."

"Yes, it is."

"I will give you some training in how to use a dirk for defense. But there isn't a great deal to learn. You thrust the blade and aim for the spot most likely to kill or at least grievously wound your opponent."

We spend the next hour or so practicing, though I can't be sure of the time anymore. The battery in my watch gave out a few days ago, and I'm not very good at gauging time based on the sun's position, not yet. When I asked Kieran about that, he informed me that he would be happy to build a sundial for me. I told him to hold off on that for now. Maybe after the big showdown on the mountain I'll want to learn about sundials.

I tried to wheedle information from him about his mysterious project, but he still won't tell me. At least he didn't turn and storm out of the room this time. Instead, he assured me that he will answer all my questions about his project once it's finished.

After my practice session, we go downstairs to look for the others. It's almost time for the midday meal. I'm dying to find out how the witches did with their task of trying to find a way to conceal themselves and Uilleam. Just as we reach the bottom of the stairs, the gang arrives.

Kieran's aunts are grinning. Uilleam remains calm, though he gives his sisters an exasperated glance.

My new husband lays an arm across my shoulders. "How did your task go?"

"Well enough," Uilleam says. "At least they didn't blow up the entire fortress."

"There were no explosions whatsoever," Efrica declares. "But we did learn that our plan will work. We were able to make Uilleam appear to vanish, while he could still see and hear us."

"You could hear me too."

"Were you able to conceal all four of you?" Kieran asks. "That was the intention, aye?"

"It was. And we succeeded in that feat as well."

"How do you know? If you were invisible, who witnessed it to prove you succeeded?"

His aunts' grins crumble. They exchange glances with each other.

"You are correct, Kieran," Lachina says. "We should test the spell with witnesses. Fortunately, we have two trustworthy people who might bear witness for us."

"Outdoors," Kieran says. "That's the safest way to test your spell."

"Oh, aye, outdoors."

We traipse downstairs and out into the courtyard, where Kieran declares that he and I should stay near the gatehouse while the others do their thing in the center of the space. Uilleam and his sisters gather there and hold hands to form a circle, bowing their heads while they whisper so softly that I think even if Kieran and I were right next to them, we might not hear it.

The air around them shimmers—and then they vanish.

"By God's bones," Kieran says in a hushed voice, "they did it. My aunts have made themselves and my father disappear completely."

I'm amazed too. Despite knowing those ladies can do real magic, since they summoned me here from the future, I still have trouble wrapping my head around the reality of the supernatural.

The air shimmers again, and the foursome reappears.

"Well?" Efrica says. "Did it work this time?"

"Aye, it did," Kieran calls out. "But I'm still uncertain of how this will help us tomorrow."

"We can cast spells to help you and Alyssa." Efrica said that as if she can't believe her nephew still doesn't get it. "Were ye not listening the first time we explained it?"

I was listening, that's for sure. More than listening, though, I saw it with my own eyes. That was no sleight-of-hand trick. They genuinely made themselves vanish. Will that help us tomorrow?

The answer depends on Simidh—and what kinds of weapons he brings.

Chapter Twenty-Three

Kieran

I was listening, Efrica," I say. "But your explanations were vague, and I never have confidence in things I do not fully understand. I know you three can do magic, and that Lachina has *da-shealladh*, but we need more than a cloaking spell and second sight when Simidh Gunn arrives. We need a battle plan."

Alyssa's eyes widen. "Battle plan? Nobody mentioned that we might need to fight an army. But that's what a battle is, right?"

"Not necessarily. I meant that we should have a plan that involves all potential contingencies. I might need to fight Simidh, but that isn't the whole plan. The cloaking spell my aunts created should give them the ability to cast more spells or enchantments to hinder whatever evil ideas Simidh has without him knowing they're in the vicinity."

"The word battle makes me very anxious."

"I know, but that's natural." I tap my finger on the sheath that holds her dirk. "You have a weapon. And if you should need to fight in close quarters, your by-knife will be your best choice."

She touches the six-inch knife attached to the dirk's sheath. "This is all getting real now. No more theoretical danger. It's here, and it's real."

"Aye, but you are a strong woman. I wouldn't have married a silly lass who would faint at the sight of a sword." I lift her hand to my lips and kiss it. "You can handle anything that comes your way."

"So can you."

We return to the house for our midday meal, then engage in a long and involved discussion of what we think might occur tomorrow on the mountain and what tactics we should use to deal with each hypothetical situation. Who knows what Simidh might bring with him. Or who he might bring. When I ask my father about that, he informs me that Simidh did not promise to come alone, though he insisted that Alyssa and I bring no one else with us. No, I do not trust Simidh. He will deceive us in any way he can.

Near the end of our discussion, my aunts retreat into the far corner of the solar to have a whispered discussion.

"What are you three doing over there?" I ask. "This is supposed to be a group discussion. If you have something to say, tell all of us."

My aunts hurry back to us and take their seats. Efrica speaks first. "We want to cast a spell that would allow us to see any cohorts Simidh brings with him, even if those men hide in the forest."

"That does sound useful. Do you have time to figure out how to do it?"

"We will work through the night if necessary."

"And into the morn," Lachina says. "However long it takes. We can't have you and Alyssa walking into an ambush."

Suddenly, my aunts are a Roman legion about to sack a Visigoth outpost. But I understand their intentions. They want to help, and I won't deny them that right. I certainly won't leave them behind in the castle. If Simidh indeed brings others with him, they might try to ambush us as Lachina suggested.

As our discussion concludes, we realize it's time for the evening meal. But after that, we go to our separate quarters. Alyssa and I head up the stair to the top floor where no one else sleeps. We have the entire floor to ourselves. On the morrow, we might walk into a battle. That means tonight I need to make love to my wife.

I shut the door behind us. "Time to consummate our marriage, *mo chridhe.*"

Alyssa turns toward me and smiles. "Absolutely."

"Shall we try that chair position you talked of once?"

"I'd love that." She meanders about the room, studying each of the four chairs as if she's making a vital decision. "This one will do."

When she tries to move the chair herself, I snatch it away. "This chair is rather heavy. Allow your husband to carry it for you."

"Please do."

"Where should I set it?"

She bites her lip while surveying the room. Then she points to the foot of the bed. "Right there. It will be good to have the bed keeping the chair in place."

I set the chair down at the foot of the bed, as she suggested. "It's time to remove your clothes, wife."

"As you command, husband."

The twinkle in her eyes assures me she's harassing me again. My wife would never do something simply because I commanded it, and I wouldn't have it any other way. The way she challenges me makes me want her even more—and love her even more.

My wife has chosen the sturdiest, widest chair in the room and in the castle. But I doubt she knows its origins. I run my hand over the arm. "I crafted this myself."

Alyssa studies the chair with a new appreciation, gliding her hands over the arms and the back. "This is a beautiful piece of art. I'm also afraid to sit on it."

"But you chose this one."

"I know. But that was before I found out you made the chair. I don't want to accidentally damage it."

"Dinnae fash, *mo chridhe*. I built this chair to be strong. If I'd gotten it wrong, the thing would have splintered the first time I sat upon it."

"Well then, there's only one thing left to do." She begins to unlace her vest. "Let's get naked, my laird."

Bod an Donais. Every time she calls me that, it makes my *slat* twitch. I suspect it's her tone of voice that does that, though. She always speaks the words in a husky tone.

I remove my clothing as quickly as possible. Alyssa is already naked by the time I finish. Watching her undress had distracted me for a moment. "Ah, *neach-gaoil*, you are the most beautiful woman in the world. Your body is a masterpiece, and when I caress your *baltan*, you will beg me to make you come."

"Tell me what those Gaelic words mean later."

"Aye, I will." I run my hand over the chair's back again. "Tell me how this will work."

"One of us will sit in the chair while the other winds up on their partner's lap. But I think you should be the one who sits down first."

I move in front of the chair and settle my erse on it.

She closes her eyes, and her lips move a wee bit. I've seen that expression before when she's thinking hard or struggling to remember something. Then her eyes open. "You're supposed to sit diagonally with your sexy ass in one corner of the chair and your knees hanging over the opposite arm."

I rearrange myself the way she had described. "What's next?"

"You stay right there while I climb onto your lap."

"Modern people certainly are creative with how they fuck each other."

"I'm sure medieval people can be pretty inventive too."

"Mayhap. But I don't think anyone has thought of this position yet."

My wife climbs onto my lap and settles her erse onto me, then she drapes her legs over the chair's arm at either side of me. "Ready?"

"Aye."

She grips the chair's arms behind her and straightens them, lifting her erse off my lap. I can't resist pushing my hand between her folds to tease her nub. She begins to breathe more heavily, and my attention shifts to her bosom and the way her breasts jiggle. "Move your hand, please. I need you inside me."

I pull my hand away and drag my tongue over each of my fingers, taking my time while I lick away all of her cream. "Ye taste like *nèamh* and feel like the soft summer *fearthainn*."

She's biting down on her lip so hard that it turns white, and her breaths have grown even heavier.

My wife gradually lowers her body onto my cock, inch by inch, her wetness gliding along my length and warming my flesh. Fuck, she feels like *nèamh* for certain, like everything I've ever dreamed of experiencing with a lass. But Alyssa isn't just a lass. She is my wife, the love of my life, and my soul mate.

When she finally has her *cìrean coilich* snugly wrapped around me, my wife keeps hold of the chair's arms as she begins to rock back and forth. My thighs and my belly serve as a cradle that prevents her from sliding off my lap. The leisure of her movements makes me breathe harder now too, and I grasp her hips to guide the lass exactly the way I want her to fuck me. I lunge my head to take hold of her nipple between my teeth. She sucks in a sharp breath. I slide my hands up to her breasts and tease the underside while I keep devouring her nipple, scraping my teeth over it, rasping my tongue across it, while desperate, hungry cries spill from her lips.

Alyssa moves faster, grinding her *baltan* into my flesh, and slaps a hand on my chest to get more leverage.

The chair scrapes across the floor.

I wrap my arms around the lass and pull her firmly against my chest, and I kiss her. She tears her palm away from my torso and grips the arm of the chair behind me, as she'd done before. I consume her mouth, nibbling on her lips briefly before I thrust my tongue deep to tease the roof of her mouth and coil it around her tongue. She moans so deeply that I feel the vibrations. All the while, my wife keeps grinding her flesh into me with a pace that grows faster and wilder with every passing moment.

The pleasure we give each other intensifies inside me, like a massive wave gathering on the ocean, barreling toward a steep cliff on the shore. I fist one hand in Alyssa's hair, at first to hold her mouth to mine, but then I pull her head back so I can scrape my tongue over the exposed column of her throat.

"Oh God, yes," she shouts. "Keep doing that, Kieran."

I lower my head to suckle her nipple.

Another cry bursts out of her, a wordless plea for me to make her come. Dinnae need to hear her speak the words. I know what my wife needs.

The chair creaks and thumps.

And I splay my other hand over her mound so I can push my longest finger between her folds and rub her nub. She comes so swiftly that her body has no chance to go rigid in anticipation of the climax. Her body clenches my cock in fierce, pulsating spasms, and that gargantuan wave out on the ocean grows higher and higher until it finally crashes into the shore. A hoarse cry borne of sheer pleasure explodes from me while I come apart inside her, unleashing my seed until I have nothing left to give.

My wife slumps onto my chest, struggling to regain her breath. "Wow, that was incredible."

"Aye, it was. I think we flew up into the sky for a moment, with the stars all around us."

"What were those Gaelic things you said?"

"I think chair sex has turned my mind into mud. But if my memory serves, I called you sweetheart, or *neach-gaoil*. Then I said you taste like heaven, or *nèamh*. *Baltan* means, ah…" I cup her groin. "This part of you."

"Uh-huh. What about that word you used after you mentioned soft summer something?"

"*Fearthainn*. It means rain." I caress her back, unwilling to move out of this position yet. "We consummated our marriage, for certain."

"Yes, we did. But I need to pee now." She grips the chair's arms but can't seem to figure out how to disentangle herself from my body. "Um, a little help would be appreciated."

"Of course." I grasp her around the waist and lift the lass off my cock, which leaves her kneeling over me. "Swing your leg over my hips."

When she tries to do that, the chair wobbles and creaks.

So I attempt to move my legs off the chair's arm.

A crack reverberates through the room.

Before either of us can react, one leg of the chair splinters, and the chair itself falls over sideways. Luckily, we were holding each other rather than the chair's arms. I know I'm uninjured, but I jump up with Alyssa cradled in my arms and set her on the bed, then I begin exploring her body for injuries.

She bats my hands away. "What are you doing?"

"Making certain you haven't injured yourself."

"I'm fine. You can stop fussing."

"Aye, of course."

When I step away from the bed, my foot strikes down on some part of the ruined chair, and I lose my balance. Staggering backward, I flail my arms but can't regain my balance. I tumble to the floor and shout rather loudly.

Alyssa leaps off the bed and rushes to me. "Are you okay? Did you hit your head?"

"No, *gràidh*, I'm unharmed." I hoist myself into a sitting position. And I smirk. "But if you want to examine me for injuries, I have no objections as long as you explore me with your soft wee hands."

She taps my nose with one finger. "You are the naughtiest man I've ever met."

Footfalls pound outside the bedroom door, drawing closer swiftly.

"Alyssa! Kieran!" Efrica shouts. "Are ye all right? We heard a fearful noise coming from up here."

"We're fine," I tell her. "A chair broke, and I tripped over it."

No, I will not admit that we were having chair sex. That's a secret between my wife and I.

"How did the chair break?" Efrica asks. "You should let us come in to see if the chair can be repaired."

"No, ye can't come in."

"Why not?"

I growl under my breath. "Because it's our wedding night, ye daft woman."

"Oh," she says with a laugh. "We'll be on our way, then. If we hear any more crashing sounds, we'll ignore it unless you scream for help."

"Aye, away with all of you." Yes, I'm certain my father and my other two aunts are out there with Efrica. I heard too many footfalls for just one person. I wait a moment before I open the door and peer into the corridor. Then I shut the door. "They've gone. We can continue with our consummation ritual."

"What ritual?"

"The one that requires us to fuck again and again until we're too exhausted to do it any longer."

Alyssa wags a finger at me. "You made that up, didn't you?"

"Mayhap I did." I saunter up to her and hook a finger under her chin. "Do you want to continue with my invented consummation ritual? I have ideas for how to make you come for me over and over and over without penetration."

"Show me."

Chapter Twenty-Four

Alyssa

Something soft and feathery tickles my cheek, rousing me from the best night's sleep I've ever had, though I can't manage to make my eyelids open. That sensation must be a remnant of the sexy dream I'd been enjoying. So I sigh and let the memory flow through me. That imaginary feather skims down my throat and chest until it meets my breast, and its silky softness tickles my nipple in the most arousing way. Damn, I need to wake my husband up and order him to screw me.

While that phantom feather skates down my belly, I start to get slick and tingly between my thighs.

Then a pair of lips kiss my tummy.

Okay, that did not feel like the remnants of a dream. I peel one lid open and discover my husband is lying beside me. He's bent over from the waist to gain access to my belly, and his tongue currently glides around my navel, then slips inside it to tease me there.

I squirm and open both eyes. My lips form a soft smile. Can't help smiling that way whenever Kieran gets playful and sweet.

"*Madainn mhath*," he says. "That means good morning."

"Good morning to you too, my sizzling-hot beast-hubby."

"Hubby?"

"It's short for husband."

Kieran smirks. "The twenty-first century sounds like a very odd place. They need a medieval Scotsman to teach them proper English."

"Ha-ha. I was thinking about going down on you, but now I've changed my mind."

"What is 'going down'?"

"That means I take your dick in my mouth and make you come."

He grins. "I would love for you to do that. When we tried the sixty-nine position, I enjoyed it. But to have your mouth on my *slat* while I can watch you doing that would be sheer bliss."

I don't know if it's a medieval thing or just a Kieran thing, but I've never heard any man talk the way he does. I like it. Modern language can be so disappointing, especially modern slang. My husband would never have described anything I did as "sheer bliss."

"Do I feel warm to you?" he asks. "You said I'm hot, but I don't feel feverish."

"That's not what 'hot' means in this context. I mean that you are the most attractive, beautiful, and virile man I've ever seen."

"In that case, you are sizzling hot as well."

"Thank you, honey. That's a great compliment."

"Honey? Is that an endearment?"

"Yep. I guess nobody uses that in this time."

Someone bangs on our bedroom door.

"Who goes there?" Kieran shouts.

"Your father, *mo mhac*. May I enter the bedchamber? I wish to speak to you and Alyssa alone. That means go downstairs, witches."

I hear women's voice but can't make out their words. Then they scurry off down the hall.

"One moment," I holler. "We need to get dressed."

"Make haste, lass. The morning meal will be served in a matter of minutes."

Kieran and I jump out of bed and scramble to find where we left our clothes last night. We get dressed as quickly as we can since Uilleam sounded serious when he issued his command. I hope nothing has gone wrong with our battle plan.

While I finish tying up my vest laces, my hubby answers the door. His father strides into the room, glancing at the broken chair. He doesn't comment on that, though his brows hike up. Uilleam sits down in one of the two chairs by the hearth. Kieran drags the chair that usually rests by the window over to the hearth too, and my husband and I sit side by side.

"Lachina had a dream last night," Uilleam says. "But you and I, Kieran, both know that her dreams are often portents of what may come."

"Aye, what *may* come. What did she see?"

"Simidh laughing while you lay on the ground. He held a bloody knife in one hand, and Alyssa's arm in the other. She appeared anguished."

Kieran rests his elbow on his chair's arm and sets his chin on his raised fist. For a moment, he just stares into the fire as if the flickering flames have mesmerized him. "It might mean nothing. But we can't risk ignoring her dream."

"I agree."

"What should we do?"

"Be vigilant. That's all we can do. We must keep to our original plan but also keep our eyes watchful and our ears sharp."

My knuckles ache, and I suddenly realize I've been gripping my chair's arm too tightly. "That's all? We stay vigilant?"

Kieran peels my hand away from the chair and clasps it. "Dinnae fash, mo chridhe. I will never let Simidh or whatever men he brings with him lay even one finger on you."

Uilleam looks at me. "Where have you left the triquetra necklace?"

"It's in the nightstand drawer."

"Please retrieve it, *gràidh*. We might need its power, and we must make certain you understand what Simidh might say."

I rush over to the nightstand, grabbing the necklace out of the drawer, and take it back to my chair by the hearth. "Should I put it on now?"

"Yes," Kieran says. "Keep it with you at all times."

As I slip the necklace on, I note the men's expressions, full of determination but also anxiety. Not the most comforting sight. But I can't expect them to be fearless. I met Simidh twice, and both times I sensed he is a dangerous man.

We head downstairs for breakfast, but there's no conversation this morning. We eat, then we gather our weapons. Even the aunts carry knives—the kind designed for kitchen use. I wish Kieran had some armor, but I asked him about that earlier, and he told me he couldn't afford such an extravagance and neither could his father. Kieran and I go upstairs to retrieve our weapons, and he helps me get the sheath for my dirk in position. It turns out Scottish warriors usually have the small sword hanging in front of their groins, and I decide to do that too. The much smaller by-knife is attached to the same sheath.

Now that I'm weaponed up, which might actually be a word, I ask, "Which sword will you choose?"

"What do you think?"

"The claymore, of course."

He kisses my cheek. "You are a proper Scotsman's wife."

I observe while he brings out the big sword and straps it on, with the sheath hanging at his hip. He wears his kilt, but with a white shirt this time, and his big boots. He also hides a dirk under that shirt, with a sheath that has a long string to strap it to his chest. I have no idea if all Scotsmen do that or if my husband is unique. Well, he's definitely unique. But maybe not in how he wears his hidden dirk.

Now that we're armed, we go outside to meet Uilleam and the aunts.

For a moment, we all gaze at each other without speaking, saying everything with our expressions and our eyes. None of us will die today. I feel it in my soul. But will we be injured? I hope not, though I realize that confronting a dangerous man might result in a tussle.

After our moment of silence, Kieran takes my hand and leads our party out through the massive doors and the portcullis, down the path through the woods. We had left the gatehouse doors open in case we need to flee into the castle. That also means our enemies could sneak in there while we're gone, but it's a chance we have to take.

Instead of going straight down the path like we had before, we turn down a narrower trail. Kieran had told me this morning that this is the way he goes when he hunts for game, so he knows it well. At the base of the mountain, Uilleam and his sisters split off and go down a different path, one that Kieran assures me curves back around to meet up with the one we will continue down. The path up Beann Dealgach becomes gradually steeper as we make our way into the higher elevations. This isn't Mount Everest, but it still offers rugged terrain that makes my muscles start to complain. But I can handle it.

Show no weakness to a foe, that's become my mantra.

We take frequent breaks to make sure we don't get exhausted before we even reach the meeting place, though I'm the one who needs to rest. He seems no less vigorous than when we left Dùndubhan. Halfway to our destination, as Kieran tells me, we take a longer break and eat the oat bread we'd brought with us. Uilleam and the aunts had taken a supply of oat bread with them too. I do feel refreshed after our snack, physically if not mentally. I keep having to fight the urge to chew my nails, though I'd never been prone to that before.

At last, we reach the end of the trail—or the beginning, depending on whether a person comes from above or below. Either way, we are here.

"Don't you want to bring out your claymore?" I ask. "To be ready for anything."

"I can quickly bring it out, but I don't wish to start this meeting at the tip of a sword."

"Guess that does make sense."

"I'm glad you approve." He kisses my forehead. "Try not to worry, *mo chridhe*. I will be here with you the entire time—and for the rest of our lives."

Someone starts clapping. "What a sweet a moment. Enjoy it while it lasts."

Kieran's jaw tightens, and a muscle ticks there.

Simidh Gunn walks out of the shadows beneath a tree and saunters up to the trail as if he knows with complete certainty that he will get what he wants today. "Give me Alyssa now, and I will vow not to execute your father."

Does he know Uilleam has been at Dùndubhan? Does he know Kieran's father is hiding the woods right now? No, he can't.

Kieran's jaw remains tight, but otherwise, he betrays no sign of his emotions. "You know I will never hand Alyssa over to you."

Simidh skims his gaze over me from head to toe, licking his lips as he studies my breasts. Then his focus lands on my left hand, and rage burns in his eyes. But he doesn't look at me. He glares at Kieran. "You married her. Since I know you can't risk going into the village for a proper ceremony, you must have gone the irregular-wedding route. That won't hold up for long. Your lass will be my wife."

"Is this why you bade me to meet you here? So you could complain that Alyssa favors me and not you?"

"She will favor me. I'll ensure it."

With magic. That's what he means. But I know, with absolutely zero evidence to back up my belief, that no spell or enchantment can erase my love for Kieran.

My husband shakes his head at Simidh. "You have no power to execute my father or steal Alyssa from me. Your impotence is legendary."

Oh, that was a nice jab. We all know Kieran meant more than Simidh's inability to get what he wants.

"Mayhap you are correct," Simidh says. "But I never come to a meeting alone. That would give my enemy the upper hand."

"You brought friends," I say. "Did you honestly think we wouldn't realize you'd do that?"

"Oh, I've done more than hope you would do that. As a *bruadarach* like me always does, I've brought reinforcements." He shouts over his shoulder, "Show yourselves, laddies!"

Half a dozen men emerge from the woods to flank Simidh. Each man wears a sword at his hip, but two also have maces.

"Go on, Kieran," Simidh taunts. "Try to stop me from taking your woman."

"You think you are a *bruadarach*, but dreamers make mistakes," Kieran says as he pulls his sword out of its sheath. "They dream too much and miss what's right in front of them."

I pull out my dirk. "Go home, Simidh. You won't get me."

"Won't I?" He grins and laughs. "Ah, you stupid wee lassie. Look at these men. I recruited them from five different clans because they are willing to do anything for the right price. They might ravage you for their own pleasure if I command them to do it."

"Swords for hire? That means they'll run away if things get too hairy. A real battle requires commitment."

Out of the corner of my eye, I can see Kieran's expression. He seems…proud. And that gives me the gumption to do whatever I need to do. "Give up, Simidh. Go home and find a very stupid woman who will marry you. That's the only way you'll get a wife."

"We shall see." The smile that curves his lips sends a shiver snaking up my spine. "Do ye think this is my whole army?"

That creepy smile makes my throat tighten.

"Come out, laddies," Simidh shouts. "Let my friends have a look at you."

A horde of men emerges from the shadows, each one carrying some type of sword, knife, mace, or crossbow. I count the men as they amble up behind Simidh. Twenty-four murderous brigands have lined up to do Simidh's bidding.

Oh, shit.

Chapter Twenty-Five

Kieran

Simidh Gunn has brought an army indeed, and I wish Alyssa weren't here. These men won't care about her safety. Simidh wants her, and they have been paid to assist him in his mad vendetta, though I still do not know why he despises me with such seething hatred. Right now, it doesn't matter. All I can do is pray that my father and my aunts can help us with their spells.

"I do love the anticipation," Simidh says, rubbing his hands together. "I think I'll give you a good long look at my men before I release my dogs to tear you to shreds."

"Even if you kill me, you will never have Alyssa."

He chuckles. "I shall have whatever and whoever I like, as often and as violently as I like. Dinnae you understand yet? Of course not, you thick-headed brute."

"Tell me and have done with it."

"I mean to kill you, your father, and anyone else who interferes with my plans." He leans forward slightly, his eyes glittering with a dark glee. "I am going to seize control of the MacTaggart clan."

"You are not a MacTaggart."

"Mayhap not, but no one will dare challenge me."

"Have ye lost your mind? It's a mad scheme sure to lead to your own death."

He shrugs one shoulder. "So be it."

"Why, Simidh? By God's bones, what did my family ever do to you?"

The *bod ceann* studies me for a moment while tipping his head side to side slowly. "You sincerely do not know." He straightens and narrows his gaze on me. "When your mother died, Uilleam was supposed to marry my sister, not Sibylla MacTavish. The alliance had already been set when Uilleam changed his mind and caused shame and anguish for Brenda."

"That is not what happened. Your uncle, whose ward you were, pulled out of the agreement in favor of wedding your sister to the chief of the Gillespie clan. No one blamed Brenda for that, nor did anyone hold my family at fault."

"Enough of this! You are a lying knave." Simidh throws his head back and screams, "*Sgaoil a mach do bhobuc!*"

The men behind him rush forward, shouting and brandishing their weapons.

I push Alyssa behind me and roar as I slash my claymore at the bastards, wounding three with a single strike. These men are not trained warriors, of that I'm certain. They were the only ones low enough to take up arms for money, which means they will likely surrender soon if I give them enough cause. But these men know Alyssa is behind me, and I can't protect her while fending them off. That means I need to trust my wife.

So I snarl over my shoulder, "Do whatever you must, *mo chridhe*. Don't hold back."

My wife turns away but remains close as she slashes her dirk at the brigands my enemy has unleashed on us. Alyssa screams like a wild she-demon, holding back nothing as she fights alongside me, and we both score multiple strikes. When one man slashes my wife's arm, I resist the powerful impulse to spin around and pierce the brigand's heart. It's clearly not a mortal wound, and we cannot be seen to back away from the fight.

A wave of invisible energy crests over me, causing me to sway a wee bit, though I remain rooted to the same spot. I freeze and glance back at Alyssa, who seems equally confounded by the sensation. It was neither wind nor an earth tremor.

Simidh and his army stand frozen as well. Unlike us, however, they sway much more noticeably, their eyes have glossed over, and their jaws hang slack. They seem to have fallen into a stupor, but whatever energy has affected them has not infiltrated our bodies or minds.

"What's going on?" Alyssa whispers. "They look like zombies without the pasty skin and hunger for flesh."

Zombies? I have no time to waste on asking her what the word means.

"I have no answers," I tell her, speaking with equal softness. "Unless my aunts have done this."

Every one of the brigands falls to the ground. Their eyes flicker closed, and their bodies go limp.

Simidh remains upright, though he staggers as he struggles against the clearly powerful command to collapse. The *bod ceann* stabs a finger in my direction. "What have you done to my men?"

"Nothing. I know naught of what caused this." That is essentially true. I know nothing, though I suspect what the cause might be. "Mayhap you simply lack the vigor to fight."

He snarls like a wild beast, his teeth clenched, and pounds his fist in the air as if he imagines he's pounding me. "You *trealaich*! This was magic!"

Simidh is the one who's behaving like a prick.

I wield my sword, rotating the blade in a winding pattern so the light glints off its sharp edge. "Be silent, ye *cacan*. You've lost the battle, however it occurred, so take the loss like a man."

"*Ith do chac*, MacTaggart. You may have prevailed this time, but I will have your woman—sooner, not later."

He sheaths his weapon but still seems shaky on his feet, which might explain why he hasn't departed yet.

My father and my aunts trot out of the trees. When they see the men who lie prone and unconscious on the ground, they all grin.

"We did it!" Efrica shouts while clapping her hands. "MacTaggart magic has won the day."

Morna gives her middle finger to Simidh. "*Falbh dàirich fhein.* I hope you learned your lesson from getting trounced by the Witches of Ballachulish."

"Aye," my father says. "Never annoy my sisters again, or you'll regret it, laddie."

Simidh grinds his teeth so hard that I can see the muscles in his jaw working.

"Enough taunts," I say. "It's time to drag his rotten carcass off our land. Try this again, Simidh, and I will murder you. Ne'er try to abduct my wife ever again."

Simidh glowers at me, the heat of anger simmering in his eyes.

"Look after Alyssa's arm, Efrica," I say, without glancing back at my aunt. "One of his men grazed her skin."

Suddenly, Simidh whips out his by-knife and throws it. A woman screams, though I can't tell who it was. Not until I whirl around.

Lachina lies on the ground, on her back, with Simidh's blade sunk deep into her shoulder. Blood pours from the wound.

I let out a wild cry and hurl myself at Simidh. With my sword gripped in both hands, I aim to pierce his chest. But a cloud of white smoke erupts between us, and I lose track of where he is. My claymore plunges into the earth.

And I roar.

The cloud dissipates quickly, but I see no sign of Simidh. He used a paltry amount of magic to effect his escape, but it was enough.

"Shouldn't we go after him?" my father asks. "Simidh needs to be punished."

"Aye, but he's well gone by now. Simidh can run like the wind, and his wee smoke trick gave him good cover."

I walk back to my family. Lachina still lies on the ground, but the knife has been removed. Efrica is wrapping a length of fabric around Lachina's shoulder, and I suspect she tore that fabric off her own dress. When I kneel beside Lachina, she tries to smile, but the expression falters.

"*Tha mi duilich*, Kieran."

"What are you sorry for, *gràidh*? You did nothing wrong."

"Because of me, Simidh was able to escape."

"No, Lachina." I kiss her forehead. "You are not to blame. Now, let's get you home where you can rest on a soft bed."

While Efrica finishes dressing the wound, I examine the unconscious men. Alyssa and my father assist me, which makes the task go much faster. The brigands are not dead, but they seem unable to awaken. No matter how much we shake them, they do not rouse. Morna suggests using a wee spell both to awaken the devils and to convince them to leave and never return to Mac-Taggart land. Efrica joins Morna in casting the enchantment. Those brigands scurry off through the forest.

I lift Lachina into my arms and carry her for the entire journey back to the Dùndubhan. Once we reach the fortress, my father raises the portcullis and closes the doors, then locks them with the wooden crossbar while I continue into the house with Lachina. Efrica, Morna, and Alyssa go with me. My father catches up to us as we start up the stair.

"Which room should we take her to?" he asks. "Lachina's bed is not well padded, and she would ne'er let anyone make it more comfortable."

"My bed 'tis comfortable, Uilleam," Lachina says. "You fuss too much."

As we reach the first floor, we halt in the hall to discuss—or rather, argue about—where to take Lachina.

"Let's put her in our bedroom," Alyssa says. "It has the softest, biggest bed and all the amenities."

"Aye, we should give her our bedchamber."

When the others open their mouths to complain, I give them a hard look intended to silence them. It works, but only because they agree with our decision. Otherwise, they would have complained in spite of the look I gave them.

"Can you carry her all the way to the top floor?" my father asks. "It's quite a long way."

"Kieran can do it," Alyssa says. "He's very strong and has lots of stamina."

My wife would know that better than anyone. Fucking her requires a great deal of stamina, and I love that my wife is so passionate.

We climb the steps up to the highest floor and take Lachina into the bedchamber. Alyssa pulls the covers back so I can lay my aunt down on the soft bed. A fire still burns in the hearth, but my father stokes it and adds more wood to ensure Lachina will stay warm. Alyssa and I offer to watch over Lachina for a while. After that, we will all take turns.

Efrica, Morna, and my father leave us, while my wife and I settle onto the chairs by the hearth.

"This is unnecessary," Lachina says. "I don't need a nursemaid, much less two of them."

"Hush, *gràidh*," I tell her. "You need rest to recuperate properly."

I can hardly suppress my shock when Lachina agrees and cuddles under the bedsheet and quilt to sleep. She only complained once, and it was a half-hearted attempt. Alyssa and I simply watch the fire, occasionally exchanging a glance but otherwise doing nothing at all. After the battle we endured on Beann Dealgach, we both need to relax. Nothing seems more soothing than a warm, crackling fire.

Eventually, we fall asleep in our chairs.

A noise rouses me some time later. I yawn and glance at my wife, but she still sleeps. The noise comes again, and I recognize it as a faint whimper. My wife did not make that sound. It originated behind us. As I rise from my chair, I give Alyssa a wee shake.

She gazes up at me with sleepy eyes. "Sorry I fell asleep."

"Dinnae fash, *mo chridhe*. I heard Lachina make a sound, and I thought to check on her."

Another whimper, louder this time, draws both our attention. We hurry over to the bed.

I sit on the edge and give Lachina a gentle shake. "Wake up, *gràidh*."

Lachina's eyes flutter and finally open. She seems only half awake as she mumbles, "Never begin a thing on the third of May."

Alyssa comes up beside me, resting her hand on my shoulder. "What did she say? Something about the third of May?"

"It's an old superstition. One should never begin anything on the third day of the month of May. I don't know where the superstition originated."

"Why would Lachina say that in her sleep?"

"Only she can answer that question. Once she wakes, we might ask her."

Alyssa leans her body against mine and slips a hand into my hair, combing it with her fingers in a soothing manner. I clasp her other hand. Lachina will recover well, though she might have a scar from the knife wound. My fear is not that she might die, but that Simidh will make another attempt on the life of someone I love.

My father comes into the room a wee while later, taking over the duty of watching over Lachina. Alyssa and I spend the night in the solar, sleeping on the floor atop a layer of rushes and my kilt. Neither of us sleeps well, but we did not expect to do so. My enemy waits out there, somewhere, plotting his revenge for a wrong I did not not commit. My father is not culpable either. He did what any good clan chief would do—accept an alliance that would serve the needs of his clan, rather than what he would have preferred.

I wish Brenda Gunn had not suffered because of that. But I cannot alter events that have already occurred.

While my wife continues to sleep, early in the morning I rise to go out into the courtyard and inspect the fortifications. I need to do more to protect my family.

But with magic involved, will anything be enough?

Chapter Twenty-Six

Alyssa

I can walk on my own, Efrica," Lachina says as she tries to bat her sister's hands away. Efrica wants to help Lachina get out of bed and dress herself, while Morna nods her head vigorously every time Efrica tells her injured sister to stay in bed. Lachina has clearly had enough babying. "Look at my wound. It's already begun to heal, which means I can walk and talk and even chew without your help."

As the youngest of three sisters, I imagine she's used to being treated like a child despite the fact she is a grown woman. I grew up without any siblings. I might not have the experience to understand what a life with siblings is like, but I can envision it thanks to the time I've spent here with the MacTaggarts.

Efrica and Morna give up and let Lachina slide off the bed on her own. She has no trouble walking, showing not even a tiny bit of wobbliness. She clearly favors her injured shoulder, though she only winces a little and only when she tries to lift her arm.

She eyes her sisters, who make no attempt to hide their disapproval. Then she sighs and lifts her gaze toward the ceiling. "Go on, help me get dressed."

I move toward the door. "I'll go downstairs and get more wrappings for her wound."

"Thank you, *gràidh*," Efrica says. "You are a sweet and thoughtful lass, and we're all so glad you came to us."

"I'm glad to be here too. Lachina, can I bring you anything else?"

She puckers her lips. "A dirk so I can wave it at these two when they get too 'helpful.' "

I assume she's joking. With the MacTaggarts, I sometimes can't tell for sure. They might be an odd bunch, but I love them all.

When I get downstairs, I head straight for the solar where I know I can find some clean fabric. Morna had been darning one of Kieran's shirts. My husband won't mind if I steal it to make bandages for his aunt. I grab scissors too. As I'm leaving the solar, I hear voices coming from the kitchen. That must be Kieran and Uilleam. The ladies wouldn't have come downstairs yet since they'll need to wait for me to bring the makeshift bandages.

I'm curious what the boys are up to, so I walk into the kitchen.

Kieran and Uilleam stand at the counter, staring down at something I can't see because their big bodies are in the way.

I clear my throat deliberately.

The men turn to look at me, both seeming surprised.

"What are you two doing in here?" I ask. "Didn't think you guys knew where the kitchen was."

"I've been known to cook a meal now and then," my husband says. "Just ask my aunts. They can verify my claim."

"Oh, so your cooking skills need to be verified. That probably means you'll talk one of your aunts into making the food, then serve it to me and claim you cooked it."

I amble up to Kieran and pretend to scrutinize the slab of meat that lies on the counter. "What is this? Squirrel?"

"No, you saucy wench." He slings an arm around my waist, then slides his hand down to my bottom. "This is *capall-coille*, a type of bird. A Sassenach like you would call it a capercaillie."

I pinch his ass. "I'm American, not British."

"Do you know what a capercaillie is?"

"Yes. It's kind of like a turkey. But you probably don't know what that is."

"Nay." He points at the meat. "I sliced this to get enough pieces for all of us to eat. Haven't had time to go hunting again."

"You shouldn't hunt anymore. What if Simidh is still out there?"

Kieran smacks his hand down on the counter. "What would you have me do? Hide in this castle? I need to go out there to hunt, yes, but also to determine if anyone is keeping an eye on us."

"No, you can't leave the castle."

His nostrils flare. "I am not a bairn, Alyssa."

I lean around Kieran to look at his father. "Uilleam, please tell your son it's a bad idea to leave the castle."

My father-in-law shakes his head. "I can't do that. I agree with Kieran."

"What?"

He shrugs. "Hiding is not the answer, lass."

"But your sister was injured yesterday."

Uilleam opens his mouth but doesn't get the chance to speak. Someone else gets there first.

"My brother is right. We cannot hide."

We all turn to look at Lachina.

She approaches me and clasps my hand. "Please don't fash yourself about this, *gràidh*. It's clear you come from a world that's much different than ours. Here, we have no choice but to fight because hiding will only prove we are weak and unwilling to defend ourselves and our loved ones."

"I get that, I do. But Simidh used magic to escape."

"And we used it to fend him off. Kieran might not like to admit it, but he also has immense power that he refuses to employ. I hope you can convince him that it's nothing to fear." She cants her head. "Or must I convince you first?"

"No, I believe it's real. And I saw what you three did yesterday. It was amazing. But I still worry about Kieran going out there alone."

"He won't be alone," Uilleam says. "I will accompany my son."

"I'm going with you guys."

My husband squints at me. "You will not leave this compound."

"Let's not go through this argument again. I have weapons, which you showed me how to use. I am going with you."

Uilleam chuckles. "You found the right lass for certain, *mo mhac*. I knew your mother was the woman for me when she fought alongside me in that skirmish with the Chisholm clan." His smile turns sentimental, almost dreamy, and his gaze goes distant. "Morainn was a wonderful woman."

"Aye, she was," Kieran says, his voice hushed. "I still miss her."

"We all do."

Kieran rubs his eyes, and his shoulders flag. "Alyssa, you can come with us."

I kiss his cheek. "Thank you."

"We will close the doors and the portcullis to protect the aunts."

"Um, won't that mean they're trapped inside the fortress? With no way out?"

"If the worst happens, they know to flee through the garderobe channel. Besides, they have magics on their side."

Yeah, that does give them an edge. But I'll still worry about the aunts—and Kieran and Uilleam too.

Since Lachina feels up to it, we gather in the dining hall for breakfast. Despite what went down yesterday, we laugh and tease each other and basically act like nothing has changed. We aren't idiots. But we can't spend every waking moment worrying about what might happen. After we eat, the boys and I discuss the problem of my clothing. A voluminous skirt isn't ideal for running away, if someone should attack us. Before I can suggest it, Kieran brings up the idea of finding braies for me to wear. I already figured out that "braies" means pants, though the medieval kind only goes down to the knees. I need tall boots too, but none of Kieran's will fit me.

"We have boots for you," Efrica says. "When last Uilleam visited us, we asked him to bring an old pair of Kieran's boots for you. The ones he wore as a young laddie ought to fit you."

Morna races off to find that footwear, returning moments later with a well-worn pair of knee-high leather boots. When I slip them on, they do indeed fit. *Nice.* Now I don't need to wear a skirt all the time. The aunts usher me into the solar so I can change into my new outfit. It feels good. I've never been a tomboy, but I prefer pants to skirts, so this is heaven for me.

When I walk out of the solar, Kieran and Uilleam are there waiting.

My husband had been leaning against the wall, but now he straightens, and scans me from head to toe. His lips curl up the slightest bit. "You look even bonnier in that clothing."

The deeper tone of his voice proves he loves my outfit. He would probably fuck me right here in the corridor if no one else was around.

I bow and flourish my hands. "Thank you, my laird."

"Stand up, before I do something that will embarrass my aunts."

"Are you daft?" Efrica asks from behind me. "We saw you and Alyssa having a good time in the courtyard."

"We heard you going at it in the stair too," Lachina says. "None of that embarrassed us. And you know that."

Kieran screws up his mouth and avoids looking at me. "Let's go. The day isn't getting any longer."

It's time to head out. So I strap on my dirk with its attached by-knife, while Kieran and Uilleam grab their claymores. We won't kill game with those weapons. They're in case Simidh makes an appearance. Instead, we'll use crossbows. As we approach the entrance, I wonder how Kieran plans to close the portcullis and doors again since they're huge and outrageously heavy and the wooden crossbar is on this side. Once we leave the fortress, we can't get back in.

But that doesn't bother Kieran. My husband heaves the portcullis up and opens the doors as usual. Once Uilleam and I have exited, my husband does not follow us. He pushes the doors closed and somehow climbs up to the top of the wall to drop down on our side. Kieran then pulls the portcullis down.

"How did you do that?" I ask, feeling baffled and horny at the same time. Damn, he is incredible in every way.

Kieran dusts off his clothes. "I climbed onto the crossbar, then stepped over to set my feet on the top hinge. After that, it was quite simple to climb onto the walkway above and then leap off it."

Uilleam chuckles. "Quite simple? No one I've ever met could do that—save for my son."

The pride in his voice is unmistakable.

Kieran ignores the compliment, the way most men would, and starts off down the path. I love the way he walks, with just enough swagger to make him hotter than hot but not so much that he seems like an arrogant jackass. I don't even try to hide the way I'm ogling his tush. I stayed a couple steps behind Kieran to walk with Uilleam since I know my hubby prefers to be at the head of the line. But I also like staying in the back for the aforementioned opportunities to admire Kieran's backside.

"Morainn enjoyed watching me walk ahead of her too," Uilleam says. "In fact, she usually insisted upon doing that."

"Yeah, I'm sure she did." My father-in-law might not be a youngster anymore, but he still has a good body. The medieval lifestyle must require a lot of manual labor, which leads to well-developed muscles. Though I appreciate Uilleam's body, I don't feel like ogling him.

Uilleam winks at me. "Morainn always wanted to go into our bedchamber after a walking session. I'm sure you will feel the same after this hunting expedition."

Am I blushing? I think so. That's not something I've ever done before, but hearing my father-in-law talk about sex, even in a sly manner, makes me feel a touch embarrassed.

I can't help asking a question, though. "Do all people of this era speak so frankly about sex?"

"Since I've not met everyone in the world, I can't answer that question."

Kieran halts and spins around to glare at us. "Be silent. We won't catch any game if you two are wagging your tongues the entire time."

I hold my hands up. "Okay, no more talking."

"Aye, no more," Uilleam agrees.

But as soon as Kieran starts walking again, his father winks at me. Not sure what that means, but he clearly thinks his son's declaration was entertaining.

Halfway up the hunting path, we stop for a rest.

"What happens when we reach your favorite hunting spot?" I ask. "Do we spread out to look for game?"

"Normally, we would do that. But I dinnae want us to separate this time. It's too much of a risk."

Uilleam nods his agreement.

"Do you have an alternative plan?" I ask my husband.

"Aye." He draws lines in the dirt with a twig, apparently laying out the plan. He points to each item in turn. "At the top of the path, we will fan out, but only a wee bit. Alyssa, I want you to stay at my right, here. I will be in the middle."

Uilleam nods again. "And I will be on your left side."

"Aye."

While Kieran explains the best techniques for finding and killing game, I listen intently. If anyone had asked me a few months ago whether I'd like to go hunting, I would have said absolutely not. I'd rather go to a grocery store to get my food. But here in the sixteenth century, we have no choice. Since I came here, I've realized that veggies alone won't sustain me. Living in medieval times requires a lot of labor, and we need meat to keep ourselves fit enough to do all that work.

Maybe if Kieran weren't banished, we might have other options. I don't know, and it doesn't matter. We can only work with what's available to us.

And hope it's enough.

Chapter Twenty-Seven

Kieran

My wife seems to enjoy hearing about how we hunt and how we will clean and prepare what we do catch. I'd thought she might be squeamish about it, since the process involves blood and entrails, but she didn't bat an eye. How did I come to have such a strong, fine lass as my wife? I don't deserve her, but I will never let her go. She has come to mean everything to me.

"Do all Scots hunt on foot?" Alyssa asks. "Wouldn't horses be better?"

"Nay," I respond. "Only nobles hunt that way. Besides, the terrain in the Highlands is not ideal for horses. Most folk don't have them. And also, I can't go into the village even if I wanted to procure a horse. I was born in Ballachulish and raised in Loch Fairbairn, but I will ne'er again see either place again."

"I forgot about the banishment. But they might lift that restriction sometime, right? They won't actually punish you for the rest of your life."

"Of course they will. Simidh Gunn will make certain of that."

My wife squeezes my hand. "I'm so sorry, Kieran. You don't deserve any of this."

Don't I deserve it? I used to be certain that I did not, but now I have no idea whether I do.

Alyssa seems to understand that I don't wish to discuss the subject any longer. She turns to my father. "Uilleam, why don't you have a horse? You walked all the way to Dùndubhan."

"Aye," my father says. "Dinnae want a horse. As long as my son is banished, I will not travel by any means other than walking when I come to visit with him."

His statement makes me freeze and stare at him. I hadn't considered the manner by which my father reaches Dùndubhan. But to hear him say that he refuses to ride a horse and make his journey easier simply because of me… Dinnae know what to think of that.

"You should ride a horse if you want to," I tell my father. "Dinnae be daft about it."

"My loyalty to you will never wane, and honor requires me to make that loyalty evident."

I have no response to his declaration. But my throat goes thick, and I feel a stinging in my eyes. I won't cry. That would be ridiculous. A grown man does not show such emotion to another man, even if that man is his father.

Fortunately, I have a valid excuse to end the conversation. I rise and stretch. "Time to continue our journey."

Our hunting expedition nets us two rabbits. I almost took down a boar, but it swerved at the last moment as I released a bolt from my crossbow. The rabbits will do for now.

I show Alyssa how to dress a carcass, and she doesn't flinch at the blood and entrails. She does exactly what I tell her and does it flawlessly.

We do not encounter Simidh on our journey back to Dùndubhan. That does not mean he is nowhere near the property. The bod ceann knows how to conceal himself in the forest, and considering the depth of his hatred for me, I can't believe he would give up so easily.

Once we return to the castle, I hand our game over to my aunts. We have arrived at the usual time for our midday meal, but my aunts will need to prepare and cook the meat. That means we have time to spare. I should go out to the courtyard to continue my repairs, but I've grown tired after our long morning of hunting. Alyssa seems tired as well, and so is my father. We retire to the solar for a wee bit of relaxation. My wife and I sit by the hearth while my father stretches across the bench by the wall.

Soon, I hear him snoring softly.

Alyssa appears to be drowsy, but she seems determined to stave off the impulse to sleep.

I lean over to touch her knee. "Dinnae fight it, mo chridhe. You need rest."

She rolls her head to the side to give me a sleepy smile. "I'll sleep if you will."

"Aye, we'll both do that."

The lass closes her eyes, and I watch as she gradually slips into slumber and her body goes slack. I'm relieved that she will get some rest, but I don't expect I will do that. I can't stop thinking about Simidh and his obsession with my wife. He blames me for what my father did, though his decision to marry a different woman, not Simidh's mother, seems to be the impetus for his rage. I hadn't known Simidh well when I lived in Ballachulish. My family had moved to Loch Fairbairn shortly after that, and I had no contact with Simidh for years. Our branch of the MacTaggart clan had split off from the rest.

Mayhap I should tell Alyssa more about my family's past. She is my wife now, and I want to have no secrets from her. That will mean telling her how my banishment came to be.

"Wake up, Kieran."

My wife's voice rouses me, though I had no idea I'd fallen asleep. She gives me a wee shove and repeats her command that I should wake up. At last, I pry my lids open, yawn, and turn my head toward Alyssa.

She plants her hands on her hips. "Finally. I thought you were going to sleep for twenty years like Rip Van Winkle."

I push up out of my chair and stretch, groaning because my muscles had grown stiff. "What is Rip Van Winkle?"

"A fictional character in a book. But I guess that story was written in the eighteen hundreds." She pats my chest. "Never mind about that."

I glance at the bench where my father had lain earlier, but it's empty. "Where did my father go?"

"The aunts wanted to go outside the walls to look for medicinal plants. They want to stock up, apparently."

"And my father let them go outside the walls? He should not have done that. It's dangerous."

"Don't you trust Uilleam's judgment? He's not stupid."

"I know that." I scrub my hands over my face and groan again. "But I worry about Simidh, that he might catch one of you out there alone."

"Which is why we don't go out alone. Uilleam is with your aunts, and you will always be with me if I go outside the fortress."

Alyssa is right. I should stop behaving like a prison guard and instead give my family the leeway they deserve. They all know the dangers and the best ways to stay safe.

"Would ye like to eat something?" I ask. "I need to discuss a few things with you, but a wee snack wouldn't go amiss."

"I think we can find something to eat, somewhere in this house."

Alyssa accompanies me to the kitchen, and we choose a few items that we put on a plate. She carries that while I hold our mugs of mead, which weigh more than the plate. Once we've sat down in the solar again, near the crackling fire, I know it's time for our talk.

But first, I eat a chunk of cheese and drink a few mouthfuls of mead. "I wanted to talk to you alone, mo gaol, without my father or the aunts here."

"Okay. I'm ready to hear whatever you need to say."

"Aye, you always are." I eat a bite of meat leftover from lunch before I begin. "I need to tell you about my banishment, how it came to be and why I was sent here to Dùndubhan."

My wife tucks her legs beneath her and turns toward me. But she does not speak. Alyssa must realize this story will be uncomfortable for me to share. I love her all the more for that.

"You know what Simidh said." I want to shove more food into my mouth to delay the inevitable, but I force myself to go on instead. "He had come to our clan as a young laddie, with his mother Clara and his sister Brenda, after his father was killed in a raid. At the same time, the Gibsons had wanted to take over the Gunns' territory, and they managed to murder a great many of them in the battle. Unfortunately, Clara died not long after that when a fever swept through the village."

"How awful. But I can't feel too sorry for that evil bastard. For his sister, sure. Not for him."

"Nor can I. But Brenda is a good lass. She bears no responsibility for what her brother has done." I lodge one ankle on my other knee and gaze into the fire as the memories assail me. "My father was more than willing to take Brenda as his new bride. I was rather a handful for one man to care for. Women are better equipped for child raising."

"I'll ignore that slightly sexist comment. Medieval etiquette is different."

"Aye, I'm sure it is." I let my head fall back against the chair. "Brenda's uncle arranged everything. The banns had been posted. The wedding date had been chosen. Then my father severed the agreement, though he did not do so lightly. He knew the Gunns would be angry, but the MacTavishes could offer more to my clan than the Gunns could. It was an important alliance that has resulted in many years of peace. And my father helped find Brenda a different husband who has made her happy."

"Uilleam did the right thing, I'm sure. He's a good man, just like you."

"The alliance was sealed by the marriage of my father and Sibylla MacTavish. Many arranged marriages are not happy, but my father grew to love his new bride, and she grew to love him in return. I'm glad that it turned out well for them. But Simidh has apparently held on to his grudge against my father for many years."

Alyssa slides off her chair and crawls onto my lap. "I don't understand how what your father did made Simidh hate you."

"I can't explain that either. Somehow, he believes I am responsible. Only Simidh can provide the reasoning behind that belief."

"How does this play into your banishment?"

To have her on my lap while I continue my story makes me feel better about everything. I still have an enemy out there plotting against us, but I feel more confident in our chances of defeating Simidh, simply because this woman loves me.

"You know that Simidh claimed I was a thief," I tell her. "He spread that rumor wherever he could and hoped to convince many people. He succeeded in convincing a good number, not all of the clan. Not even the majority of them. But Simidh would not give up. He railed against me at every turn, whenever he saw an opportunity to do so. My father had no choice but to send me away, permanently."

"You came to Dùndubhan because your aunts live here. But why did they move to this place?"

"Dùndubhan was built by a MacTaggart, my ancestor Ruiseart. Our clan had lived in a disorganized village that had no name, until Ruiseart came along and brought the people together. He made us a cohesive clan. He made us MacTaggarts."

"Why was the castle abandoned?"

"Another clan laid siege to Dùndubhan and caused much damage, though the castle did not fall. Ruiseart negotiated a peace treaty that required the MacTaggarts to abandon the fortress and swear never to return. Many of my ancestors died in that siege, though not Ruiseart. His life was taken years later when bandits attacked his new home. His wife and three children survived, but they did not wish to live there any longer. They moved on and rebuilt their lives in Ballachulish, and later, Loch Fairbairn. They did not, however, return to Dùndubhan."

Alyssa brushes her fingers through my hair and rubs her cheek against mine. "Your clan survived, and I'm so grateful for that. I would never have met you otherwise."

"Marriage to a disgraced and banished man is nothing to be grateful for, though I am grateful that you came into my life."

"You need to stop blaming yourself for what happened. You did not fail your family."

"What if I can't protect you from Simidh Gunn? He might go after my aunts too, or my father."

Alyssa glances past my shoulder. "Maybe you can convince him, Uilleam."

"It's doubtful. My son is determined to shoulder all the responsibility for everything bad that happens."

My wife hops off my lap.

I heave myself out of the chair, feeling as if I've gained a thousand pounds in the past few minutes, and turn toward the doorway where my father stands.

He strides over to me. "If you're going to take credit for the bad things, at least also give yourself credit for everything you have accomplished."

"Such as what?"

"Taking care of your aunts. Repairing the castle. Standing up to Simidh." He slaps a hand on my shoulder and smiles. "But your greatest accomplishment was convincing Alyssa to marry you."

No, I won't dispute that claim. My father is correct. I still have no conception of how I came to have a wife such as Alyssa. She saved me in ways I cannot even articulate.

"I need to return to the village soon," my father says. "But I would like to help you with the repairs here first."

"Any assistance is greatly appreciated."

My wife raises her hand. "I can help too."

"I would prefer it if you did not, but I know you will simply follow us about while we do our work. So you might as well assist us."

She takes my hand, threading her fingers with mine, and leans against me. "Thank you, Kieran. You're becoming a well-trained husband."

"I doubt I will ever train you properly."

"Luckily for you, I know you're joking. So was I, by the way."

On our way out of the castle, we come upon my aunts in the hall on the first floor. They're cleaning the floors, though that seems like a pointless task to me. Won't the floors simply attract more dirt? But I suppose it's no different than repairing the castle. That will need work again in the future, just as the floors will require more cleaning.

I share my notion with Alyssa.

She laughs. "So true. But in the twenty-first century, there are machines that will scoot around cleaning the floors for you."

"Machines?"

"Oh, that's way too complicated to explain right now."

"Aye, I'm sure it is."

My wife does indeed assist us in our work on repairing the courtyard walls. She hands us tools and brings us buckets of mortar. Alyssa also helps guide us as we move wooden beams into position. Aye, my wife is wonderful. She hunts, she knits, she participates in repair projects, and she lets nothing ruin her good spirits.

When we open the doors partway and raise the portcullis to effect repairs there, Alyssa asks a question.

"Shouldn't there be an easier way to open and close those things? It's not very helpful."

"Mayhap not," I say. "But the gatehouse was built to withstand an invasion, not for ease of use."

"Couldn't they do both?"

My father and I exchange glances. He shrugs. And I turn back to Alyssa. "Mayhap the doors could be altered to serve dual purposes. Let's all think on that this eve in the solar."

"Great. I'm so glad you liked my idea."

"I haven't said we'll implement it, only that we will think on it. Dinnae get too excited."

She sets her hands on her hips. "Oh, come on. Let me get as excited as I want. It won't hurt anything."

I exhale a long sigh. "Have it your way. Get extremely excited."

Alyssa runs straight at me, leaping into the air at the last moment, and I'm forced to catch her. Must I hold her tightly to my body? Nay, but I enjoy it more that way.

She kisses every inch of my face and then begins to paddle her feet, though she's hanging in midair. The lass acts like an excited child, not a forty-year-old woman, but I dinnae care.

Happiness should be clung to for as long as possible.

Chapter Twenty-Eight

Alyssa

During the evening meal, I regale Kieran's aunts with kind of exaggerated tales of how I helped the men "spruce up the fortress." I'm not lying. We've all had a lot of stress lately, and a good tall tale makes everyone relax and enjoy themselves. Even my husband seems to be entertained by my stories. I have fun too, spinning yarns and spicing them up with hand gestures and noises that accompany my tales. I never would've imagined I'd behave this way. But with this family, I feel more at home than I ever had in the twenty-first century.

But as my stories wind down, the MacTaggarts keep up the boisterous atmosphere with tales of their own. Listening to them, watching how they interact with each other, I get a lump in my throat. Does anyone back home know I'm gone? Or am I in some kind of alternate timeline? Maybe one day I'll be hurtled back to my own century and find out I returned to the moment right after I'd left. I had friends in my time. Do they realize I'm gone? Do they think I just abandoned my job and moved to Tibet?

My parents will have noticed I'm gone for sure, though they will have no idea that I was hurtled into the past. Then again, we lived on different sides of the country, and I didn't call them as often as I should have. It might take awhile for them to notice anything amiss.

When I landed in this medieval world, I thought I'd never have a family again, but now I do. I have Kieran, his aunts, and his father. Will the rest of the clan ever accept me? I'll never know the answer if we can't prove Kieran never stole anything. Does he want to prove that? Or would he rather live here in this ancient castle for the rest of his life?

We have so much to talk about.

After dinner, the aunts announce they're going to bed. Uilleam prefers to go outside and look at the stars. It's kind of chilly out there tonight, so I try to talk him into taking a small quilt with him. He smiles and pats my cheek, then tells me that he can handle a "wee chill." Once Uilleam has left the dining hall, Kieran and I make our way upstairs to our bedchamber. As we cuddle up under the covers, I rest my head on his bare chest and listen to the rhythmic sound of his heartbeat.

Kieran caresses my hair. "May I ask a question?"

"Since when do you request permission?"

"I was trying to be delicate."

"Oh, I see." I trace circles on his chest, mesmerized by the soft little dark hairs that pepper his skin. "Go on, ask me a question."

"Do you miss your family? They're still in the twenty-first century."

I rest my cheek on his chest. "Yeah, of course I miss them. "

"Do you have no one else at home who will miss you?"

"I had friends, but they were more like work buddies. I doubt anybody has noticed I'm gone. They'll just be annoyed that I'm not there and they'll have to take on my workload."

Kieran grunts. "Those are not friends."

"Yeah, I know. Since I came here, I've become part of a family and realized that none of the people back home who claimed to be my friends even knew what that word actually means." I cuddle up to him even more, loving the scent of him and the warmth of his body. "I don't ever want to go back to the twenty-first century. I belong here with you."

"Aye, lass, ye do."

"I wish I could've met your mother. She must have been quite a woman to raise a son like you."

"Morainn Ross was a force of nature but also a kindhearted woman. She never disliked anyone, not even Simidh Gunn. But she was too intelligent not to realize Simidh had secret motivations."

When he used his mother's full name, first and last, I remembered something. "When we got married, in the vows I gave my family name, Vescovi, and I noticed you called your mother Morainn Ross. Do all women in this century keep their family names after marriage?"

"Aye. It's traditional."

"So, I can't really be a MacTaggart. I stay a Vescovi."

Kieran folds his arms around me, hugging me close. "You are a MacTaggart and a member of the family."

I rub my cheek on his chest to inhale another deep breath of him. I might have a different last name, but I've joined a new family and I never want to leave them.

A long day of hard labor outdoors has left Kieran more tired than he'd like to admit. He falls asleep long before I do. I keep thinking about Simidh and his vendetta. What will he do next? He got Kieran banished and tried to abduct me, injuring Lachina in the process. That seems like an escalation. What would the next logical step be for an evil cretin like Simidh Gunn? I need to know more, but my husband prefers to obsess over refurbishing the castle. We each have different ways of dealing with stress.

By the time I fall asleep, it's so late that I don't wake up until later than usual. Kieran is no longer in bed with me. He probably went downstairs to avoid disturbing me. But as I get out of bed and begin to assemble my clothes, I hear the soft sound of the doorknob being turned. Someone eases it open a few inches.

And Kieran peeks through the gap, like a burglar casing the joint.

"I see you, Kieran. Might as well come in."

My husband pushes the door open, walks inside, and kicks the door shut again. Then he pulls me into his arms and kisses me deeply. While I struggle to regain my wits after that kiss, he palms my breast. "Good morn, Alyssa. Care for a wee morning fuck?"

"Afraid not. I need to talk to you about something. It's important."

"We are alone. You can tell me anything you like."

I finish lacing up my vest and slip into my ankle boots. "I had a horrible nightmare. It was so realistic that I needed to tell you about it."

"An evil spirit harassed you while you slept? But I did not feel anything of the sort last night."

"Evil spirit? I guess the word nightmare has a different meaning in this time."

"What does it mean to you?"

I wrap my arms around myself. "A horrific dream. It felt real, but it couldn't have been because…I saw you being hanged. Then your body was burned at the stake."

He folds his arms around me. "Dinnae fash. It was nothing but a dream. I haven't been accused of witchcraft, much less convicted of it."

"I don't know if you'd been accused of witchcraft in my dream."

"Mayhap not, but you described the usual method for dispatching a convicted witch here in Scotland."

Despite his warm body wrapped around me, I still feel cold. The horror of that dream has left a stain on my soul. I need to know more, though Kieran probably won't like my questions. "Have there been a lot of witch trials in Scotland?"

Kieran stiffens the tiniest bit. "Aye, there was a fervor last year. It swept through the whole of Scotland like a demonic plague. Hundreds of people were murdered, though most of them had never gone near witchcraft."

"But you and your aunts have."

"Aye." He curls his fingers, the nails scraping on my vest. "I worried my aunts might be swept up in the tide, but no one comes to Dùndubhan. The only people who know that I've dabbled in white witchcraft are my father and my aunts. They would never tell anyone. My aunts have been more open about their witchcraft, but still, no one in the clan would betray them."

"Does Simidh Gunn know about you and your aunts?"

"Not that I'm aware of. But he is a guileful *bod ceann*." Kieran takes a step backward and takes hold of my shoulders. "Let's go downstairs and eat breakfast. Try to forget about your nightmare."

"Yeah, okay. I'll try."

By the time we walk into the dining hall, I feel a lot less unsettled, though not entirely free of the memory. I've never had a dream as vivid and disturbing as the one that plagued me last night. Unlike Kieran and his aunts, I don't have any special powers, which means that was nothing more than a horrible nightmare. I need to forget about it, just like Kieran said.

Fortunately, Uilleam and his sisters know exactly what to do to cheer me up, though they don't know why I'm less talkative this morning. Their jokes and teasing help me crawl out of the mental muck and rinse off my psyche. The dream recedes from my awareness, and I jump right in to make wisecracks. I will not let Simidh Gunn, or his nightmare doppelgänger, drag me down ever again. I bet that creep won't have the nerve to harass us again, not after his epic failure on the mountain.

Yes, everything will be fine.

Uilleam pushes his chair back and stands up, then claps his hands. "I'm afraid it's time for me to go home. I've enjoyed being here with all of you, but as chief of the MacTaggart clan, I mustn't neglect my duties."

"We understand," Kieran says. "And we would never ask you to shirk those duties for us."

Kieran rises, and I do the same. His aunts follow suit, and we all traipse down the staircase and outside to the gatehouse.

Uilleam hugs his sisters, then pulls me into a firm embrace. He pats my back and whispers into my ear, "You are the angel my son has needed for so long. Take care of each other. Whatever might happen, you can handle it together."

He pulls away, winking at me, and hugs his son.

Kieran seems somewhat baffled. The two men probably don't show their emotions often, if ever. But while I watch, Kieran's eyes begin to shimmer with what seems like gathering tears. I don't know what his father is saying to him, since he must be whispering, but it clearly affects my husband deeply.

Uilleam touches Kieran's cheek, then walks down the drawbridge.

Kieran stares out the gap between the doors to watch his father amble off down the path. Then he pulls the portcullis down and pushes the doors shut, lowering the crossbar.

The rest of us turn to walk away, but Lachina remains rooted to the same spot where she'd stood when we all watched Uilleam departing. She doesn't move, doesn't speak, but just stands there like a statue with her eyes glossy and her gaze distant.

Morna touches her sister's arm. "Lachina? What is it, lass?"

Still her sister does not move.

Efrica approaches too and gives Lachina a gentle shake. "What are you doing, standing here as if you've left your body?"

Kieran and I walk back to the spot where his aunts are, halting directly in front of Lachina. "Wake up, *gràidh*. Can you hear me? It's Kieran." He waves a hand in front of her face. When that doesn't work, he snaps his fingers. "I said *wake up*, Lachina."

His voice booms through the courtyard.

Lachina blinks once very slowly. Her body sways a little. Kieran grasps her shoulders to keep her from falling over, though she doesn't really seem like she might do that. Lachina blinks again, several times, but still does that as if she's trapped in a pool of molasses.

"Will she be okay?" I ask. "It's almost like she's in a trance."

Lachina jerks and blinks rapidly. Then her gaze lands on me, and I swear I see swirling pools of darkness inside her pupils. "When the fire-haired demon comes again, the trial by fire shall begin."

We all exchange confused glances.

And Lachina abruptly returns to normal. She scrunches her brows and flicks her gaze from me to Kieran and then to each of her sisters. "What on earth are you doing? Staring at me as if I've grown several more limbs and a coat of green hair."

"You went into a trance," I say. "We tried to snap you out of it, but nothing worked. You finally snapped out of it on your own."

"That's not entirely true," Efrica says. "Lachina roused from her trance when you spoke to her."

"Aye," Kieran agrees. "And she gave you a message."

Yeah, and it made so much sense. "Lachina, you said 'when the fire-haired demon comes again, the trial by fire shall begin.' What did that mean?"

She shrugs. "I haven't a clue."

Efrica puckers her lips. "I called Simidh Gunn a fire-haired fiend. But I ne'er called him a demon, though I certainly should have."

Kieran's body goes taut, and he straightens with his shoulders rolled back. "If Simidh ever comes again, he won't get the chance to initiate any sort of trial. I will run him through with my claymore."

That strange, disturbing feeling I'd had when I woke up from my nightmare this morning has begun to seep into my soul again. I grip Kieran's hand. "What if 'trial by fire' means a witch trial?"

"Let's not assume the worst based on a vague vision or intuition or whatever Lachina had. The witch trials were last year. No one wants to repeat the horrors of those days. And besides, I am not a practicing witch, and my aunts have been careful about how they practice. Aye?"

"That's right," Efrica says. "We are discreet, and so are the folk who come to us for help with their ailments."

"See?" Kieran says as he nuzzles my cheek. "Nothing to fear, *mo chridhe*."

A shiver rushes through me, and I huddle closer to Kieran, needing the comfort of his warm body. I want to believe that nothing bad is coming, but I can't shake this eerie sensation that has wormed its way into my psyche. I'd thought I got over it earlier, but Lachina's entranced warning has brought it back. And something that Lachina murmured on the night when Kieran and I watched over her comes rushing back to me.

"What day is this?" I ask. "Does anybody know?"

"I do," Efrica says. "I mark each of my entries in my book with the date. It's the third of May."

"Never begin a thing on the third of May." A rougher chill rattles me down to my bones. "Lachina said that while she was convalescing in our bedchamber. Kieran told me it's an old superstition."

"It means nothing," Kieran says. "Besides, we haven't started anything today."

"But your father has. He started walking back to the village."

Everyone goes silent, and none of us speaks for a moment that seems to drag on into eternity. We glance at each other, and everyone else looks as confused and unsettled as I've felt. Could an old superstition be true? Will something happen to Uilleam because he began his journey home on this date?

No, it's crazy. I've never believed in bad omens.

Kieran hooks a finger under my chin. "Would you like me to go after my father and bring him back here."

Efrica shakes her head. "Dinnae bother. 'Twill do no good. His journey has already begun, for better or worse, and all we can do is pray for his safe arrival at the village."

A sense of unease seems to have infiltrated the air itself, spreading outward to encompass the fortress and the woods. I close my eyes and pray we are all being paranoid and nothing bad will happen to Uilleam. But if I've learned anything over the past few weeks, it's that no one can control the fate of another person.

We split off individually, each going somewhere to do something that will feel like the least important task in the world. But we can't just sit around worrying. We need to keep busy. But as I get to work on learning to knit, one thought keeps haunting me. Should we have gone after Uilleam and made him come home?

Sooner or later, we will know the answer.

Chapter Twenty-Nine

Kieran

I do not believe in curses. The only magics that truly exist are the sort that help heal folk. My father has not wandered off into oblivion by heading home on a specific day. My aunts have always been rather superstitious, but I never thought of their ramblings as anything more than idle talk. What Lachina muttered in her half-awake state the other night did not mean anything. And her trance today… Aye, that also meant nothing.

Once when I made love to Alyssa, I was certain I had employed some sort of magic to make us both come more slowly. It was a ridiculous notion. I no longer believe that's what happened.

Days go by, though I don't bother to count them, while we go about our lives as normal. Even my aunts return to their enthusiastic selves, and Alyssa once again insists upon helping me with my repair work. She is a fine assistant. But I can't continue my secret project with her following me about like a lost lamb. So I conspire to distract her. That means I ask my aunts to keep my wife busy while I do something that I refuse to explain to them. They're accustomed to me not speaking much. It isn't a surprise when I have no desire to explain my intentions to them, except to demand that they keep my wife away from the walled-off area I've been creating.

How do they distract Alyssa? I haven't a clue. But they do manage to prevent her from spying on my "secret project." That's what my wife calls it. But this will only be secret until I've completed the work.

One day, I realize my wife isn't eating her food at the morning meal. She picks at it and moves the bits around on her plate, but she consumes only the smallest amount.

"Are you unwell?" I ask her. "You normally eat your entire meal."

"I'm feeling queasy, that's all. I'm sure it will go away."

"Would you like some bread rather than porridge?"

She rests a hand over her belly. "Yeah, that might be okay."

Morna bustles off to the kitchen to get bread for Alyssa. When she returns, my wife breaks off minuscule pieces and chews them slowly. After a wee bit, she begins to eat larger bites, and finally, she picks up her spoon and begins to work on her porridge. I know it's not the most interesting food, but Lachina makes good porridge. Mayhap Alyssa simply ate something that didn't agree with her. For the rest of the day, and for two days after, she suffers from no queasiness. And I cease worrying.

Until the following morn, when Alyssa and I rise from a good night's slumber. I get up and stretch, feeling quite good. Alyssa shambles over to the chair on which she had left her clothing and picks up her chemise. But she freezes, wincing and puckering her lips.

"Alyssa? What is it?"

"Oh, God, I think I'm going to—"

She pitches forward and clutches her belly as she vomits all over the floor.

I rush to Alyssa and lay a hand on her forehead. "You don't feel warm. Mayhap you ate something that didn't agree with you at dinner last eve."

"This is so embarrassing." She straightens and wipes a hand across her mouth. "I actually feel a lot better now. Guess I just needed to get rid of whatever it was."

I smooth hair away from her face. "Mayhap you should rest, *mo chridhe*. My aunts can take care of the housework."

"You're very sweet, but I'd rather be useful. I've been practicing my knitting, and that's not a strenuous activity."

"As you wish. But if you begin to feel ill again—"

"I'll yell for you."

She suggested that because she knows I will worry and because she realizes I might annoy her with my need to check on her incessantly. If I know she will do nothing more than knit, I won't need to annoy her.

Most likely. I can't vow it won't happen.

A few days later, a visitor pounds on the castle doors. I trot out there with my claymore gripped in my hand and raise the crossbar so I can open the door a wee bit. The man standing on the other side of the portcullis wears a grim expression, and I recognize him.

"John?" I say. "What brings you to Dùndubhan?"

Alyssa trots up beside me. "Do you know this guy?"

"I do. He's my cousin John." I face our visitor again. "You must have had a reason to travel all this way. Why don't you come into the house and we can have a drink while you tell me whatever it is."

John's expression turns pained. "I'm sorry, Kieran. Your father died yesterday."

I stare at him, unable to comprehend what John said. The world seems to have vanished, leaving me inside an empty room in the pitch dark. Alyssa grasps my hand, and that's the only thing preventing me from bellowing like a wounded bear. I can't understand the words my cousin spoke. Dead? My father? No, it can't be.

Alyssa begins to cry, but she doesn't sob or even hiccup. She grips my hand so tightly that it hurts, but I dinnae care.

By rote, I lift the portcullis and move aside to let John pass through the doors.

"I shouldn't stay," he says. "You know I never believed the lies Simidh told about you, but I can't be seen with a banished man. I needed to give you the news, but now I should go. We all grieve for Uilleam, but none as deeply as you."

"How—how did it happen?"

"Uilleam's heart gave out. He clutched his chest and collapsed."

The world spins around me in the most disorienting way, but I somehow sound calm when I tell John, "You may go now. Thank you for letting us know."

"You cannot attend the funeral."

"Aye, I know."

I watch as John walks down the path that leads to the village. Once he has gone out of my sight, I shut the portcullis and the doors, then lower the crossbar. Alyssa and I shuffle into the house. I hold Alyssa tightly to my side as we enter the kitchen where my aunts have been cooking the midday meal. They smile at first, then their happiness crumbles away.

"Oh, no," Efrica says. "What is it, Kieran?"

"My father is dead."

Her lips quiver, and her eyes shimmer with tears, but Efrica remains as stoic as anyone could be under the circumstances. When Lachina and Morna begin to sob, Efrica wraps her arms around them. Alyssa clings to me with her face crushed to my chest, her shoulders heaving with every sobbing breath.

Aye, my father is gone. I will never see him again.

For days after we heard the news, the castle becomes as silent and hollow as a tomb. We hardly speak to each other. But we can't simply wallow in our grief because life must go on as before, else we will all starve and wither away. Eventually, our conversations become less stilted and more normal, though we avoid talking about my father.

After what feels like ages but was only a month, we do talk about my father. We remember his humor and his ability to lead his people no matter what came to pass. I share stories from my childhood that involve my father, and Alyssa enjoys that very much. Aye, it still feels as if someone has taken a knife to my chest and carved out a hole that will never be filled. But every day its gets a wee bit easier.

Then one day, my wife finds me in the bakehouse where I've been cleaning things up to make room for another surprise for Alyssa. I haven't purchased the surprise yet, so she can't tell what it might be.

I draw my wife close and kiss her. "Welcome to the bakehouse, *mo chridhe*. It finally resembles one of those, doesn't it?"

"Yes, it does. What are you going to put in here?"

"I haven't decided yet." Of course I have, but she won't find out yet.

She bites her lip and studies my shirt, picking at the buttons. "I figured out why I keep getting queasy sometimes."

"What caused it?"

"It's, um…" She rests her forehead on my chest. "Oh, God. I can't figure out if it's too soon to tell you, considering that you lost your father a month ago."

"Tell me, *m'eudail*."

Alyssa lifts her head and aims her bonnie blue eyes straight into mine. "We're having a baby, Kieran."

"What?" I gape at her, uncertain if I imagined she said that. "A bairn? Are you sure?"

"Yeah. I haven't had my, um, monthly flow since a few days after I arrived here."

Though I understand the words she spoke, my mind seems to have trouble accepting that I'm not imagining it. Alyssa said we are having a bairn. Mayhap I shouldn't feel happy, considering that my father died only a few weeks ago, but the feeling that sweeps through me now is not anguish or guilt. It's joy. I should experience that. My father wouldn't want me to languish in grief for months or years. He would want me to live my life, and the news my wife just shared convinces me.

I pull Alyssa into my arms and kiss her.

When I finally give up her lips, I grin and throw my head back to shout with joy. The sound echoes off the castle walls as my wife joins me in celebration, and the echoes grow even louder as her cries mingle with mine. I hoist her off the ground and spin us round and round.

When I finally stop whirling about, I notice my aunts are sprinting across the courtyard toward us.

"Kieran!" Efrica screams. "Alyssa! Are you injured?"

"Nay," I shout to her. "Dinnae fash. We are unharmed."

My aunts halt near us, all of them breathing hard and their faces flushed. They must have run here from somewhere on the upper floors of the house.

Morna regains her breath first. "We heard screaming, then saw you holding Alyssa up as if she couldn't stand on her own feet."

"Calm yourself, Morna. We are both well. But my wife shared a bit of news that made us both feel so happy that we needed to express that joy aloud."

Morna lays a hand on her chest. "Oh, Kieran, you gave us all quite a fright."

"I apologize for that. But you will agree the shouting was appropriate once we share the news."

Efrica scowls at me, but it's a halfhearted expression. "After the way you frightened us, you need to share the news right now."

I glance at my wife and nod.

She grins at my aunts. "We are having a baby."

My aunts do not shriek or leap about with joy. Instead, they shake their heads at each other.

Efrica folds her arms over her chest. "Did ye think we didn't know that already? We are witches, after all. And we are also women. That means we recognized the signs when Alyssa began having fits of queasiness."

Lachina whispers into Efrica's ear.

"Oh, aye," Efrica says. "We agree that is the appropriate next step."

My aunts rush at us while screaming and babbling nonsense. They hug Alyssa and me, several times each. Then we go into the house for a celebratory snack in the solar. Morna brings mead too, but Alyssa declines the beverage.

"In the twenty-first century," she tells us, "it's believed that drinking during pregnancy is bad for the baby. Alcohol can cause physical and mental problems."

"We have many things you can drink," Efrica says, "that have no alcohol in them. Lemon drink is delicious, then there's barley tea, sage water, rose and clarea of water. We also have our own concoction of honey and herbs."

"Thank you. I'm so glad to know I can stay off alcohol for the duration of the pregnancy. I was afraid I'd have to drink the garderobe water." Alyssa gives me a sly smile, so I know she's teasing me. "I wonder if we'll have a boy or a girl."

"Would ye like me to ask the spirits of our ancestors?" Efrica asks. "They might give us the answer."

"No, I'd rather be surprised. What about you, Kieran?"

"I dinnae care if it's a boy or girl, as long as our child grows up safe and happy. But if we should have a girl, I know the lass will be as brave, intelligent, and kind as her mother."

Mayhap I wish my father could be here to see his grandchild. But I know he will be watching over us and our children. And aye, I'm sure we will have more than one bairn. Our line will continue down through the centuries, giving birth to new generations who will have opportunities I could never dream of, though my wife knows exactly what the future will be like.

But the only future I want to think about is the day months from now when our child will be born.

Chapter Thirty

Alyssa

When I first arrived in this century, at this big old castle, I had felt like a prisoner. Sure, Kieran had locked me in that dank room for a while, but I soon realized he had reasons for his behavior. I also realized that I had been more of a prisoner in the twenty-first century than I ever would be here at Dùndubhan. I'd spent my days glued to a computer screen, crafting social media strategies for products and services that would never elevate people's souls. It was all about profit.

Now, I live in a world where none of that exists. I'm free to do things I never would have tried before, like knitting and swordplay. Kieran has been teaching me how to better use my dirk. I'd gotten a crash course in using a crossbow too, on that day when we went hunting with Uilleam. I got a longer introduction to crossbows after that.

God, I miss Uilleam.

He was such a good man. Kieran has been surprisingly willing to discuss his feelings for his father ever since I told him I'm pregnant. I think he realizes now just how precious those memories are, and he wants to make sure our child knows Uilleam through the stories we share with our "bairn."

I'm learning the Scottish words now.

Today, I'm under orders to relax and do nothing strenuous. Yes, my husband issued that decree. But I'm happy to follow his orders because I've been feeling tired lately. At least the morning sickness has gone away. Since I'm not allowed to do anything strenuous, I head for the solar to work on a baby blanket I'd started knitting a few days ago.

When I walk into the solar, Efrica is already there. She sits by the hearth, scribbling in her journal. When I enter the room, she looks up. "Oh, there you are, *gràidh*. Come sit with me."

I settle onto the chair opposite her. "How long have you been writing down all your experiences?"

"Since Kieran came to live here. I suddenly felt it was important to document our daily lives."

"Kieran thinks you write things down because you're turning into a dotty old woman who can't remember anything. But I think he's joking."

"Aye, he is. The laddie loves to harass me."

"Now that Uilleam is gone, he worries even more about us ladies."

Efrica sets her book on her lap, face-down. "He worries most about you and the bairn. But Lachina assured me you will both be fine."

"What about Kieran?"

"I haven't cast the runes for him yet. Mayhap I will later."

The solar door opens, and Morna and Lachina come inside. They talk me into playing a game of fox and geese. Do future people play this game? I'd never heard of it before, but maybe it's a Scottish or British thing in the twenty-first century.

"You can play against Lachina first," Morna says. "You can easily beat her, and that will encourage you to take part in more games with us."

Lachina fake-scowls at her sister. "I am not easy to beat. I have *da-shealladh*, you know, and that means I foresee every move you are planning to make in every game we will play."

"Oh, is that why ye lost the last three times we played? Your *da-shealladh* seems to need a good washing to get rid of the grime that's fogging it up."

I love listening to these ladies rib each other. It feels like we've gotten back to normal at last.

While Morna sets up the fox and geese board, I absorb everything she tells me about the game. It's played on a square wood board with a cross-shaped center area created by thirty-three holes that each hold a peg. Morna insists that Lachina should be the fox while I will be the flock of geese. The fox is supposed to try to capture the geese, but all I can do as owner of the geese is to try to hem in the fox so he can't get away. The fox can move in any direction as long as it's a straight line. My geese, however, can only move forward or sideways.

This is a very strange game.

Lachina wins the first game, and Morna pretends to be offended that "the worst player in the world" prevailed. I'm now the worst player. But nobody really cares who wins or loses. We just want to have fun. Once I get the hang of the game, I win a few rounds. Fox and geese is kind of addictive. I'm a little disappointed that the fox and geese aren't pieces carved to resemble those animals. Instead, they're pegs in holes.

Kieran comes in just as Efrica beats Morna by capturing all the geese. He stands on the open threshold to the solar doorway, leaning against the jamb with a slight smile on his lips. He's watching his aunts and listening to the jibes they throw at each other.

"You cheated," Efrica says. "I saw you move your geese backward when you thought I wasn't paying attention."

"I did no such thing. You are getting senile, that's the problem. Ye can't tell the different between forward and backward anymore."

Kieran saunters over to the table where the game board is still set up. "Do I need to separate you two?"

"Nay. Not as long as Efrica apologizes for slandering me."

Efrica leans toward her sister. "The word you're looking for is slaughtering, not slandering. My fox ate all your geese, and they were delicious."

Kieran snatches the board away from his aunts. "Enough. I know you lasses are only having fun, but your shouts can be heard in the courtyard. Time to settle down. Dinnae want my wife to get overexcited."

Morna smirks at him. "Then ye best sleep in separate bedchambers. We all hear you two, at night and during the day. Your outdoor adventures are legendary."

"According to whom? Only you three live here with us."

Efrica smiles at him. "Aye, and we say it's legendary. I've ne'er met a couple as…energetic as you and Alyssa."

Oh yeah, we are definitely energetic. My husband and I keep in great physical condition with all our sexual exercise. I'll need to tone it down a bit as I get into the later months of pregnancy since we've come to love all the varieties of chair sex as well as stair sex, corridor sex, and even garderobe sex. That involved Kieran sitting on the wooden seat while I climbed onto his lap and rode him like a "wild Highland lassie," as my husband phrased it. We only did that once. Ever since, I've been afraid we might break that wooden seat and go tumbling down into the channel far below.

Kieran and I know how to find new ways to get it on, so we won't be deprived of excitement.

My husband leans over my chair from behind, setting his hand on the table in front of me. "May I take my wife for a walk outside the walls?"

"I'd love that."

Kieran doesn't wait for me to get up. He shoves his hands under my bottom and lifts me out of the chair, straight into his arms. He damn well knows I can walk under my own power, but he enjoys carrying me whenever I'll let him do that. This time, I give in. He transports me out of the house in his arms, and I love the little smile that curls his lips at the corners. The hilt of his claymore bumps into my bottom with every other step he takes. He always brings a sword if we're going outside the compound.

"You should've let me get my dirk," I say as he marches out the door and across the courtyard. "Then we'd both be able to protect each other."

He smirks but says nothing.

That always means he's up to something, and that usually means he wants to have sex.

But Kieran surprises me. He takes us toward the walled-off area where he's been working on his secret project. At the door to the new section, he has hung a large, well-worn bedsheet to hide what lies inside.

He stops there. "We need to go through the area where I've been working, but it's not ready for you to see yet. Please close your eyes and dinnae peek."

"I won't. Cross my heart." I make that gesture with my finger. "How soon will I be able to see what you've been doing in there?"

"Soon. Be patient, *mo chridhe.*"

I close my eyes and let Kieran take me through the secret area. I can hear it when he opens another door, but I hadn't realized there was one. Before he began his project, there wasn't a door in the outside wall in this spot. I'm sure of that. Asking him about that will get me nothing, I know. My husband has been completely mum on the subject, not even accidentally blabbing a clue, and even my seduction doesn't encourage him to spill the beans.

Once I hear the door shut behind us, I ask, "Can I open my eyes now?"

"Not quite yet. Patience, Alyssa."

"You know I'm terrible at being patient." I wrap my arms around his neck more tightly as he breezes around a corner. I feel like I might tumble out of his arms, but I know he would never let that happen. "When I was little, I used to sneak into my parents walk-in closet at Christmas because I knew they kept my presents there. I'd carefully peel the tape off the wrapping paper so I could get a peek at the booty."

"Did your parents realize what you'd done?"

"I thought they didn't. But when I was all grown up, they confessed that they knew I'd been sneaking a peek every Christmas."

"And they never minded. I wish I could meet your parents. They are clearly good folk, just like their daughter."

He finally stops walking and sets me down. "You may open your eyes now."

We're standing under a tree that has long branches that spread out like a canopy above us. Near the base of the trunk lies an ornate wooden cross with its end stuck in the ground.

I look at Kieran. "I don't understand. Why did you plant a cross here?"

"For my father. My aunts were allowed to attend his funeral, but I couldn't be there." He crouches in front of the cross. "I wanted to have a small memorial for my father, so I could visit with him in my own way. It's daft, I know."

"No, it isn't silly at all." I kneel beside him and hold his hand in both of mine. "I think it's beautiful, Kieran. Uilleam would approve."

He bows his head and wipes at his eyes, trying to chase away the wetness in them. "At least I was able to spend time with him in the weeks before his death."

"Uilleam loved that. He was very proud of you."

"For being an outcast? Dinnae see what there is to be proud of."

"The man you've become, that's what." I lean against him, resting my head on his shoulder. "We can stay here as long as you want."

He rests his chin on top of my head, and for a while, we simply stay here gazing at the beautiful cross he'd made. Birds sing in the bows above us, and a gentle breeze rustles my hair. I can hear the burbling of the river, though I can't see it from here. My husband chose the best spot possible for his private memorial to his father.

Finally, Kieran rises. He takes my hands to help me up.

"I need to examine the walkway atop the wall," he says. "I've ignored that section of the compound, but now it's time I inspected it to make certain there are no weak spots that an enemy might exploit."

"May I go with you?"

"Up there? The walkway is on the highest part of the wall. I will need to go up through the tower to get there. The steps leading to it are rather steep."

That doesn't sound like fun, but I would like to see that part of the fortifications. I can't help worrying about what Simidh Gunn might do now that Uilleam is gone and can no longer protect his son in any way. I suspect Kieran and his aunts feel the same anxiety. From what they've all said about Simidh, I know Uilleam had done a lot to keep that creep away from his son.

"Please take me with you," I say. "I'd like to know more about the walkway."

He studies me for a moment, then sighs. "You may accompany me."

"Thank you, honey."

Kieran scrutinizes my clothes. "You should wear your braies instead of a skirt. 'Twill be easier to climb the tower stair that way."

"Good idea."

He cups my breast in his hand, and even through my vest and shirt, I can feel his touch. "I prefer you dressed thus, but it isn't practical for climbing up to the walkway."

"We can have sex later. I can tell that's what you have on your mind."

"I won't deny that."

Chapter Thirty-One

Kieran

Mayhap I did want to ravish my wife, but I do indeed have a serious task in mind, namely ensuring the compound will be safe and ready for whatever might come. The fact that Simidh Gunn has stayed away for this long makes me worry more, not less. He must be plotting, seeking a way to destroy me, and that method will involve Alyssa. Without my father here to tell me what my enemy is doing, I should journey out into the world to seek information via reconnaissance. But I cannot leave Alyssa and my aunts unguarded.

We return to the confines of the fortress, but before I take my wife up to the walkway, I realize it is time to show her what I've done for her. Alyssa has waited long enough. To ensure it is a surprise, I once again order her to close her eyes. She doesn't complain. But then, she rarely does that. I pick her up and carry her through the doorway, then kick it shut and set her down.

"You may open your eyes now, *mo chridhe*."

Alyssa's lids flutter open. She swivels her head left and right. Her jaw falls open, and her eyes widen. "Kieran, this is incredible. How did you do all of this? It looks like something that would require a crew of workers."

"It took months and a great deal of labor, but you are worth the cost in time and strained muscles."

My wife turns in a circle, slowly, as she sees for the first time what I had hidden in this corner of the castle. She throws her arms around my neck and kisses me. "It's the most beautiful thing I've ever seen."

We stand inside a walled garden filled with lush greenery and blooming flowers.

I take Alyssa's hand to lead her through the wee sanctuary I created, showing her plants along the way. "This bush holds red carnations, which are said to represent true love. And here is the Damask rose, a bonnie flower for certain but not as beautiful as you. The bushes you see along the periphery are sage, rosemary, cotton thistle, and Cupid's dart. I placed the hollyhocks along this back wall."

As we reach the end of our journey around the garden, I stop us in front of a wooden bench. "I crafted this for you, Alyssa. You may sit on the bench to appreciate the garden's beauty and the many scents that fill the air. The corner beside this spot holds various medicinal plants as well as those used in white witchcraft."

She settles onto the bench, still seeming stunned. "Kieran, this is the most amazing gift. I love the garden. Thank you for creating this little sanctuary."

I sit down beside her. "Living in a fortress is not the most enjoyable experience. The least I can do is give you a refuge where you might read or knit or simply relax."

She rests her head on my shoulder. For a length of time I don't even try to count, we enjoy the tranquility and beauty of this space. Then, Alyssa suggests we should invite my aunts to see the garden too. They are, naturally, overly excited by what I have built and grown inside these walls.

But now I need to inspect the walkway.

Alyssa still wishes to come with me, and I do not argue. By the time we reach the top of the tower stair, she's breathing hard and needs a rest. I could use a rest as well, though I'm not breathing as heavily as Alyssa is. We took the steps slowly, but it was still a long way to go up the steep rise. Alyssa did not complain even once, but I hadn't thought she would. My wife is strong and resilient.

I might never have gotten through the loss of my father without her.

"Okay, I'm ready now," Alyssa says. "What did you need to do up here?"

"Check the walkway. I told you that before we climbed the stair."

"Right." She straightens and rolls her shoulders back. "Lead the way, Laird of Dùndubhan."

I would prefer that she not refer to me as the laird, though I once told her to do so. Much has changed since then. She has become my wife, and I can't imagine my life without her now.

We inspect the entire walkway, but I find nothing that needs immediate attention. Alyssa asked questions during our inspection, but I didn't mind that. She seemed genuinely interested in castle construction. The crenellations especially roused her curiosity, and I can understand why. Each crenellation consists of a solid block between slits in the wall, which allow archers to fire off arrows while hiding behind the blocks. Will it help Alyssa to know that? I doubt it. But at least it made her feel more secure.

My wife has become proficient with a crossbow, so mayhap the crenellations will be of use to her. But I pray not, for that would mean enemies have assaulted the castle.

We now stand directly above the gatehouse, between the towers, gazing down at the drawbridge below us. It lies empty since for many decades no one has needed to fend off an enemy here at Dùndubhan. Even during the witch fervor of last year, we had not worried about an invasion.

"Mayhap I should fill the moat," I tell Alyssa. "That would provide another barrier between us and the rest of the world."

"You're that worried? Is this a reaction to your father's death?"

"No, I don't believe so. But I feel a coldness inside me and a weight bearing down on my chest." I pull her close to my side as I study the forest. "Something or someone is coming, and it will not be a happy occasion."

"Maybe you should fill the moat, then."

I look down at her upturned face. "You believe in my premonition? Or whatever you'd like to call it."

"Yes, I trust your instincts. I wonder if your aunts have felt the same thing."

"But you have not. The terrible dream you once had seems to have faded away."

She hunches her shoulders. "Once in a while, I get a bad feeling similar to what that dream caused, but I always brush it off as nothing."

"Do not dismiss it. Intuitions can be subtle but powerful."

"You once told me that you thought you had slowed down time while we were making love. That would mean you have magics inside you." She stares out at the forest. "Maybe you should try to use that power again."

"Let us return to the house and discuss this with my aunts."

Alyssa has less trouble walking down the stair than she had going up it, and we reach the ground floor within minutes. Though I had suggested we should speak to my aunts first, I change my mind once we reach the bottom step. I grasp her hand to stop her from continuing into the ground-floor corridor.

"Will you come out to the garden with me now, *mo chridhe*?"

"Of course I will. But I thought you wanted to talk to your aunts."

"That can wait a wee while. I've had an intuition, and it tells me I should make love to my wife in the garden I made for you."

She smiles. "Is this an excuse for sex? You don't need to make up stories to get me naked."

" 'Tis no excuse. Please, come with me."

"You know I'll go anywhere with you, Kieran."

We make our way to the garden, and I lower the bedsheet to cover the doorway again, though I no longer need to hide what lies inside this space. But I dinnae care to have my aunts glimpsing our lovemaking. While Alyssa undresses, I remove my kilt and lay it out on the grass in the center of the garden. I need only remove my boots, and that takes but a moment.

My wife stretches out on the kilt, on her back, with her hands linked above her head. She is the most beautiful creature on earth, an angel who has deigned to touch her feet on the ground so I might give her pleasure.

She gives me pleasure too, and so much more.

I lie down beside her and trace the backs of my fingers over her cheek. "*Tha thu bòidheach, mo chridhe.* That means you are beautiful, my heart. You bring light and sweetness to my world."

"I can't remember what my life was like before I met you. None of that matters anymore, it's like a dream that faded away."

"Aye, I feel the same." I smirk. "Even when you try to kick me in the erse and curse at me, you're still my angel."

"Shut up and make love to me."

I roll over to lie atop her, pushing her legs apart with my knee, and settle my arms at either side of her shoulders. I need to feel her skin on mine, everywhere, while I take her body. She skates her palms up and down my back, over and over, every stroke gentle and as light as a feather. My cock is firm and swollen, throbbing with a need I can no longer restrain. I touch my forehead to hers as I slide my length between her folds and into her waiting channel. The velvety warmth of her body surrounds me.

A soft sigh whispers out of her when I begin to thrust at a leisurely pace, taking my time so we can both relish the sensations and the intimacy of this moment. The scents of the flowers and bushes mingle as they spread throughout the garden, but one aroma rises above the others—the sugar-and-clove scent of red carnations.

While my hips pump in and out, I lift one arm so I can duck my head and latch on to her nipple. But I don't devour her flesh as I've done before. This time, I lavish her taut peak with slow swipes of my tongue, coiling it round and round until she clutches my arms and arches her neck. Her breaths come faster in time with my own, as if we have become joined deep inside ourselves. Our mouths fall open, and our breaths mingle, as we keep our foreheads touching and I push deeper inside her.

Alyssa wraps her arms and legs around me as if she wants our bodies to become one. "I love you, Kieran, I love you."

Warmth rushes through me, but it's a sweet and gentle sensation that feels like Alyssa. While the scent of red carnations swirls around us, I have no need to tap into my willpower to keep up the measured pace because the feeling I'd experienced that night in our bedchamber has returned. Time seems to slow, and I swear my heartbeat thumps in time with hers.

She comes with such slowness that I can feel every spasm of her climax, and it seems as if we're floating above the earth, caught in a web of sweet magics. When I come, it happens as gradually as her climax had. I unleash my seed little by little, then I push inside her once more with a single, powerful thrust.

We gaze into each other's eyes, and I know she felt what I had experienced. No words could describe it, so we don't even try to summon our voices. I rise and take Alyssa with me, cradled in my arms. I need a long moment before I can convince myself to set my wife on her feet. Then we dress and walk toward the doorway that remains shrouded by a bedsheet.

"Wait," Alyssa says. "Do you see that?"

"See what?"

"That over there."

I look at the corner of the garden she had pointed out and realize the red carnations have grown taller and thicker just since we entered the garden. "What does it mean?"

"Your love made this garden, and it's a part of us both now."

"Are you suggesting it was magic?"

"I think you know the answer to that question."

Aye, I do. But I have trouble believing that I, a banished man, have been gifted with magic and the love of a good woman. But with Alyssa, I do feel that way.

"You are correct as always," I say. "The sensation I experienced on that other night grew stronger today in this garden. You are the reason that Dùndubhan blooms, and nothing will ever take us away from each other for more than a wee while."

The castle that had become my private prison has been transformed into a home at last—because of Alyssa.

Chapter Thirty-Two

Alyssa

I can't believe what happened in the garden. I'd known Kieran and I shared something special, something amazing, but I never imagined we could cause flowers to bloom just by making love. It sounds insane. But since coming to medieval Scotland, I've learned that magic is real and what seems crazy often turns out to be a wonderful gift.

But now, we have to tell the aunts about our premonitions.

When we walk into the solar, Kieran's aunts are gathered at the hearth watching the flames flicker and listening to the crackling of the fire. They've dragged another chair over there to accommodate all three of them. When they notice us, the aunts turn their grave faces our way.

"We knew you would be coming," Lachina says. "And we knew it would be bad news. But we have no conception of what has happened or might be soon to occur."

"Bring two chairs over here," Efrica says. "Then we might discuss the matter by the warmth of the fire."

Kieran drags two chairs over to us, but Lachina insists on trading places with me because her chair has more padding. She says that I should have a softer seat because I'm "with child." I won't bother to point out that I'm barely pregnant and not even showing yet. Lachina means well, and I don't want to upset her by refusing to accept her gracious offer.

My husband sits beside me in a less cushy chair. "Several weeks ago, Alyssa suffered a terrible dream. It has haunted her ever since."

Efrica sits up straighter, her gaze intent on me. "Tell us about this dream, *gràidh.*"

"In my dream, Kieran was hanged and then burned at the stake."

"That is the standard method for executing a witch."

My heart thuds, and a wave of cold sluices through me. "Does this mean—Is Kieran going to die?"

He grasps my hand. "Nay, Alyssa, I will not die."

"But you can't know that. And you agreed that my premonition might be real."

"Aye. But we will remain here inside Dùndubhan until we are certain any danger has passed."

Lachina has begun to wring her hands. "Kieran, I'm afeard for you terribly. Dreams can be powerful premonitions, and we need to find out if this is an omen we should not ignore."

"How do we do that?" I ask. "I can't crawl back into that dream to get more information."

Efrica sits forward, and her eyes light up. "Mayhap you can do that. We are spellcasters, after all. We hid ourselves from the view of Simidh and his *bod ceann* army. The *Fath Fithe* charm that made it possible came from white magics, not the dark sort."

"Okay. But I still don't see how I can recapture a dream. I'm not trying to hide anything, so that charm won't work."

Efrica smiles with a depth of satisfaction that suggests she believes she has found the key to everything. "We summoned you here from a time far removed from our own."

"I remember that."

"Well, dinnae ye think if we could do that, then we could also send you back to the moment when you suffered that terrible dream?"

Kieran huffs. "But you don't know how you brought Alyssa from the future. It was an accident, aye?"

"What if it was?" Efrica says. "Let us try to recreate the summoning spell. It involved several charms combined to craft the magics."

Morna nods. "One element of the spell was the Triple Threads charm."

"We borrowed many of our incantations from Hebridean witches who traveled through the Highlands the year before Kieran came to us. Those lasses remained with us for a fortnight, and we shared many ideas with each other."

"Oh, aye," Lachina says. "That was a wonderful experience. We shared the *gradh a's fuath* charm with the Hebrideans. That one was included in the spell we cast to bring you here, Alyssa."

I raise my hand, which is kind of silly but has become a habit since I arrived in this century. "Um, all this discussion of spells and charms is fascinating. But it doesn't get me any closer to reenacting my dream."

"Enough of this nonsense," Kieran snarls. "I will not have you reenacting any sort of magics that involve my wife. She might be injured if you cannot accurately reproduce what you did the first time."

I lay my hand over his, which is gripping the arm of his chair so tightly the tendons are visible. "Relax, honey. Your aunts would never do anything to hurt me. I trust them—and their magics."

Those are words I never would have imagined I'd ever speak. But I mean it.

Kieran's muscles have slackened, and he slumps back in his chair. A weary sigh gusts out of him. "I trust them as well. But where you are concerned, I have little patience for any suggestions that might have any chance of harming you or our bairn that's growing inside you."

"I would never risk our baby's life. You know that." I lean over to kiss his cheek. "Trust me, trust your aunts, and trust in the power of white witchcraft."

"Once, I did place my faith in such things. My banishment eroded that belief. And since my father left this world, I've had trouble holding on to that faith."

I want to crawl onto his lap and just hold him. Of course he's had a crisis of faith since Uilleam died. Even though Tony had betrayed me, I still grieved when he passed away, though that grief was nothing compared to what Kieran must be feeling these days. I knew Uilleam for a short time, but he became like a father to me. I loved him, and I miss him. Uilleam would want his sisters to try to recreate my dream, I know that. Can't explain why I believe it, but I do. That's what faith means.

Kieran kisses me, then pushes up out of his chair. "We will do this thing. But I will remain with Alyssa at all times."

"Aye, you will," Efrica agrees. "And I believe we should attempt the spell in your bedchamber, where the dream was hatched."

Efrica leads all of us upstairs to the room Kieran and I share. A fire still burns in the hearth, though it has burned down quite a bit. Lachina suggests we should reproduce the conditions inside this room as they had been on the night of my dream, as much as we can remember it. So Kieran stokes the fire and adds more wood, then we both change into the clothes we'd worn on that night. I always sleep in a chemise while Kieran prefers to go nude. His aunts turn their heads away while he gets into bed.

Then we cuddle up the way we always do. That means we spoon, though I don't want to try to explain that term to Kieran or his aunts.

"Close your eyes, Alyssa," Lachina says. "We need all the conditions to be the same. That means you should also close your eyes, Kieran, if that is your usual manner."

We do as she said, and I hear the aunts bustling around, probably getting their spell ready. My curiosity gets the better of me, and I open my lids a sliver, just enough that I can see what's going on. They're kneeling on the floor beside the bed, directly in front of me, sprinkling herbs or something onto the floor. Lachina sets three pendants on the floor, one each for herself and her sisters.

"Eyes closed, *gràidh*," Lachina murmurs. "We are about to call on the *daoine maithe*, the good folk or fairy folk. They will guide our spell."

I shut my eyes and listen while the aunts begin to chant in another language that I assume is Gaelic. The lyrical way they chant lulls me into a form of twilight sleep, not quite awake, not quite slumbering. The feel of Kieran's body snuggled up to mine provides warmth and security, and I slide deeper down toward sleep every second. I feel as if I'm floating on a warm ocean with waves lapping against me while the scent of herbs and spices wafts through the air inside our bedchamber.

My eyes open, though I hadn't consciously tried to make my lids part. I don't feel as if my eyes are open either, though I can see my surroundings. I'm no longer in the bedchamber I share with Kieran. I stand in the courtyard of Dùndubhan, alone, wearing only my chemise. The cold air raises goosebumps on my arms, and my exhalations release a cloud of mist. I rub my arms and look around, trying to understand what's going on.

Footfalls behind me draw closer. I whirl around to face the visitor.

Simidh Gunn smiles at me with feral hunger. "There you are, Alyssa. I have been waiting for you."

"Where is Kieran?"

"Do not trouble your mind with thoughts of that one. I will give you everything you could want or need." He rushes at me so fast that I don't have time to react and lashes me to his body with both his arms. *"An toir thu dhomh pòg?"*

"No, she will not kiss you." Kieran's voice reverberates through the courtyard. He comes up behind me, and I can see him peripherally. "Release her, Simidh, or I will run you through."

He brandishes his claymore and sets the blade's tip against Simidh's throat.

The scumbag laughs. "I have cast a charm on your woman. Several charms, actually. Soon, she will be mine."

I ram my knee up into Simidh's groin. He doubles over, losing his hold on me, and I ram my knee up again—this time to smack the underside of his chin. His teeth clack shut. I scuffle backward.

And Kieran thrusts his claymore into Simidh's chest.

Well, he tries to do that. But his blade snaps in two, leaving the end ragged. When Kieran thrusts his blade again, the claymore flies out of his hands and clatters to the ground behind me.

The redheaded asshole laughs again, louder than before. "You cannot win the battle. I am too strong and too knowledgeable. Would you care to see a demonstration of what lies ahead for you, the illegitimate laird of Dùndubhan?"

A gallows appears directly behind Kieran with the noose already around his neck. His hands are bound, and a wooden block has appeared beneath his feet.

Simidh kicks the block away.

Kieran gasps and gurgles, flailing but unable to get free. The scene shifts into fast-forward as I watch my husband dying and can't move a muscle to help him. The moment his life is snuffed out, flames erupt around him and consume his body.

I scream.

And Simidh chuckles.

Suddenly, the gallows and the flames vanish, along with Simidh Gunn. My heart thrashes in my chest, and I can't catch my breath. My ears are ringing. I feel like I might faint.

Uilleam appears before me. He grasps my shoulders and kisses my forehead. "Take it easy, *gràidh*. You have not lost Kieran. But he will be in grave danger soon, and you must save him."

"This is a dream. You aren't really here."

"Aye, of course I am. The *daoine maithe* have sent me to give you a message."

"What?" I'm still struggling to understand what's going on. The moment Uilleam had touched me, I relaxed and my heart rate slowed.

He bends his knees just enough to level our gazes. "You are the greatest charm any man could have and the best defense against the evil Simidh will unleash upon my son. Believe what I've said. It is true, and all that I can say."

"But what about Kieran?"

"He must die, but 'twill not be as you might believe."

Uilleam disappears.

I jerk upright, suddenly back in the bed I share with Kieran. The aunts are still kneeling on the floor, but they've stopped chanting. A puff of smoke is dissipating inside the circle they had created, and I smell incense or something like it.

Kieran bolts upright. When he sees me, he pulls me onto his lap. "What did you see, *mo chridhe*?"

"Uilleam. He gave me a message." I swallow, but the lump lodged in my throat won't soften. "He said you have to die."

Chapter Thirty-Three

Kieran

I must die. That is what Alyssa claims my father said. I would ne'er doubt anything my wife tells me, but I cannot believe my father would predict my death and not offer some insight into how I might avoid that fate. Not that I've accepted Alyssa's vision as truth. Simidh Gunn might have somehow tricked her into seeing what he wished, so that she might share the news with me in the hopes I will be weakened by it.

"Are you certain he said that I must die?" I ask her. "Did you once again watch me being hanged and burnt at the stake?"

"It was slightly different than before. I saw you hanging from the gallows, dead, and then flames erupted around you."

"So, 'twas not the same. The differences might matter."

"You may be right, but knowing that doesn't help. What your father said in the dream was vague and not very useful."

Alyssa is not accustomed to magics, especially the sort that manifest in dreams. The fact that my father entered the dream when he had not done so before makes me wonder. "You did not see my father in the first dream. Aye?"

"That's right. But the spell your aunts cast was supposed to drop me back into the nightmare by sending me back in time."

"Only your mind, dearie," Efrica says. "Your body and soul remained rooted to the present."

"*Mhac na galla*," I say. "Must you three always be so cryptic? Either my wife traveled back in time or she did not. You can't have it both ways."

Morna chuckles. "Of course we can. Magic cares nothing for years or minutes or locations. How can you still not accept that after living with us? And you have evinced magics of your own."

"That's true," Lachina agrees. "Kieran, you admit you have used white magics in the past. Don't dismiss Alyssa's dream so swiftly."

"I have dismissed nothing." Should I tell them that I felt magics inside me on two occasions? To do so would mean I must explain the circumstances, which involve fucking my wife. No, I will not describe those events. Yet I should tell them some bit of what occurred. "I have twice felt magics inside me, but I dinnae know what it means."

Efrica smiles and shakes her head. "Oh, Kieran. You are the stubbornest man I have ever known. It near pains you to admit there might be magics inside you."

Alyssa touches my hand. "Maybe we should talk about this alone. Or at least not while we're in bed with your aunts watching us."

Efrica stands up. "I will make barley tea for the lass. Morna and Lachina, you will cook the evening meal. When Kieran and Alyssa are ready, they will join us in the dining hall to discuss matters."

My aunts leave the room, shutting the door behind them.

Alyssa and I dress to avoid speaking to each other, at least that's how I perceive the situation. Her dream disturbed her greatly, and I worry for what might occur if Simidh attempts to enact the events my wife had foreseen.

I've just grasped the knob, ready to open the door, but I stop.

Alyssa stares at me, and her brow gradually wrinkles. "What is it now, honey?"

"I do not wish to die at all, but most of all I do not want that to happen before our child is born."

She wraps her arms around me. "I don't want you ever to die."

"Everyone must shuffle off the mortal coil eventually."

My wife gazes up at me with such grief in her eyes that my throat constricts. "I can't watch you die for real. There must be a way to save you."

"We don't even know if what you saw was more than a dream."

Alyssa opens her mouth but does not have the chance to speak.

"Kieran!" Morna shouts. "Hurry, Kieran! 'Tis someone at the gatehouse. They are pounding on the doors."

I hasten down the stair and burst out of the door on the ground floor, pelting across the courtyard. Someone is indeed pounding on the doors to the gatehouse. I halt and open the wee window to peer out at the visitor. But I do not recognize him.

"Who are you?" I demand. "Why have you come here?"

"I am Guarin Abadie. Do you not recognize me? We met many years ago when your father went to Edinburgh to find a wife."

Guarin Abadie? I recall the name, but I have ne'er seen him since I was a young man. And I dinnae trust anyone strange who comes to Dùndubhan. "How did you know where to find me? And why would a Frenchman travel all this way?"

"I have been seeking a place to live, a place where I might make a new life." He smiles, but the expression seems too charming, as if it might be artifice. "I have, you might say, been too friendly with women who are closely associated with the king."

"What king?"

"Henri. The king of France."

Aye, his manner is too casual, too comfortable. No stranger shows up at a fortress behaving in this manner—particularly someone who claims to have known me. "You did not come here to renew our acquaintance or to hide from your indiscretions. Be on your way."

I shut the window.

Guarin raps on it three times.

He is unusually determined. So I shout, "Be on your way, Guarin. No shelter will be found here."

"At least come out here to speak with me. For the sake of old times."

I trust him even less the more he speaks. But I sense that I will not be rid of him until I appease the *cacan*. Yet I cannot under any circumstances allow him inside the walls of Dùndubhan.

Opening the window, I say, "I will meet you on the other side of the drawbridge. Step away now."

"*Merci*, Kieran."

I wait and watch as he crosses the bridge and halts on the other bank of the moat. I should have filled the moat before I made love to my wife, but I can't bring back the time I wasted. Not that I regret pleasuring my wife in the garden.

As I lift the crossbar and open the doors, I suddenly remember the premonition I suffered recently. *Something or someone is coming, and it will not be a happy occasion.* I had not only thoughts the words but had also spoken them to Alyssa.

Is Guarin Abadie the someone who heralds danger?

The sound of footfalls draws my attention to the area behind me. My aunts and Alyssa have entered the courtyard. I gesture for them to halt where they are. They remain close to the house, exactly as I had wished them to do. Alyssa hugs herself.

I open one side of the gatehouse doors enough that I might slip through the gap. As I march across the drawbridge, I move only my eyes to survey my surroundings. I can't see anyone other than Guarin, but that means very little. The forest can hide so many things—and so many men.

I halt a few yards from the visitor. "Explain yourself."

"I have fallen upon bad times, and I need somewhere to stay, only for a while."

"Nay, you may not stay here."

"But I saved you from mariners who would have slit your throat. I ask only for a small favor in return."

I cross my arms over my chest. "You did not save me. We fought our way out of their clutches together. That means I owe you nothing. Be on your way now, or I will drag you out into the forest and toss you into the river. The current is swift and will tow you into a loch. There, you shall drown."

Guarin raises his hands. "I mean you no harm, *mon ami*."

"If that is true, head back from whence you came."

He seems about to speak when something past my shoulder catches his attention. "*Mon Dieu*. What a fortunate man you are, Kieran."

I turn only my head to glance at the woman who is walking toward us. My hands clench, and I snarl, "Come no further. Return to the courtyard."

My wife ignores my command, coming up beside me. "Who's your new friend?"

The uninvited guest bows. "I am Guarin Abadie, an old friend of Kieran."

"We are not friends," I say, squeezing the words out between my teeth. "Leave this place now or drown in the fucking loch."

Alyssa eyes Guarin with no small measure of suspicion. "Better do what Kieran says. He always makes good on his threats."

Guarin bows again. "Forgive me, I shall go."

As he strides off down the path that eventually leads to the village, I round on my wife. "You should not have left the castle. That man is not my friend, and I dinnae know what he wanted."

"I'm sorry, Kieran. I shouldn't have ignored your wishes. I just had a weird feeling and needed to make sure you were all right. That dream still makes me feel uneasy."

"Aye, I know." I take her hand as we cross the drawbridge. "I love your courage, but events of late have given me cause for concern."

Only once we're inside the walls of Dùndubhan, with the portcullis and the doors closed, do I discuss our visitor. I lead my wife into the garden so we may sit on the bench to have a private conversation before I speak to my aunts. They had tried to follow us, but I waved for them to go inside. Miraculously, they did so without complaint.

"I wish you had not approached the visitor, Alyssa. I know nothing of his motivations."

"But you know who he is."

"Aye. We met when I was a young man, during the time I spent in Edinburgh with my father. Guarin gave me the coins to pay for the French whore, whom I once mentioned to you."

"Yeah, I remember the French hooker." She turns toward me. "But you didn't tell me about this other guy when you talked about Edinburgh."

"It seemed irrelevant. I apologize for not being forthright about the entire circumstances of that time in my life."

She lays a hand on my thigh. "I'm not upset about it. You weren't required to tell me everything back then since we weren't a couple yet."

Alyssa always understands and accepts me, and I no longer feel as if she shouldn't do that. Despite my behavior when first we met, she saw something in me and loved me. I am a fortunate man to have such a woman as my wife.

"How did Guarin find you?" Alyssa asks. "There's no Google to give him directions."

"What is goo-gall?"

"Never mind. Once in a while, I still forget that you don't know anything about the twenty-first century."

And I ofttimes forget that she is from another century.

"I do not know why Guarin came here," I tell her. "However, I can surmise how he found me. Everyone in the village knows that I was banished, and they would likely know that I came to live at Dùndubhan with my aunts."

"Do you think your father told everyone?"

"He would have no reason to do so—until recently. His visits to Dùndubhan would have necessitated sharing his plans."

"So, anyone could have found out where you live."

"Aye, 'tis possible." I reflect back on my conversation with Guarin, and I experience a sudden memory. "Simidh lived in the village of Loch Fairbairn with my clan for many years. And he was very curious about my time in Edinburgh. When I shared the tale, I embellished it somewhat to make Simidh jealous and also told him about the Frenchman who paid for the whore. I remember telling Simidh that the man's name was Guarin Abadie."

"That's one mystery solved."

I thread my fingers through Alyssa's as I gaze across the garden at the red carnations I had planted for her. "If Simidh sent Guarin, then grave danger must await us."

"What do you think he'll do?"

"He wants you. Simidh brought bandits with him when we met on the mountain, the sort who expect to be paid for their service. He will not come alone the next time either."

"What if Simidh has convinced everyone in the village that you're a black witch?"

I stare intently at the red carnations as I consider her question. "Mayhap I should have taken his lies more seriously. But I could not believe his dislike of me had turned to treachery."

She wraps both her hands around mine while we sit here contemplating the dangers. What can we do? Mayhap I should visit the village to explain the situation to the clan.

"Kieran!"

The woman screaming my name sounds like Efrica. Her cry sounded as if it originated from the walkway atop the wall.

I leap up and keep Alyssa's hand firmly in mine as we race into the courtyard.

Efrica stands on the walkway high above us. "Kieran! An army of men from the village are coming up the path. They have torches and weapons."

"Come down from there, Efrica."

Morna and Lachina race out of the house, meeting me and Alyssa in the courtyard. Morna speaks first. "This is Alyssa's premonition come to pass. You must flee through the garderobe channel, both of you, immediately. Please, Kieran."

"I will not flee. But you three and Alyssa should do so."

"Like hell," my wife says. "I am not running away while you get attacked by angry villagers."

Efrica bursts out of the house and halts in front of me, gasping for breath. "The villagers have not yet come close enough to see the moat. Fill it now, Kieran, whilst you still can."

"I must raise the drawbridge as well."

"Hurry, Kieran."

How much time do we have? Not enough. "Stay with my aunts, Alyssa. I must go outside the walls to open the dam."

My wife does not argue with me. She huddles with my aunts as I open the gatehouse doors and raise the portcullis. Then I race across the bridge to run down the length of the moat's bank, trying not to glance down at the thirty-foot drop mere feet away. I reach the dam and struggle to open it since no one has attempted to do this in many decades. No one had needed to do this. Finally, I succeed in my task and water pours into the moat from the river.

Do we have time to fill it? Or had I waited too long?

I rush back to the gatehouse and raise the drawbridge, then close the portcullis and the doors too.

The enemy is nearly upon us, and all we can do is wait.

Chapter Thirty-Four

Kieran

I have no armor, but I retrieve my claymore and give Alyssa her dirk. She knows what to do should the worst happen. Simidh wants her alive and me dead. I will never allow him to take her, which means I must stay alive to protect her and my aunts. Though desperation has taken hold of me, I struggle against the impulse to give in to it. That will accomplish nothing. I once vowed to protect Alyssa at any cost, and I shall not renege on that promise.

"Into the house," I say. "With an army approaching, we must turn to our last resort."

Efrica seems to understand what I mean, since her face goes pale. " 'Tis that dangerous?"

"Aye. Let's go."

None of the women complain as I lead them into the house. We avoid the stair and go into the ground-floor section of the castle, where I march straight into the solar.

"Efrica, gather whatever you need to cast spells," I say. "Do it now."

While Efrica hurries out of the solar to do as I commanded, I push all the chairs out of the way to create an open space in the center of the room. The women watch without comment. I try to ignore their expressions, for seeing their fear and worry will only hinder me. The last resort shall not be what Efrica assumed. 'Twill be far deadlier. But I don't care if I die as long as my wife and child survive and are able to flee from Simidh.

Might I convince his army to turn back and leave us be? If they are indeed villagers from Loch Fairbairn, mayhap I have a chance of accomplishing that feat.

Efrica returns with a large bag that I know contains all her witchcraft supplies. "We will cast a protection spell so that—"

"No," I snap. "You four will remain in the corridor while I do what must be done."

"But you wanted me to retrieve my spellcasting tools."

"Aye, I did. Now leave the room."

Lachina shakes her head slowly, clutching her hands to her belly. "No, Kieran, you mustn't."

"What mustn't he do?" Alyssa asks.

"The black arts are not the way."

I summon my most fearsome voice and shout, "Get out!"

My wife lifts her chin. "I am not going anywhere. Shout and snarl all you want, but I'm staying here with you."

Efrica lifts her chin as well. "None of us are leaving. Aye, sisters?"

Morna nods her agreement.

Lachina nods too, though she still appears deeply troubled. "Please, I beg of you, do not go down this path. Once you allow the darkness inside you, 'twill never leave your soul."

Alyssa stares at Lachina for a moment, biting her lip. Then she strides up to me. "Don't do it, Kieran. I trust your aunts, and I know you're only doing this because you're terrified of what might happen to me and our baby if you're killed."

I snatch Efrica's bag away from her. "Leave the room. If you will not, then stand beside my aunts."

Alyssa does not move.

Morna drags my wife away to join herself, Lachina, and Efrica near the hearth.

I peel back the rug and kneel in the center of the room, pulling from the bag all the tools I need to accomplish my task. Now I must cast my spell. *"Am fear nach abair mi—"*

Efrica rushes up to me and kicks me in the gut hard enough that the blow steals my breath for a moment. "We did not take you in so that you could become a demon. There is another way."

"What did Kieran say?" Alyssa asks. "It sounded like Gaelic, but my pendant won't translate."

"That is because he invoked the one who shall not be spoken of. He who fell from Heaven."

"You mean the devil."

"Ne'er speak that word again. The beliefs of our people forbid it."

"Sorry. I didn't know that." Alyssa kneels beside me and flings her arms around my neck. "Please don't do this. We'll find another way."

I fist my hands as I glare at the witchcraft tools laid out before me. 'Twould be so simple to invoke the dark arts. Simidh Gunn would do that for certain.

"Listen to me," my wife says. "You can't do this. I don't want to have to explain to our child why her father made a literal deal with the devil."

As I sit here with all the ones I love most around me, I recall the moment not long after Alyssa came to us when I promised to protect her because I claimed she was my property. I also vowed I would invoke black magics if necessary. I realized soon after that I had been wrong to do so, but now, I kneel here about to enact that vow. Will I become as vile as my enemy? To do so would taint my family too.

I slump and exhale a ragged breath. "No, I will not do it. You are correct, *mo chridhe*, there must be another way."

When I glance at my aunts, they each wear a relieved smile.

Alyssa hugs me tightly. "You are a good man. Don't ever let anyone make you think otherwise."

"We must flee through the garderobe channel."

Efrica shakes her head. "No, dearie, we can't. You filled the moat, and the garderobe channel goes through the bottom of it."

"*Mhac na galla.* I forgot about that." I drop onto my erse, my knees bent in front of me, and shove my hands into my hair. "I have failed all of you."

Alyssa peels my hands away from my face. "You haven't failed us. You did the exact opposite by refusing to invoke black magics."

What I almost did no longer matters. My wife would not console me if she believed I had committed a heinous act. I stopped short of summoning the one who shall not be named, yet I have failed to spare the ones I love from whatever ordeal awaits us.

I rise and fix my kilt, which had fallen out of position. "There must be a way to spare all of you from harm."

Lachina cries out and falls to the floor.

Efrica and Morna rush to her side, helping Lachina get to her knees.

I approach my aunts with Alyssa beside me. "Is Lachina ill?"

"No," Morna says. "She suffered a powerful premonition. Can you tell us what you saw, *gràidh*?"

Lachina's eyes had been half-closed. But now, she parts her lids to stare directly at me. "Simidh comes. He has persuaded many of our kinsmen that you are in league with he who shall not be named. Nothing can stop what is about to unfold."

I bring my keys out of my pocket and give them to Alyssa. "Take my aunts into the room where I locked you in on the day you arrived. Lock it from the inside. Our enemies may not realize the room exists, since it appears to be simply part of the wall."

"No, Kieran. Not without you."

"Please, Alyssa." I grip her upper arms tightly. "You are my wife and my heart and soul. I must know you and our child will be safe."

"What will you do?"

"Go now, I beg you. Hide yourselves in the secret room."

Tears trickle down her cheeks, but she does as I asked. Alyssa takes my aunts upstairs to the hidden room. I follow them until they've climbed up the stair and out of my sight. My throat tightens. I clench my fists so tightly that my nails dig into my flesh.

But I need to know what awaits outside the walls of Dùndubhan.

So I dash through the house and up the tower stair, emerging onto the walkway. But I keep going until I stand directly above the gatehouse with a clear view of the moat and the path that leads into the forest—or in this case, toward the castle. Flashes of light among the trees tell me all that I need to know. A horde of armed men are preparing to descend on Dùndubhan.

My claymore will not be enough.

I wait atop the gatehouse as the figures once cloaked in shadow gradually emerge from the trees. Dozens, mayhap more. Each man carries at least one weapon. And at the front of the group stands Simidh Gunn. He holds no torch and seems to have only a claymore with which to defend himself.

He halts on the other side of the moat. "Surrender now, Kieran, and mayhap I will spare your aunts. Alyssa will be mine either way."

"Your *sanntachadh* shall be your undoing, ye *olach*."

He chuckles. "I do covet your woman, but I am not a eunuch. Rest assured that Alyssa will be well satisfied when I fuck her."

My wife would rip his cock off with her teeth if he tried to take the lass against her will. But I will never let him get close enough to touch her.

"Come down from there, Kieran. Else I will be forced to lay siege to your fortress." He waves toward the horde behind him. "These men, your kinsmen, have made a sacred vow to end your reign of terror. We all know you have kept four women in this castle. How many times per night do you defile your aunts? It doesn't matter. You surely copulated with all four women during vile orgies designed to summon the one who shall not be named."

Simidh has clearly studied the history of witch trials. He knows precisely what to say. How did he convince my kin to support him in this madness?

The despicable coward flaps his arm as if he's calling in one of his horde. A blond man pushes through the crowd, halting beside Simidh. The stranger wears lavish clothes of the sort only a wealthy man could afford, complete with a feather-capped hat and an ornate walking stick.

Simidh claps a hand on the man's shoulder. "Kieran, meet the witch-finder."

An icy chill rushes through me. I do not fear for myself, though, but for my wife and aunts should my enemy discover their hiding place. Even if I surrender myself to the witchfinder, I can't be certain they will be spared.

"Come down here," Simidh shouts. "You have until the count of thirty. Then we will destroy your home. Bring in the battering ram!"

The crowd splits in two, and I soon see why. Six men push a cart down the path, though it's slow work since the cart holds a tree that has been cut and pruned specifically for this purpose. How long had my kinsmen worked to create a battering ram? I cannot fathom what Simidh must have told them to make them turn against me in this manner.

Lifting the battering ram off the cart, the men set it on the ground. I watch, stunned, as they leap into the water and swim across the moat, crawling onto the opposite side of the channel. I can't see what they're doing now, but I hear pounding and creaking sounds. A man shouts with what seems like triumph.

And the drawbridge falls.

I should do something. What? I am one man against an army.

The men with the battering ram lift it up and charge the portcullis.

I break out of my stupor and race down to the tower stair, bursting out into the courtyard. I don't stop until I reach the gatehouse. The pounding and yelling outside seems loud even with the thick wooden doors between me and Simidh's men. I risk opening the window in the gatehouse doors—and see men trying to heave the portcullis up. They've succeeded in raising it nearly halfway. Only one option remains for me. I bring out my claymore, about to stab at one of the men who is trying to raise the portcullis. But I can't do it.

The vacant look in the man's eyes has stopped me.

Everyone in Simidh's army wears the same look, and all of them move as if someone has bespelled them. Though I've not seen anything like this before, I can think of no other explanation for their behavior. Mayhap I should fight them, but I doubt I could overcome a horde of bespelled men.

With no weapon and no army on my side, I have but one choice.

"Stop!" I roar. "Stop! I surrender."

I lift the crossbar and open the doors.

The men at last succeed in hoisting the portcullis, then they use their battering ram as a brace to hold the metal grille up. For the first time in hundreds of years, Dùndubhan has been captured by the enemy.

The horde floods into the courtyard, and three men seize me. The others mill about as if they have no idea what they're meant to do, and I'm certain that's because their master has not entered the fortress yet. I make no attempt to resist. With Alyssa and my aunts hiding in the house, I will do whatever is necessary to ensure neither Simidh nor his men will discover them—even if that means I must die.

Now that the bespelled army has taken the castle, Simidh and his chief cohorts amble into the courtyard to approach me. I expected to see the witchfinder, but now I realize Guarin Abadie accompanies Simidh as well. What grievance does he have against me? I suspect I will find out soon enough.

Simidh leans in to snarl at me while spittle flies from his lips. "Where are the women, Kieran? Tell me now, or I shall ransack the castle until I find them. Can't promise that I won't defile the lasses forcibly, or that the witchfinder and my friend Guarin won't do the same."

I grind my teeth, spitting my words at him. "When I am free, I will hunt you down and strap you to a rack to watch your limbs being pulled apart."

He chuckles. "You won't live long enough to try that. Witchfinder, 'tis time to prove this man is guilty of witchcraft."

The witchfinder steps forward and shouts, "This man has been accused of the vilest crimes of witchcraft. Strip him so I might conduct my examination."

Simidh gives the order, and the bespelled men begin to tear my clothes off.

Chapter Thirty-Five

Alyssa

I can hear most of what's going on down in the courtyard, though I can't understand what Kieran is saying. He speaks in a low, snarly voice. That much I can hear. The witchfinder just ordered Simidh's men to strip Kieran, and I know it's the witchfinder speaking because he has a British accent. Did Simidh bring someone here all the way from England? Or has this creep been prowling the Highlands in search of victims?

Kieran surrendered. I know he must have had good reason for doing that, but I want to scream anyway. That would give away our hiding place, though. So instead, I jump up and try to get hold of the window ledge so I can find out what's happening now. But I can't get high enough.

Screw this. I am not hiding in this room while my husband is out there alone, about to be tortured by an evil bastard.

I spin around and race past the aunts, who are kneeling on the floor while softly chanting words I can't understand. I don't care what they're doing. They seem too absorbed in their task to notice me as I unlock the door and tear it open, sprinting down the stairs and out into the courtyard. I'm breathing so hard that I need to stop and recover, bent over with my hands on my knees. The second I'm able to do it, I march over to Simidh.

"Alyssa, *mo gaol*," Simidh says in the most insincere voice I've ever heard. "Come forth and watch as we find the evidence that Kieran is indeed in league with *Dòmhnall Dubh*."

"That must be the name of the man you've been having carnal relations with. Huh, Simidh?"

He grabs my upper arms and drags me toward him. "*Dòmhnall Dubh* is another name for the one who shall not be mentioned."

The devil, that's what he means.

Simidh shoves me in front of him and lashes one arm around me, pinning my backside to his front. "You will watch whilst the witchfinder performs his duty."

Kieran stands naked before us with his torn clothes lying on the ground at his feet. He remains impassive yet holds his head high and refuses to look away from the witchfinder. When he saw me, he gave only the faintest hint of emotion. No one else would have noticed it.

I try to kick and bite Simidh, but he simply laughs. "You'll be punished for this, you bastard. Mark my words."

The witchfinder begins his routine, exploring every inch of Kieran's body to search for who knows what. I'm not an expert on witch trials, but from what I saw in a documentary once, I think the witchfinder might be hunting for any little mole or discolored patch of skin that he will claim is the mark of Satan. The pervert even examines Kieran's genitals.

"Turn around," the witchfinder commands.

Kieran obeys, but I swear I see a spark of rage in his eyes.

When I'd left the secret room, the aunts had been chanting. Are they trying to cast a spell that might stop this madness? I don't dare glance up at the window, and I keep my gaze on my husband.

The witchfinder kneels before his prisoner to study Kieran's ass, parting the cheeks as if he thinks he'll find a miniature demon in there. Then the pervert spots the brown smudge that lies just above the crease of Kieran's buttock. I'd noticed that spot once but dismissed it as a birth mark. Never thought to ask my husband about it.

My heart beats so hard and fast that I feel a little faint. But I will not pass out. I need to witness whatever happens to Kieran.

The witchfinder springs upright and whirls around to face us. He stabs one finger straight up into the air. "This man is the devil's disciple. The mark of the witch is plain to see on his flesh. He is guilty and must be punished."

Simidh sneers as he shouts, "Turn around, Kieran, and face your fate."

My husband shuffles around to face us.

Run, Kieran, run, get as far away from here as you can. But I know he won't do that. The Laird of Dùndubhan would never abandon his charges—me and his aunts.

Simidh keeps his arm lashed around me as he turns toward the entrance. "We shall hang him from the gatehouse. Get a rope, witchfinder. I will execute him myself. You may find what you need in the old bakehouse."

The witchfinder heads for that building and returns with a long length of sturdy rope. Simidh orders his lackeys to get a chair from inside the house, and they return with it a moment later. The men attach the rope to the raised portcullis and set the chair beneath it.

Kieran calmly follows the witchfinder to the makeshift gallows.

A strange sensation flows through me, raising goosebumps and making the hairs at my nape stiffen. I instinctively glance sideways at the window of the secret room, realizing too late that I shouldn't have done that. Fortunately, it seems like nobody noticed. What was that weird feeling? It reminded me of something I'd felt in the moments right after I materialized in this century.

Simidh drags me closer to the gatehouse. "Watch whilst your beloved strangles to death. Then we shall roast his body in the flames of perdition."

I swear I can hear more chanting coming from up in the secret room. It grows louder and louder every second.

Hot tears roll down my cheek, and the saltiness infiltrates my mouth. It feels as if a giant rock has been dropped onto my chest. I can barely breathe. A single sob rushes out of me.

Kieran stares straight into my eyes. "Hush, *mo chridhe*. Close your eyes."

"No, I have to watch."

"Please, Alyssa. Close your eyes."

I do what he asked, but the tears keep flowing. My breaths have become so shallow and quick that my ears begin to ring. Though I recognize that I'm on the verge of passing out, I can do nothing to stop it. I hear the crack as the chair is kicked out from under Kieran and the gurgling as he strangles. Then everything goes black.

"Wake up, dearie, it's over."

Efrica's voice rouses me, but I feel too groggy to understand what's happened. Slowly, I open my eyes. The sun blinds me.

"That's right, lass. 'Twill take a moment to adjust. You gave us quite a fright when you collapsed, and Kieran was terribly worried about you."

"Kieran? But he's—" The words get choked off by a sob.

"He is not dead, *gràidh*."

Her matter-of-fact tone snaps me out of my stupor. As my eyes adjust to bright sunlight, I see Efrica crouching beside me while someone else stands behind her.

"Kieran!" I shriek, leaping to my feet. I nearly stomp on Efrica's hands as I throw myself at my husband. "You're alive."

He wraps his arms around me. "Aye, I'm alive. Are ye feeling better now? You had me worried for a moment."

"*I* had *you* worried?" I smack his chest. "You were on the gallows. Why didn't you tell me you had a plan to escape?"

"Because I had no such plan. I believed I was about to die."

He hugs me firmly to his muscular body and kisses me like the world might explode any second. His kiss takes my breath away. The simmering warmth of desire sifts through me, awakening me in ways I thought I'd never experience again. Kieran is alive.

Once he gives up my lips, I have to ask a question. "What the hell just happened? How did you survive?"

Efrica smiles in her motherly way. "Morna, Lachina, and I cast a *seun* that made Kieran invulnerable, temporarily. A *seun* is a charm, which is a kind of spell."

Her sisters come up beside her, and Lachina says, "While we were ruining Simidh's attempt to murder Kieran, we also discovered that he had cast *eòlas a chronachaidh* on our beloved nephew. That is the evil eye. Removing that curse brought many good things."

"Like what?" I ask.

"Look behind you, *gràidh*."

I wriggle out of Kieran's embrace and turn around. What I see amazes me. The army Simidh had brought with him now mills around in the courtyard, all of them seeming confused to varying degrees. Simidh and his witchfinder lie on the ground, hogtied and gagged.

As I turn back toward Kieran and the aunts, I probably look as confused as those men behind me. "Okay, somebody needs to tell me what on earth went on while I was unconscious."

"Oh, quite a bit, dearie," Efrica says. "But Kieran should explain."

My husband clasps my hands. "After my aunts cast their charm to save me, Simidh's horde no longer obeyed him. They have no memory of being in his service because Simidh bespelled them, and now they are free. I then tied up the red-haired savage and the witchfinder too."

"Why did Simidh do any of this?"

"Let me tell you about that," Efrica says. "Whilst Kieran was taking care of the blackguards, we cast a spell to encourage Simidh to speak the truth. He admitted that he had orchestrated a campaign against Kieran because he was jealous. He coveted the lass to whom Kieran had been betrothed, and he employed the *gradh a's fuath*, which is an herb used to cast a spell that encourages love. But it can also warp itself into hate depending upon the intent of the one who casts it. If they harbor evil in their heart, such as Simidh did, the *gradh a's fuath* will sour into malice."

"Wow. All of this happened because one jerk screwed up a spell." I lean against Kieran, grateful beyond measure that he's still here with me. "What about Simidh's army?"

Kieran nods toward the shuffling, confused men. "Those laddies are MacTaggarts. The depth of Simidh's hatred, warped by the *gradh a's fuath*, grew beyond his own mind and infected those who encountered him. My kinsmen had no free will, but now we have liberated them."

"Can we trust them?"

"Aye. The magics are gone. I also discovered another man among the horde who had been bound by Simidh's magics but now is free."

He leads me through the crowd to someone I recognize. "Guarin. He's not an evil prick after all?"

Kieran chuckles. "Nay, he is merely a formerly bespelled man."

"Does that mean he's your friend again?"

"Mayhap. We shall see. It has been years since I set my eyes upon Guarin, so I will wait until I've had time to judge his character."

"Good idea."

In the aftermath of Simidh's attempt to murder my husband and sack Dùndubhan, we learn a lot about the "fire-haired fiend," as Efrica once called him. He has lost his mind, for one, though not in a dangerous way. He has lost his hunger for vengeance and now cares more about growing vegetables than destroying Kieran. My hubby's kinsmen know something strange happened, but they can't remember what. They want to give Kieran the job of clan chief, but he declines. All we care about now is our child, who will be born in about six months.

Guarin does indeed become a good friend to Kieran—and to me. I'm glad for that. Simidh will never be a friend, but at least he's no longer an enemy.

When I asked Efrica about Simidh's mental state, she told me, "I'm afraid he will never fully recover his wits, but neither shall he harm anyone. Henceforth, any male progeny he might beget will suffer from a similar illness of the mind once they reach their twenty-eighth year. But the spell may be broken by a MacTaggart when the time comes."

We also summon my parents from the future and give them the choice to stay with us here in the past or go home. They choose to stay with no regrets about that decision.

More changes keep coming, all of them good. The clan finally lifted Kieran's banishment and welcomed him back into the fold, but we decided to remain at Dùndubhan. It's become our home. His kinsmen insist on helping us to rebuild and expand the castle, and it has become the unofficial seat of the MacTaggart clan. Even the clan chief has no problem with that.

And weirdly, the chief's name is Ruairidh—Rory, in English.

So I've come full circle. My odyssey began when I met Rory MacTaggart in the twenty-first century and now ends when I'm introduced to his ancestor who shares the same name. My odyssey might have concluded, but my life's journey has only just begun.

Yet we have one more adventure to undertake before we can close the book on time travel. And it involves a book, appropriately. Efrica has written the final entry in her journal, relating the tale of Kieran's execution and resurrection. When I suggest that she should indicate in her book that Kieran's death was a ruse, she gives me a surprising response.

"Let the MacTaggarts of the future unravel that mystery. If I should write that in my book, 'twould mean you never came to us."

I hadn't considered the time-travel ramifications. But she's right. The mystery of Kieran MacTaggart must live on.

And our final odyssey is about begin.

Love the

Hot Scots

series?

Visit
AnnaDurand.com

to subscribe to her newsletter
for updates on forthcoming books in the series
&
to receive free gifts for signing up!

Anna Durand is a bestselling, multi-award-winning author of contemporary and paranormal romance. Her books have earned bestseller status on every major retailer and wonderful reviews from readers around the world. But that's the boring spiel. Here are the really cool things you want to know about Anna!

Born on Lackland Air Force Base in Texas, Anna grew up moving here, there, and everywhere thanks to her dad's job as an instructor pilot. She's lived in Texas (twice), Mississippi, California (twice), Michigan (twice), and Alaska—and now Ohio.

As for her writing, Anna has always made up stories in her head, but she didn't write them down until her teen years. Those first awful books went into the trash can a few years later, though she learned a lot from those stories. Eventually, she would pen her first romance novel, the paranormal romance *Willpower*, and she's never looked back since.

Want even more details about Anna? Get access to her extended bio when you subscribe to her newsletter and download the free bonus ebook, *Hot Scots Confidential*. You'll also get hot deleted scenes, character interviews, fun facts, and more! Plus you'll receive audio bonus content narrated by Shane East, Vanessa Edwin, and Ava Lucas.

Visit AnnaDurand.com to sign up.